ALL THAT SHINES

Glitter Bay Mysteries, Book 2

Published by Escape With a Writer Publishing

Print ISBN: 978-1-7383328-8-5

Digital ISBN: 978-1-7383328-9-2

Cover by Diane Bator

All That Shines

Glitter Bay Mysteries, Book 2

Diane Bator

Escape With a Writer Publishing

Chapter One

"**A** fashion show?" I gawked at my supermodel sister like she'd popped out of the ground in front of me and grown purple petals around her face. "Is that really the kind of retirement party you want to throw for Gill?"

"Think about it, Sage." Laken placed her hands on my shoulders. Her green eyes mirrored mine as they shone brightly with excitement. "What a better way to say goodbye to the Sweet Eden Tea House and hold a grand opening bash for Vintage Sage? Gill would love it. We can serve some of his famous teas and those yummy little cakes from the bakery, while we showcase the great items you've collected for the shop."

My sister knew the right thing to say to set my imagination off and running. A fashion show wasn't the worst idea Laken ever had. Heaven knows she'd walked down enough runways in her modeling career to pull it off. While she was jet-setting around the world, I'd moved from Seattle to Glitter Bay and started Vintage Sage in a badly lit building to sell gently used designer clothing, accessories, and other items. These days, I ran the store with her help.

"I'll think about it," I told her, glancing down at my paint-splattered overalls.

"What's there to think about?"

I rolled my eyes envisioning dollar signs flying out the open windows. We were already knee deep in repainting and doing repairs to the former Sweet Eden Tea House. Adding more to my to-do list would have me bordering on insanity.

"Think fast. I told Gill the show is Friday night at seven." Laken curled her shoulder-length red hair around one ear. She was tall, thin, and stunning. A natural both in front of a camera and on a runway.

I was a shorter, "healthier" version of Laken, according to our Grandma Sadie. The Supermodel and the Boho girl. Total opposites in many ways, yet we managed to work together in the boutique without causing each other bodily harm.

So far.

"You already told him? But today's Saturday."

"Then we'd better get a move on. There's a lot of take care of," she said, turning to leave. "Oh, I'm going to get my nails done before I meet Cameron for dinner. Could you let Sammy out later?"

Sammy was my sister's English Sheepdog who seemed to grow at a phenomenal rate. He thrived on a steady diet of table legs and couch cushions as well as my sister's unmentionables.

"Sure." I hid my hands behind my back, so she didn't see my jagged nails.

"See you later." Laken wagged her fingers as she reached for her Coach bag, which held her wallet as well as dog poo bags, toys, and treats for Sammy. Basically, it was an expensive doggy travel bag.

I glanced around at the large soon-to-be showroom where I'd spent the past two days painting Buttercream yellow. "Yeah. You go on ahead."

Our original plan was to open the new store a week from Monday. Now I had less than a week to finish painting, redo the floors, and set up the airy vintage boutique I'd only dreamed about until recently.

Typical Laken. She'd become the ideas part of the team, while I did the grunt work.

What were sisters for?

I sighed as I climbed back up the ladder, stuck my roller in the paint, then let it drip into the tray while I gazed around the room. Buttercream yellow. At least the name sounded tasty. My stomach rumbled for food.

"So, we're doing a fashion show, are we?" a tall, dark-haired man asked as he stepped out of one of our new change rooms.

"Yup." I leaned into the ladder before I glanced behind me.

Andy Briggs was a local paramedic who'd become my good friend over the past couple months—thanks to Laken meddling in the death of Gill San Vicente's wife, Tilly. Even though Andy had worked alongside me all morning, I completely forgot he was in the building.

"That sounds like fun." He set his hammer on the counter and adjusted the tool belt that sat low on his narrow hips.

"Don't kid yourself. Laken's on a mission, which is never fun." I descended the ladder to inspect his handiwork. "The dressing rooms look great. All they need is a coat of paint and curtains."

"Which I'll leave in your capable hands, Miss Miller." He grinned, flashing his perfect teeth. His face was tanned from spending more time outdoors than in whereas my face was alabaster white with tan and new yellow freckles. He'd make a great model in the show.

"Yellow's a good color on you, Sage. It brings out your freckles." Andy dabbed a spot of paint on the end of my nose with one finger. He ran his other hand through his dark hair leaving a streak of pale sawdust behind.

My face grew warm as I smeared a blotch of yellow across his cheek. "It looks good on you, too."

Andy chuckled as he rubbed his cheek. "Just when I was going to treat you to a coffee."

"Good thing you can wash it off. You just spread it all the way to your chin." I traced the line across his stubbled jaw which made his face flush. For a moment, he gazed into my eyes. I wasn't sure if he contemplated kissing me or adding more paint to my face.

When he didn't make a move, I led him into the kitchen where Gill San Vicente used to make soups and sandwiches for guests of the Sweet Eden Tea House, while his late wife guarded the cash register like a fire-breathing dragon. Lucky for me and Laken, Gill kept the fridge and tea cupboard fully stocked out of habit. Mostly since he and his new love, Enid, enjoyed cooking.

I ran the water until it grew warm, then wet a cloth. "Thanks for your help. I'm glad you didn't have to work today."

"So am I." He hovered nearby as I wrung out the cloth. "I would've missed building change rooms, fixing stairs, and—"

"Hey, I bought you breakfast. Besides, you did volunteer. I could've asked Laken to put up the walls."

Andy raised his eyebrows and waited for a punchline. Finally, he burst into laughter. "You know that would never happen. She might break a nail."

"Then I'd do it myself."

"Not on my watch, pretty lady." He pulled a few strands of my hair out of a gob of paint on my forehead. "You're lucky to have a sister who's worth a fortune. It was nice of her to buy this place for your store."

I grimaced. "You know Laken bought the building so she could move into the apartment upstairs, and we could move the store. I pay rent." I paused. "Once she accepts my money."

The handsome paramedic met my gaze. "It's great she believes in you. Once she moves in here, you'll have your house to yourself again."

Was he insinuating something? Sure, we'd hung out together several times, but we'd agreed to take things slow. Sloth-paced at present. Mostly on my part after my ex-boyfriend, Jonathan, moved to Los Angeles.

Privacy was one thing, but I'd miss my sister horribly once she moved out. I kind of liked having a roommate. For now, she lived with me while she waited for a contractor to renovate the apartment upstairs. Whenever the guy showed up that was.

"If we're planning a fashion show for Friday, I'd better get back to work." I glanced at the clock while Andy wiped yellow specks off my face. "It's already two? No wonder I'm light-headed."

"Stop moving," Andy said, then held my chin in place with one hand while he finished cleaning my face. "Why don't I grab us lunch? Then we can sit out front and breathe some fresh air. The paint fumes are making us both light-headed."

That explained the funny feeling in my head. It wasn't just having Andy less than a foot away. I wiped my hands on the cloth on our way back to the showroom. "It's a date."

When Andy glanced at me and chuckled, I winced. Finding romance after my last breakup didn't seem as far from my mind as I tried to convince myself. It was odd how my ex had started texting me out of the blue once we'd started renovations. As far as I was concerned, our relationship was over. I never replied, nor did I mention his texts to Laken. What was the point?

Andy left in search of lunch, leaving me to paint my way toward the three new dressing rooms while my thoughts roamed.

The demise of the former Sweet Eden Tea House was swift and painless. Gill moved in with Enid Walsh, Glitter Bay's own gossip columnist, which seemed kind of abrupt, but who was I to judge? Apparently, they had a sordid history.

Moving Vintage Sage from the grungier side of Glitter Bay had several hiccups with town bylaws, but now all we had left to do was polish the wood floors, move in some merchandise, and throw open the doors. Laken and Sammy would move upstairs. Muumuu and I would have our house back. Then we'd all live happily ever after.

Until Friday.

I deflated as the front door opened.

"Can you believe some woman screamed at me because I sold the tea house?" Gill let Sammy's leash go, so the pup could run toward me. He straightened his khaki pants and plaid dress shirt with a huff.

"Hey, Gill. Why do you have Sammy?" I climbed down the ladder in time for the puppy to grab hold of my shoelaces.

He ran a hand over his thick, silver hair. "Laken asked me to drop him off. She figured you'd forget about him."

"She's probably right."

"I've been thinking about that fashion show thing she wants to do," he said.

I wiped paint off my hands. "She told you about that already?"

Gill waved a hand. "We talked about it last week. Anyway, I had this great idea."

"Last week? I just found out half an hour ago."

"Figures. She's been a bit distracted," he said. "I was thinking, why don't we set up a tea table? Like a wine and cheese event, but with tea and sweets like I used to sell at the tea house?"

Since I'd sampled every tea Gill used to sell, the idea excited me. "Anything that can bring new customers into the store can't be all bad. I have no idea what she has in mind though."

His eyes crinkled in the corners. "We can make a few teas and serve them with desserts and hors d'oeuvres. Maybe you can convince the bakery to donate dessert."

Sammy snuffled around the empty shop dragging his leash behind him.

"Gill, I don't know anything about fashion shows or tasting events. I have no idea where to start."

"Good thing Laken's done a zillion shows and I know food." He shrugged. "What more do we need? You stay open late Friday evening, make some tea, and let people buy old clothes. We rake in a few bucks while people check out your new store."

"Now you sound like my sister."

Gill winked. "That's because this was her idea. We were brainstorming ways to get good publicity. When she brought up the fashion show, we went with it. What do I know about clothes except what Enid tells me?"

Deep down, I had a feeling I was being set up. Laken probably asked Gill to soften the blow and make the fashion show seem like a good idea. "I wish she would've talked to me before telling everyone else."

"Any idea where to start?" Gill asked, as Sammy nipped his pantleg.

"Not a clue. We'll need extra staff. There's no way Laken and I can pull off an event like that off alone. Maybe Abbie and a few of his friends could help." I leaned on the counter. "Could you ask Enid to run an ad in the newspaper or mention it in one of her blog posts?"

Sammy gave a bark before he curled up at my feet.

I leaned over to stroke his back. "If we ask local shops to donate desserts and appetizers, people could pay twenty dollars admission. That would cover the tea and expenses."

"I'd suggest fifty dollars a ticket. You have to make them think it's the one event of the season they can't miss." He folded his arms across his bright blue and yellow shirt. "I'm retired now. I need the money to move somewhere they cater to me."

"You moved in with Enid. Doesn't she cater to you?"

"That's different."

I picked some dried paint off the back of my hand. "If it's a Vintage Sage event, you might a cut. I guess you'd better start by asking around town for donations. Not only food, but maybe some raffle prizes we can sell tickets for."

He tapped my head. "Now you're starting to think like your sister."

"At least she knows what she's doing. I've only done bake sales for the yoga studio. I'm at a loss."

"People love a good banana bread," Gill said.

Sammy made an odd noise between a yip and a yawn.

"We're not doing a bake sale on top of everything else. I barely have time to breathe this week let alone bake. I take it Sammy's my responsibility now."

"Looks like," he said. "I have to run errands. Enid's cooking seafood stew in the crock pot, so I need to get a baguette. I'll ask her about ad space and text you later. Hopefully, you can decipher my message. I hate those tiny buttons."

"You know you can record a voice message instead of typing, right?" I asked. "Get Abbie to show you how."

He narrowed his eyes before he seemed to consider the option. "I'll check it out."

On his way out, Gill passed Andy on the steps. When Andy strolled onto the porch with a paper bag, Sammy and I scurried toward him.

A little sunshine and fresh air turned out to be exactly what we all needed. Re-energized, we worked until seven o'clock, then knocked off for the night. We took Sammy for a run on the beach between Devil's

Peak Bluff and the marina a mile away on the far side of Glitter Bay from Vintage Sage.

Andy walked us home to the cottage-style house Grandma Sadie sold me before she retired to a beach house in Santa Monica where she taught kids to surf. He kissed my forehead leaving a spot that tingled before whispering, "Have a good night, Sage."

My face grew warm. "Thanks for your help."

"Any time," he said, giving a wave as he strolled away.

Sammy jumped at my legs, knocking me into the door jamb.

I covered my face with both hands even though I doubted anyone but Sammy noticed me stumble. As I unlocked the front door, I sighed. "He's a good guy isn't he, Sammy? Why he hangs out with me is baffling. He could do a lot better."

After grabbing a cup of tea, I sat at my desk with a sandwich to sort through a mound of paperwork. Generally, I was good at keeping my finances organized, but this move coupled with the renovations were throwing me for a loop. It didn't help when Laken paid for things then tossed random receipts on the pile with no notes. We needed to move into the new location so I could return to yoga classes before I had a severe anxiety attack.

When my phone dinged, I smiled expecting it to be Andy saying goodnight. Instead, it was Jonathan asking, *"How was your day?"*

Part of me wanted to block him. Had I overreacted when he left for Los Angeles? Some long-distance relationships worked. Ours had for a long time when he lived in Seattle, but I grew tired of not being one of his priorities.

"Hey, Sage," Laken called out from the front door and saved me from my thoughts. "I'm going to work on some things for the fashion show tonight if you want to help."

"I'm juggling the books if you want to help with those."

"Ha. Maybe some other time," I replied. Taking a deep breath, I returned to the stack of receipts.

I'd managed to get by thanks to both a small loan from Grandma Sadie and a settlement from a court case that still haunted me. Case closed did not mean the victim didn't have to live with the aftermath. It hadn't done much for my ability to trust people or my anxiety. I found some relaxation music on my phone and stuck in my earbuds. For now, I needed to take life one receipt at a time.

That is until I came across a peculiar receipt that punched every ounce of breath straight out of my lungs. I stared at the five-digit number in the lower right corner as a shower of miniature fireworks popped in front of my eyes. Usually, those lights signaled the onset of a migraine brought on by either a panic attack or hyperventilation. Tonight it was both.

"Thirty thousand dollars?" I rubbed my eyes in case I'd misread the number. Nope. "What did she do, buy a company car?"

Next, I gawked at the letterhead for a company in Los Angeles. More specifically, on Rodeo Drive. I'd never spent thirty thousand dollars on anything aside from my house. Not in one lump sum anyway.

Grasping the invoice, I stormed into the living room. "Can you explain this?"

My sister glanced up from her laptop. Sammy lay nestled into a six-inch gap between her legs and the arm of the couch. "Since you're doing the books, I'd say offhand it was a bill."

"Yeah. For thirty thousand dollars from the House of Hayward in Hollywood." I shook the paper at her.

"Oh. That." She reached out a hand as she leaned forward. "It must've stuck to something I threw on your desk."

"If that invoice is for the store, I need to know what it's for before my accountant hyperventilates like I nearly did." My voice crackled and I grew hoarse. A sure sign I was overtired. "This could break me before we even open the new location."

Laken nudged Sammy to one side then set her laptop on the coffee table. She strolled toward me, taking the paper from my hand. "Remember how I promised to get some beautiful display cases a guy I knew was getting rid of?"

"You also said they were cheap. This isn't cheap."

"They were cheap." She pointed to a single line on the page. "Six glass and chrome cabinets at a hundred dollars apiece."

I was so upset my hands shook. "How many pieces are they in? Even at a hundred dollars each, that's six hundred dollars I don't have. What about the rest?"

My sister read the invoice line by line. "Shipping and handling from Los Angeles to Glitter Bay. Oh, and he threw in a couple mannequins for fifty dollars each."

"Fifty dollars I can live with. How many are we talking about?"

"Ten."

My jaw dropped. "What do we need with ten mannequins?"

"Oh, my mistake," she said. "Ten males and ten females."

Dizzy, I slumped into the armchair and cradled my face in my hands as my phone dinged again. I ignored it. "I don't need six display cases or twenty mannequins. I need room for people to browse."

Laken sighed. "You're forgetting that you have three times the space you did in the old store. You're moving from a postage stamp to a business card."

"The cabinets and mannequins add up to two thousand dollars," I said. "What else did you buy, Laken?"

She bit her lower lip as she read some more. Finally, she shrugged. "I think he messed up and added a couple extra zeros. He's a designer, not an accountant. Let's call it three grand, including shipping, and I'll deal with the rest in the morning."

Despite the stiff muscles from painting, I jumped from my chair. This time I moved toward her slowly in the hope she wouldn't run off before I got some kind of explanation. "What rest? Laken, what did you do?"

Her face reddened and her mouth twitched. At first, I thought she'd burst into tears, then she pulled out her phone. "Sebastian was clearing out his old fixtures to update his studio. He had a few pieces no one wanted, so I told him to give us a deal and throw them in."

"Throw them in with what?"

She made sure I was sitting on the couch before she showed me photos of the new-to-us fixtures scheduled to arrive the next day. The twenty mannequins were faceless and thin. They looked like weird alien beings. The next photo showed a display case filled with glittering necklaces and gold coins.

My head pounded. "Fake gemstone necklaces and gold coins. What kind of place does your friend run?"

"It's a fashion design house." She swiped to the next photo.

"Of course, it is."

The next glass cabinet encased a fully dressed mannequin, her ensemble colorful, frilly, and feathery with pyramid-shaped headpiece. Something only either an eccentric woman or a drag queen would wear. While inappropriate for the streets of Glitter Bay, it was vaguely familiar, but I couldn't place it.

I shook my head in and asked, "Are you out of your freaking mind?"

"I owed him a favor," she said quietly.

"What kind of favor's worth that?" I stomped into the kitchen for a strong mug of chamomile tea and a cold pack for my neck.

Laken joined me. "Sebastian helped to me get away from my ex. Well, not so much my ex as the paparazzi. Those guys are like wasps. They hunt you down and swarm you like heat-seeking missiles. I couldn't have escaped Hollywood and moved here without his help."

Only half convinced, I turned on the kettle.

Laken switched it off, then opened the fridge. She handed me a well-chilled, half-full bottle of pinot grigio. "You'll probably want this instead."

"There's more?" I asked as I leaned against the cupboard. While my migraine would prefer chamomile. I couldn't take any more of Laken's surprises without a little support. Pinot it was.

My sister wasn't stingy when she filled my glass. It seemed I was in for more revelations. Since she no longer drank alcohol, she filled a second glass with sparkling water.

I took a large gulp before I dared to ask, "What's going on?"

"We need to sit." Laken half-dragged me back to the living room. She turned off her laptop before we sat in front of the fireplace. "I'm sorry I didn't talk to you about off of this first." She hesitated. "Sebastian is... Well, he's..."

"He's what?" I growled.

Laken chugged her sparkling water before she sighed. "He's part of the package."

My eye twitched. I grasped my glass with both hands. "Who is Sebastian and what package is he a part of?"

"He's the fashion designer who owns House of Hayward. That thirty thousand dollars includes his expertise to help us set up Vintage Sage like a shop on Rodeo Drive."

I stared in the hope she'd crack a smile or laugh and say she was joking. When neither came, I shook my head. "No, no, no, no, no. Send it all back. The cases, the dummies, the snooty designer… Especially the snooty designer. Laken, I've done fine without Hollywood intruding before now."

"No, you haven't," she said. "If it wasn't for me, you'd still be stuck in that dingy building with those ugly Antique White walls and abandoned shops all around you."

Ouch. I sipped my wine for the sake of my sanity and to keep from swearing. I needed to let this battle go before my head exploded. "How long will he be here?

"Six weeks max."

My phone dinged as my mouth fell open. "Six weeks? Are you crazy?"

She held up her hands between us. "Any more than that and I will personally toss him into a rowboat and launch him back to the city."

"Since I'm stuck with him, I'll listen to his advice. But don't expect me to do everything he says. It's my shop. I get final say. Plus, this guy is your headache, not mine."

She gave me a hug. "I promise you won't regret this."

I sipped my wine. "Too late."

As my sister ran up the stairs with her cell phone, Sammy chased after her nipping at her bare heels. A door closed before her voice became an excited hum.

My phone dinged once more. This time it was Andy saying goodnight. I send a message back then deleted the texts from Jonathan without reading them.

*****

I got up early Sunday morning despite having two glasses of wine the night before. I met Andy and his electrician buddy, Brad Angler, at the store shortly before seven o'clock. The two of them had met in detention while in high school years ago. Something to do with cherry bombs and an anxious teacher. With Andy's part-time passion for carpentry and Brad's full-time electrician gig, they were able to do a lot of the work without costing me a small fortune.

Like Andy, Brad ran every day and worked out religiously. I found myself surrounded by more testosterone than I'd anticipated.

Our mission for the day was to polish the old barnboard floors. Rumor had it, those floors came from an old farm north of Glitter Bay where Gill's grandfather raised horses and held illegal races. Neither of the stories were substantiated.

While they moved the ladder and the front counter into the kitchen, I vacuumed any debris and grumbled about my sister hiring the designer behind my back.

By ten, Andy ran up the street to the café. He'd probably had enough of me complaining.

"This is a bigger job than it looked." Brad sat back on his heels and arched his back as we paused from scrubbing each floorboard to get rid of mystery stains. "I never thought Laken would pull something so sneaky. I had a business partner once, but it didn't work out so well."

"Did your partner make deals behind your back?" I asked.

He grinned, dimples burrowing into his tanned cheeks. "Nope. She left me for an electrical contractor and took me for half of everything I owned. I had to start from scratch."

"That's awful."

When Brad shrugged, the small hole in the shoulder of his dusty peach t-shirt seemed to grow. "I had the last laugh. The guy left her with nothing."

"Sounds like good karma." I laughed.

The corners of his brown eyes crinkled. "She begged me to take her back, but I'd already moved on. Speaking of. What happened to that guy from Seattle you were seeing? Jonathan, right?"

"He moved to California." Right on cue, my phone dinged. I deleted Jonathan's latest message. "He became a trainer to the stars and tried to convince me he'd see me on weekends."

"Sounds like a match for my ex," Brad said. "If he ever comes around, give me a call. I'll set them up. Might be good payback for both of us."

"I like that plan, especially since he keeps texting me."

"What for?"

"No clue. He wants me to call him, but I'm ignoring his messages."

Brad studied me for a moment. "If you want my two bits, either block the guy or see what he wants, then block him. Have you told Andy?"

"Why would I?"

"Aren't you guys, uh...?"

Since my hands were wet, I made a mental note to block Jonathan later. "Andy and I are just friends. Besides, I was hoping Jonathan would go away on his own."

"I suggest you do something about him. The sooner the better."

When Andy tapped on the glass, Brad opened the front door, then shooed me out for a coffee break. Andy waited until I was sitting before he handed me a coffee. Brad took his cup down to the beach to check his phone.

I sat on the top step in the sunshine and closed my eyes. As I stretched a kink from my neck, Andy rubbed my shoulders.

"I'm not surprised you're achy after all the work you've done on this place," he said.

"Yoga helps. You should come to a class sometime." I closed my eyes to savor the warmth and pressure from his hands on my aching muscles.

"Oh, yeah? And when's the last time you attended a class?"

"The day Laken bought this place to surprise me. I've been cleaning and renovating since." The pressure on my tight shoulders made me moan. "I've done Sun Salutations on the deck every morning. Okay, most mornings."

Andy raised his eyebrows as if he didn't believe me.

"Twice in the past week?" I winced.

"That I believe. You know you can take the day off, right? Brad and I can finish up on our own." He sat back in the sunshine.

"Yeah? What else would I do?" I asked, turning my face toward the sky.

"Pack up the old store and find some lackeys to move it all," he suggested, then nudged me. "Oh, right. You already have lackeys."

"Who?"

"Me and Brad. I'll bet we could even get Laken's boyfriend to help. If Cameron can lift a full-grown Saint Bernard, I'll bet he can lift a box or two."

"True." I yawned.

Andy averted his gaze. "Did you get any sleep last night?"

"A few. After all the surprises Laken threw at me yesterday, I'm surprised I got any. I had visions of fashion designers dancing through my head all night. There's so much left to do, and that's without the fashion show. Plus, she invited that know-it-all designer I told you about."

Andy sipped his coffee before he met my gaze. "You know, having him here might get you out of helping her with the fashion show."

He had a point. "Which means I can focus on getting the store ready for our opening."

"Isn't that why you're doing the fashion show on Friday?"

I bowed my head, then covered my face with both hands and wanted to scream. "That's not funny."

Andy chuckled. "There's a lot more to do by Thursday, or you'll be sending models down the runway while you're covered in paint and varnish."

"Thanks. That'll be tonight's nightmare." I grinned. "You know if I didn't need your help so badly I'd send you home, right?"

"But you won't because you like me." He met my gaze. There was a twinkle in those hazel eyes that made me smile.

"It's only been a couple months. I'm not completely attached to you yet."

Andy leaned against my shoulder and murmured, "Are you sure about that?"

Who was I kidding? Two months felt more like two years. Technically, we'd known each other longer, even if I used to find him arrogant and annoying.

"What's happening with Laken's apartment?" he asked. "Did she find someone to do the renovation work she wanted?"

"Garnet Noire." Who was notorious in town for taking money, then leaving jobs half done. "I tried to warn her, but she insisted. She hired him a couple weeks ago and he's been out of town ever since. I doubt we'll see him again."

"Are you talking about Laken's renovations?" Brad strolled up the sidewalk in his steel toe boots and faded jeans. "I offered to help, but she said she found someone."

"Garnet," Andy said.

Brad burst into laughter. "Of course."

If my sister wasn't dating Cameron Dale, I'd happily set her up with Brad. Except that she had an aversion to pickup trucks, construction boots, and would've found several faults with him. She was better off with the veterinarian and his little red Corvette. They were a better fit.

Brad leaned against the railing sipping his coffee. "About those spotlights you wanted. I can come by Monday afternoon if that works."

"Sounds great. I'll show you before we wax the floor in case I'm at the other location on Monday." My phone rang just as I got up to go inside. I waved the guys to go ahead while I answered it. "Hey, Laken, what's up?"

"How are the floors?"

"We're just starting on the wax. What's up?"

"Remember how I told you that designer is coming to help?"

My forehead tingled. "Yes."

She seemed to hesitate. "He'll be here tomorrow afternoon and will meet us at the new location. Don't worry, we won't be underfoot."

"*We* won't be underfoot?" I asked. "Laken, you want to do a fashion show in five days. I don't have time to deal with a designer. There's still an entire store to move and organize."

"Relax," she said. "You won't even know he's here."

"Right. Famous last words."

My sister groaned. "I know I said that when I found Sammy, but he's a dog. How was I supposed to know he'd grow to be the size of a small horse?"

"By talking to your boyfriend the vet and looking at his paws. Those things are nearly as big as my hands." I glanced inside to where Andy was showing Brad where I wanted the spotlights installed. "I have to go. Andy and Brad are taking over. At least they're doing a better job fixing this place than I am."

"You're doing a great job," Laken said. "It'll look amazing once the floors are done."

I smiled. "They'll be so shiny and smooth we'll be able to dance on them."

"Or bowl."

"You haven't bowled since we were kids. It took two of us to roll Grandpa's favorite ball across Grandma Sadie's hardwood floors, and she nearly killed us both. I'll see you later."

She spoke fast before I hung up, "I'll make pasta primavera for dinner tonight."

That caught me off guard. She was buttering me up with my favorite meal. "Don't you have a date tonight?"

"Cameron had to go to Portland to see his parents."

I raised my eyebrows. "And you didn't go with him?"

"There was a family emergency, and he didn't want me to feel out of place." There was a catch in my sister's voice as though she was ready to burst into tears.

After all of Emery's lies, she'd become better at listening to her gut instincts. My instincts, however, said Cameron was no player. The man had definite quirks though.

"Gotta go," I told her.

I wasn't always a horrible sister, but Laken's pity parties could drown an Olympic swimmer. Sink a canoe. That sort of thing. Besides, who was I to turn down her amazing pasta?

Andy tossed me a can of wax. With a groan, I got back on my hands and knees to prep the floors the old-fashioned way. Wax in a thin layer that Brad could polish and smooth to a shine with the buffer.

Once that was done and everything put away, I tried to stretch out a kink in my back with every muscle aching.

"I know how you feel," Andy told me, rubbing one of his bulging biceps.

Then he pulled me into a hug and lifted me off the wraparound porch. My back let out a pop, which helped.

"Thanks," I said, as Brad started his truck and honked.

Andy kissed my forehead. "Get some rest. We have a long week ahead."

"You know I don't expect you to help every single day, right?"

"Too bad. That's my plan." He grinned, then planted a soft kiss on my lips. Rather than wait for me to respond, he left.

Shuffling home, all I wanted was a nap, pasta, and a cold shower. Until I discovered I'd missed three more texts from Jonathan and was ready to toss my phone in the ocean.

I kept my mind occupied with something besides renovations, ex-boyfriends, and fashion designers. Thinking about Andy and that brief, soft kiss did nothing to help.

Lucky for me, my sister had the perfect Sunday afternoon cure. A pint of ice cream, a glass of wine, and an afternoon of romantic comedies while my muscles twitched. I set my phone face down on the table, then cuddled up with my heating pad to watch a couple sappy movies.

Chapter Two

Monday morning, I was greeted by a ding and a text saying, *"Call me when you get up."*

I barely had enough time to delete that and the three next texts from Jonathan before my sister hustled me out the front door while I ate a handful of granola for breakfast. She left Sammy at home in his crate, so he wouldn't be underfoot when our shipment arrived.

My phone dinged again as we opened the front door. *"Where are you?"*

Just as I went to block Jonathan, there was a rumble outside as the truck filled with fixtures from Rodeo Drive pulled up to the curb. I was impressed. Either they took turns driving all night or they'd stayed in a nearby motel and got up early.

I'd have to take care of my annoying ex-boyfriend later.

The driver reeked of cigarette smoke and beef jerky. His two assistants, one short and stocky and the other about fifteen and cranky, helped move the furnishings inside. Six white and chrome display cases with glass tops. Two shorter, upright, glass-front cabinets filled with flat velvet cases. A tall glass cabinet complete with a fully dressed mannequin packed with several yards of bubble wrap. All twenty black plastic mannequins stood in stark contrast to the white furniture and yellow walls.

Thankfully, the men also helped to put felt pads on the feet of each case, so Laken and I could slide them around the room without scratching the polished floors. We were careful to keep everything away from the freshly painted walls.

Once the movers left, I studied the mannequins and muttered, "It's an alien invasion."

Ten wide-shouldered, narrow-hipped plastic men and ten thin, less than curvy women took up more space than either of us expected. They also sent goosebumps up my arms. We needed to figure out what to do with them before they scared anyone else.

"Think of how many more outfits we can display," Laken gushed as she tore bubble wrap out of the glass cabinet. "They'll make it easier to show those beaded gowns and tailored suits."

"That's true." As I approached the upright glass cabinet, I cringed. The mannequin inside wore a lace and feather ensemble that reminded me of someone in the Seattle Pride Parade. She was garish and colorful. I kind of liked her, especially since she was the only mannequin with a detailed face. Someone had made her up to look like Greta Garbo in *Mata Hari*, complete with the bejeweled headpiece.

"This place looks great." Laken strolled through the showroom then spun around. "Sage, you're a genius. I had no idea you had so much interior design talent."

"Obviously not since you went and hired Sebastian. What do you want now?" I bumped into one of the mannequins.

Two of them teetered before they collided with the others, then began to fall like dominoes. They each leaned into each other until Laken lunged to grab one in the middle to stop their momentum. We hurried to straighten them.

"I'm sorry, Sage. I know it was one of those decisions I'll regret, but it's too late now. He'll be here in a few hours."

I folded my arms across my chest. "Why don't I go back to the old store to do some packing before I wreck anything? You can help your designer friend here."

"This is your shop," Laken said. "You should be the one to explain your vision."

"I don't have to explain anything to some guy I don't even know."

"At least help me fill him in on our plans for the fashion show," she pleaded.

"What plans?" I asked, letting out a frustrated laugh. "This whole fashion show was your idea. Besides, he probably knows more than I do already. Why don't you focus on that while you figure out how to set thing up in here? Oh, Gill's asking Enid about doing a free ad in the newspaper to invite all of Glitter Bay to check us out."

My sister huffed. "In the meantime, you're jumping ship."

"No. I'm packing up the old store, so we can move things here before my lease ends." I frowned. "Do you mind hanging out here today? Andy's friend Brad is going to drop by this afternoon. The two of them had some ideas to upgrade the lighting. Maybe Brad can help you figure out how to create a runway."

"You didn't ask him yesterday?" she asked, raising her eyebrows.

"We were a bit busy doing the floors." I texted Brad to let him know we'd received the furnishings, and he was safe to come by in the afternoon.

Unless Laken's designer friend became an issue.

"Sage, don't be like this," Laken told me. "We still have time before Sebastian gets here. Let's figure out where to put things. I could also use your input about the fashion show."

My shoulders sagged. "Okay. Maybe we should see what's in those cabinets before he gets here. I hope he's not trying to pawn any crap off on us. We barely have storage space for the stuff we already have."

"Sebastian wouldn't—"

"Look around. That's exactly what he's done." I waved toward the alien army.

Inside Mata Hari's case, we discovered a small yellow envelope taped to the glass that contained several keys along with a handwritten note. I handed the note to my sister while I figured out which key unlocked what. The same key unlocked every cabinet.

"That's strange." I set the keys on top of the front counter, then opened the door to reveal dozens of black velvet jewelry boxes.

"What are those?" Laken asked.

"You tell me. What does his note say?"

"Just that he'll see us soon." She reached for one of the boxes.

When she opened it, we both gasped at the sparkling diamond and citrine necklace inside.

I stood and took a couple steps back. "Please don't tell me those stones are real. I don't want to be part of some jewelry smuggling ring. There's no way I can afford the insurance to sell real jewels."

My sister lifted the necklace out of the box, then took it to the window for better light. "It's a convincing fake."

I blew out a relieved breath as she opened more boxes. Worry lines deepened in her face.

"I don't remember these listed on the invoice."

"He'd better not charge us after the fact." I snorted with my hands on my hips.

"We should keep them locked in the cabinet until we can sort this out." Laken held out a large, square box. "Wow."

I peered around her and asked, "Are those gold coins?"

My sister shrugged. "Decorations. He's a designer. Maybe they're for his new line."

"Why send them here if he'll need them?"

Mata Hari must be his inspiration. The coins weren't as heavy as I expected. They were thin, like aluminum, and each had a head on one side that resembled an alien mannequin with various flowers on the other. I returned the box to the cabinet with the necklaces.

She locked the cabinet. "Let's tuck them away until I can talk to Sebastian face to face."

"He'll definitely want those back."

The front door opened. Before we could turn around, a man gasped and wailed, "That is the most hideous shade of yellow I have ever seen."

I bit my lip. Hard.

The man in the doorway was slim, but of average height. He wore a short, black Liza Minelli wig and had pasty skin that, judging from his sharp incisors, hadn't seen sunlight since the early 1500s. His pointy face reminded me of a hairless gerbil. He wore a loose, white shirt, a pair of tailored, knee-length pants, and bright yellow, three-inch heels covered with sequins. His lips were pinker than my sister's cheeks. The only consolation was that his handbag matched his shoes.

"Oh, dear." The figure who strolled in behind him was taller and wore hot pink, tailored pants. His broad shoulders and hint of a belly stretched his yellow dress shirt to its limits. His fingernails resembled short daggers painted the same hot pink as his pants. He wore a platinum, bobbed wig and his jawline bore the hint of a five o'clock shadow.

Laken cleared her throat. "Sebastian. You're early."

"No way. Seriously?" I gawked.

It was a good thing the furniture was already in place. From the waif-like look of Sebastian, we would've had to move everything on our own if we'd waited for his help. His sidekick would've worried about breaking a nail.

"What are you talking about, darling?" Sebastian asked. "We said noon. I'm here at noon. Good thing, too. This place is a complete disaster."

"The only disaster is your furniture," I grumbled.

"It's already noon?" Laken stepped between us. "No wonder I'm hungry."

Sebastian's sidekick nodded. "Me, too."

"Hungry?" Sebastian handed his handbag to the man with the pink nails before he strutted closer to give my sister air kisses. "Darling, Laken, you're a model. Hunger is a perpetual state of being."

"I'm a former model. I eat real food now," she reminded him.

"Tell me why you would want to live in an awful place like this? You haven't lost your looks, but have you lost your valuable senses?"

I cleared my throat which probably sounded like a growl.

Laken's face reddened. "Sebastian Hayward the Third, this is my sister, Sage Miller. She not only owns this shop, but she's spent days painting and polishing it. I'm just the hired help."

Yeah, the hired help who chose the Buttercream paint to brighten the walls. With a huff, I held out a dusty hand to Sebastian Hayward the Third and lied through my teeth. "Pleasure to meet you. Laken's told me great things about you."

"Oh, really?" He raised his thin, perfectly shaped eyebrows as he studied me. "The dear girl never had anything nice to say about me before."

"Now there's a two-way street," my sister muttered.

"You begged for my help, darling, don't ever forget that." Sebastian pointed out. He glanced over his shoulder, then pointed with his thumb. "This is my protégé, Hamlet."

I tried not to smirk. "Hamlet?"

"Actually, I—," the platinum blond started to speak, but Sebastian silenced him with a look that made us all shudder.

"Hi, Hamlet, nice to meet you," Laken said. "What happened to that other guy you worked with? Michael, wasn't it?"

Sebastian waved his hand. "Mishel grew woefully tiresome. I tried to mold him into the best version of a fashion designer that I could, but he rebelled at every step. Finally, he left my employ to strike out on his own. I'm happy to report that he failed miserably."

My sister grinned in amusement. "That's odd. I heard his new designs are amazing. His latest line was picked up by a high-end department store."

"Don't do that, darling." He punched a clenched hand to his hip.

"Do what? Be right?"

That seemed like a good time for me to speak up, "Thank you for selling us the display cabinets and mannequins. Laken says you're renovating your shop on Rodeo Drive."

Hamlet cringed and took a step back which seemed like an odd reaction.

"I am recreating everything from the roof down." Sebastian waved a hand as he strolled to inspect Mata Hari before looking directly at Hamlet. "Everything. My last ungrateful protégé not only took my best designs, but most of my loyal customers as well. It was horrifying. I need a fresh start to regain my mojo."

My sister folded her arms across her chest. "That's not the way I heard it."

Sebastian flicked his hand toward her. "No matter. We are here to discuss this eyesore. So, about this fashion show. It seems I have arrived in time to avert an epic disaster."

I glared at my sister. How did this creepy little gerbil know all about the fashion show when I just found out yesterday?

He walked between Laken and I, stopped, then huffed. "If you want my honest opinion, I suggest you burn this place down and start over."

"Sebastian," Laken warned.

I chuckled. "By Friday?"

"Sage." She turned to me.

"It was a joke, darling. We must be realistic here." He shot her a scowl. "Since total demolition is out of the question—for now—we need to hire a crew to repaint the walls electric blue, then—"

"The walls are fine. No one's touching them."

His impossibly violet eyes grew wide. "Pardon me."

I spoke slowly to make sure he could understand. "We are not painting the walls."

Sebastian puffed out his chest before strutting through the store. "Young lady, are you an internationally renowned designer? Were you paid to come to some hole in the wall town to give your rather golden advice on this dump?"

"I'm not the one paying you," I told him. "I don't even know who you are."

Hamlet gasped as Sebastian's thin eyebrows twitched like gerbil whiskers.

Laken put an arm around me and whispered, "Please just let him do what he does best. Once he's gone, we can do things your way."

"Six weeks from now, you mean?" I asked.

"Sage, calm down."

I shrugged off her arm. "I don't have to listen to this, clown. I'm going to finish packing."

My sister's mouth fell open. "What am I supposed to do?"

"Take notes," I told her as I headed toward the kitchen to grab my things. "Then burn them."

Sebastian tutted after me. "Young lady, you are being childish. Did you really think I would show up and fall in love at first sight with this monstrosity? Honestly. The natural light is lovely, but you need more track lighting and spotlights. There should also be a more dramatic color on the walls. By the way, I also want to see the designs Laken is going to model."

I stopped so fast my shoes squeaked on the freshly waxed floors. "Laken?"

Sebastian grimaced. "Well, who else did you have in mind? Certainly not her small-town sister who looks like she works in a horse barn instead of a high-end design boutique."

"This is a vintage shop, not a designer boutique," I announced, glaring at Sebastian Hayward the Third before I turned to Laken. "Brad will be here at one to install the lighting. You need to turn off the breakers in the kitchen. I'm sure he can show you how. He knows where everything goes. You also need to deal with the gerbil."

"What gerbil?" She frowned.

I motioned to Sebastian.

Hamlet flashed a small smile before he caught Sebastian's angry gaze. He was probably glad I didn't call him a rodent.

"Where do you think you're going, young lady?" Sebastian snapped.

"To pack up the old store. Deal with my sister." I tossed my long red hair, then pushed open the kitchen door.

"As I was saying..." Sebastian's voice was muffled as the door closed behind me.

"A horse barn. Who does that pompous gerbil think he is?" I ranted as I set my phone on the counter.

I tried to scrub the ick off my hands from meeting him, but what I needed was a hot shower. As I stormed out of the building via the rear exit, my stomach growled. The last thing I wanted was to go back inside to raid the fridge. I jogged home with too much pent-up energy to walk.

While I checked in on the animals, I made a veggie wrap and grabbed an apple. I managed to coax Sammy into his crate before returning to the original Vintage Sage. Turning the sign to open was a reflex. With any luck, I could sell a few items and have less to move.

A wave of emotion washed over me. I paused to blow out a long breath.

Setting up the original Vintage Sage was less lonely than dismantling it. Back then, I had a partner to split the work and the bills with. Delia Reeves and I met at yoga after I moved to Glitter Bay from Seattle. Back then, my life was kind of like a Hallmark movie. I was tired of big city life, had broken up with my high school sweetheart, and needed a fresh start. While I'd wandered from shop to shop looking for work, I fell in love with what would become my new store.

Cue the new best friend and business opportunity...

"What was I thinking?"

The neighborhood was thriving when Delia and I had first opened Vintage Sage. After the man from the antique shop next door died, the owner of the bookstore across the street moved to another town. Tourists stuck to the main street and the big box stores on the outskirts rather than take a stroll in the rundown part of town.

I gazed out the large front window at the silent street. This time next week, my view would be the Pacific Ocean. My rent would remain the same, thanks to my sister, but my bills had already tripled. Again, thanks to my sister.

"I'm so in over my head," I whispered.

Several garments still hung on racks around the quiet store. I bundled the outfits we'd discussed for the fashion show and hoped Laken had reached out to her list of potential models. If no one accepted, she and I would end up not only organizing but strutting our stuff down the runway, which I dreaded. I was a behind the scenes girl. Definitely, not runway material.

Although if Sebastian had his way, there'd only be one model anyway. Laken. He'd even asked to see which designs she'd model. I paused near the computer and held the tip of my thumb between my front teeth while I thought. Packing could wait. I dove into research on Sebastian Hayward the Third and the House of Hayward, which I should've done last night.

The House of Hayward boasted a bright, airy showroom adorned with the same chrome, white, and glass cabinets that now resided in Vintage Sage. Some contained jewelry. Others, bits of fabric. Scarves, maybe? Ten of the plastic alien mannequins stood around the showroom. I noticed the rest tucked in other rooms. It seemed the House of Hayward was a large operation. was still amid renovations. There were no updated photos. The display cases were the exact same ones that currently sat in Vintage Sage.

I clicked on the Events page seconds before the front door opened.

"Ah, this is where you're hiding." Andy strolled inside and handed me a paper cup. The scent of peppermint tea mingled with soap from his post workout shower.

"Hey. What are you up to?" I asked, closing the website as my heart skipped a beat.

"Didn't you get my messages? I've been texting you all afternoon."

"No, I…" I patted all six pockets of my cargo pants. "Uh-oh. I must've left my phone at the new place. I left in kind of a hurry."

"That's what Laken said when I stopped by." He leaned against the counter in front of me. "Are you okay?"

"That designer Laken hired to help us is annoying."

He grimaced as though unconvinced. "Yeah. Brad sent a text saying something similar. The guy's assistant hit on him the entire time he was installing your lights."

I chuckled. "Poor guy. I can't see Hamlet being his type."

"Hamlet, huh? No kidding." Andy nodded toward the door. "My truck's out front. I thought you might need help bringing things over."

"Depends. Is Sebastian still there?"

"Didn't Laken pay for his services for six weeks?" he asked.

I leaned over and thumped my head on the glass-topped counter. "Ugh. Thanks for reminding me. That guy is so obnoxious. I don't know how I'll survive six weeks with him around."

Andy chuckled as he reached for a box. "I'd run interference, but I can't take six weeks off. Why don't we haul a truck load to the new store, then grab a pizza and hang out for a while?"

That sounded like a good distraction. I sighed. "The boxes in the change rooms are done. I'll put the more delicate items in garment bags."

"Excellent," Andy said, opening the curtain covering the farthest change room. He took a step back. "You have been busy. I'll load the truck while you take care of the rest."

As I focused on bagging beaded gowns and bespoke suits, I pushed—no, shoved—Sebastian and his sidekick out of my mind. Andy emptied the change room before he helped me fill several more boxes. Some items had probably been here since me and Delia opened the store five years ago. My sister had pointed out several times that I needed a better system for keeping track of inventory.

"Did a mouse die in one of these boxes?" Andy asked fanning his nose. "Something smells funky."

I sniffed. "Mothballs. I've asked the woman who dropped it off to pick it up twice now. I have half a mind to leave it at the curb."

We locked the front door at five o'clock sharp, then drove toward the new location. I fell in love with the former Sweet Eden Tea House building the first time I saw it. The bright white veranda and weathered yellow exterior made me happy, especially since it overlooked the Pacific Ocean. Now I'd get to work there every day.

As I unlocked the front door, I was grateful to be met by silence. Andy hauled in boxes while I hung the bagged items to steam tomorrow.

My phone was right by the kitchen sink where I'd set it when I'd scrubbed my hands. I'd missed three texts and two calls from Jonathan, plus several messages from both Andy and Laken. I shoved my phone into my pocket, then went to help Andy empty the truck. My phone dinged three more times.

Andy placed a hand on my shoulder once we were done. "Laken felt bad you and Sebastian didn't hit it off."

"Hit it off?" I asked, raising my eyebrows. "The guy was rude and insulting. I don't care if he doesn't like the color of the walls."

"He said that?"

"Yeah. His shop was the exact same color. Or that he said I should work in a horse barn instead of a boutique of any sort."

He shrugged. "Sage, honey, you have an amazing location, plus you get to work with Laken, who he thinks of as his muse. Once this place is set up the way you want it, Vintage Sage will be just as beautiful as any shop on Rodeo Drive.

"I suppose so."

Andy pulled me into a bear hug. "I know so. Don't let the guy get under your skin. Personally, I like the color. Those mannequins scare the crap out of me though."

"Me, too." I flashed a smile. "Thanks. Let's go get that pizza. I'm starving."

"Did you find your phone?" he asked. "I don't want to text you goodnight later, then lay there all night wondering why you're not speaking to me."

I fished it out of my pocket. "It was on the kitchen counter. I washed my hands before I left. Sebastian had me so wound up I forgot it."

We made sure both entrances were locked before leaving to pick up a couple of pizzas. Heaps of meat for Andy, and vegetarian for me. Now that we'd moved a lot of the merchandise, I felt a thousand times better. Relaxed and smiling, I opened the front door of my house.

"Who decorated this place, Frankenstein's monster?" Sebastian's voice rang down the hall from my office. "There are no clean lines and far too much texture. It looks like a blind old cat lady lives here."

"What the...?" I started, then shouted, "What's he doing in my house?"

"Breathe, Sage," Andy whispered and grasped my elbow while Sammy hopped at my leg for attention, or a quick escape route. "Let's sit outside and pretend he's not here."

My cat, Muumuu, wove between my legs until her fur stood upright from rubbing against my pantlegs. I was torn between avoiding Sebastian Hayward the Third, and physically throwing him out of my house. To preserve my waning peace and sanity, I followed Andy. We each grabbed a can of sparkling water on our way through the kitchen to the deck.

Sammy and Muumuu raced to join us. The dog lay with his head on one of my feet until we opened the pizza box. The cat settled in the chair beside me sniffing before she sneezed. She seemed to scowl at Sammy, who begged for melted cheese and thin crust.

My stomach growled as I reached for a slice. "I didn't realize how hungry I was."

"You worked hard today," Andy reminded me. "What's left on the to-do list?"

I savored a mouthful before Muumuu tapped my arm for a bit of cheese. "We need to finish moving everything, then get set up for the fashion show Friday, which is Laken's job. Heaven knows what'll happen with Sebastian here."

Andy nodded. "And I'm on days until Friday, so I can only help once I get off shift, if I'm not ready to collapse."

When the patio door slid open, we all jumped.

"Pizza?" Sebastian's squeal nearly pierced my eardrum. "You play host to an internationally renowned fashion designer, and you serve him pizza?"

Sammy growled.

I stared. "What makes you think you're getting our dinner?"

Hamlet peered over Sebastian's shoulder to ogle our food.

Laken herded Sebastian and protégé back inside the house before she paused in the doorway. "Sorry about that. Enjoy your dinner. We'll be back later."

"Why are those vermin in my house?" I asked, marching toward her.

Laken batted her eyelashes. "They need a place to stay, so—"

"No." I shook my head so hard I grew dizzy. "Not a chance. Forget it. It's bad enough that I'm expected to work with him, I do not want that gerbil in my house. Get him a box and put him in the backyard."

Andy stifled a chuckle.

My sister placed her hands on my shoulders. "Come on, Sage. It's only a couple weeks."

"Six weeks. Isn't that what you agreed to?"

"Yes." My sister paled.

My nostrils flared. "Then you'd better find somewhere for them to stay because there's no way I can both work and live with that man. I'd probably strangle him."

Laken nodded. "Fine. I get it. I'll call around. Worst case, they'll be here one night."

"And where will they sleep?" I asked. "You live in my guest room."

"I'll figure it out." She hugged me. "They can sleep on the hide-a-bed tonight."

"I don't have a hide-a-bed. I don't even have an air mattress, and those two self-important clowns are not getting my bedroom."

"Good point." My sister glanced at Sammy. "I'll take Sebastian and Hamlet out for dinner, then find them somewhere to stay. Can you look after Sammy?"

Andy attacked another slice of pizza. "Sure. We can take him for a walk before I go. I have to work early tomorrow anyway."

Still on edge, I returned to my chair. "I could use a good walk. I have a wee bit of frustration to burn off."

"Didn't notice." Andy grinned.

I threw a wadded napkin at him. "Sorry about all that."

"I'd offer my place, but my roommate snores."

"You don't have a roommate," I said.

Andy shrugged. "Oh, then it must be me."

After a couple more slices of pizza, we cleaned up before I snapped Sammy's leash onto his collar. He strained against the leash before we got close to the beach. The second I unhooked his leash he took off running. Andy and I chased him, then we played fetch with a large stick as the sun went down.

On the walk back to the house, Andy kept one arm across my shoulder. "It'll all work out, Sage. Just don't let that clown get to you."

"That's easy for you to say. Once we finish the move, I won't have anywhere to hide." I unlocked the front door, happy to hear nothing but a meow as Muumuu greeted us.

"Except in Laken's apartment."

"That's not a bad idea," I told him as Muumuu and Sammy butted heads. "Or I could turn that pantry into a panic room for whenever Sebastian's in town."

Andy kissed the top of my nose. "Now you're thinking. Take a better look tomorrow. Maybe we can figure out some options. At least, Laken's getting rid of them for tonight, so I won't have to bail you out or anything."

"There is that."

Andy cleared his throat as I turned to go inside. "I guess I'll see you tomorrow night then."

I smiled, then gave him a hug. "Thank you for your help."

"Aww, shucks, ma'am. It's all in a days' work." He pulled me close and kissed my forehead. My breath stuck in my throat, and I wanted…

"Have a good night," I whispered, then went inside and locked the door behind me. Leaning against it, I blew out a long breath. "What a weird day."

When Sammy headed for his water bowl, I poured a small glass of wine and grabbed a slice of leftover pizza. We curled up together on the couch and I turned on the television while I tried to shake off the day. Tomorrow had to be better.

Didn't it?

Chapter Three

As I approached the new Vintage Sage Boutique Tuesday morning, I clutched the rose quartz pendant wrapped in brass wire that hung around my neck. I still couldn't believe how lucky I was to have such a great location. Not to mention a sister who supported me enough to fulfill my dreams. The only drawback was she'd brought in that no-it-all creep from Rodeo Drive and his odd sidekick, which gave me nightmares most of the night. I needed time to wake up and think.

My first mission was to unpack the boxes we delivered yesterday.

Second, was to avoid Sebastian, who hadn't returned to the house with Laken. Since the gerbil's whereabouts were currently unknown—to me anyway—I was a titch on edge.

When I walked into the building, my gaze fell on Mata Hari. Her elaborate dress and makeup made the rest of the mannequins look even more alien. It didn't help that someone had lined the army of mannequins along the far wall beneath the new spotlights. They looked like spies waiting for a firing squad. All they needed were blindfolds. And clothes.

I itched to find a paintball gun. Although I didn't look forward to dressing them, I hoped clothing would make them appear less...alien.

Today was a new day. Taking a deep breath, I vowed to give Sebastian Hayward the Third a second chance.

Since the store was quiet, I hummed as I slid a beaded white cocktail dress off a hanger, then tugged it on a mannequin. I partnered her with a male in a gray, pinstriped bespoke suit. The fedora that matched the suit didn't sit well on the model's oblong head. It slid forward to cover where his eyes should be, which wasn't a bad thing. It made him look like an old-time gangster. Just like that I had my own Bonnie and Clyde. All I needed to finish off their look was to find the felt hat I had in a box at the old store.

"Ooh, those two look good together," Laken said, as she strolled in carrying a cardboard tray with two cups. "Do you need a hand, or should I focus on the show?"

She wore a sleek, black pantsuit I hadn't seen her wear since she first moved to town. Her pantsuit was in sharp contrast to my faded denim coveralls and tank top. That's probably why Sebastian thought I was better suited to a horse barn.

"Since you're the fashionista, you should focus on the show, just tell me what you need."

"You know I will. I bought you green tea as bribery. Oh, and I made a list of everything we have to do before Friday," my sister said, then sniffed. "What's that weird smell?"

"Did you bring Sammy?" I asked, unable to smell anything unusual.

"He's in his crate. Sebastian's allergic to animals." She sniffed the air again. "It smells musty."

"Mothballs." I pointed to the box I'd set aside last night.

Laken covered her nose as she backed away. "Ew. Mothballs are only good for keeping away moths, dogs, and fashion models."

"Multipurpose. I'll keep that in mind. Do they work on designers, too?"

"Not funny. What's in there that's worth the smell?" she asked, keeping her distance.

As I opened the flaps, my eyes watered as the scent overpowered me. "Some dresses Enid dropped off. I told her to pick them up, but she hasn't called back."

My sister removed the tea bag from a cup and dropped it in the trash. "I'll call her. She'll jump at the chance to interview a world-renowned fashion designer. It would also give us some free publicity."

"Just don't forget about her box of mothballs," I reminded her, reaching for my tea. "Where did you manage to hide Sebastian and his sidekick?"

"I ditched them and about ten suitcases at one of the hotels on the outskirts of town," she said. "Sebastian was thrilled with the ocean view but threw a tantrum when they wouldn't repaint his room before he'd set foot in it."

"There's a surprise."

My sister groaned. "I get it. You're mad at me for inviting Sebastian here to help."

"Which I never asked you to do."

"But I paid big money for him to teach us some tricks of the trade, so please promise to listen to what he says."

I slid a couple hangers along the nearby rack. "It's too early for a guilt trip. I get that you're trying to help, and I appreciate the gesture."

"But?" she asked.

"I promise to listen, but I don't have to like him. Did you have the same chat with Sebastian?"

Laken averted her gaze.

"Of course you didn't. He can say whatever he wants, but I need to make nice. If your buddy comes back in here like a bull in a china shop, I'm leaving. I have enough to take care of."

"I'll take notes." She raised her cup. "I doubt you'll have to worry about him for this morning though. He rarely gets out of bed until early afternoon."

"Lucky me." I reached for an emerald satin gown to adorn the next mannequin. For full effect, I planned to situate the mannequin, so the gown was the first thing customers saw when they walked inside. Now that we had those necklaces, I could add some bling.

"Ooh. I forgot about that one. It's gorgeous," Laken gushed, as she reached over my shoulder. "Can I try it on? I'd love to wear it in the fashion show."

"Knock yourself out."

Her eyes lit up. "I get to be the first person to use the new change rooms. Woohoo!"

"Andy was first since he built them."

"I know, but he was fully dressed." My sister paused to glance back at me. "He was fully dressed, wasn't he?"

"Yes, he was." I chose a different outfit.

"Why don't you two just admit you're dating? You spend more time together than me and Cameron."

"We agreed we're not dating. Neither of us is ready for another relationship yet." I slid the smoky blue dress with silver overlay off its hanger.

"And yet you're together constantly."

"So?"

My sister poked her head out of the change room. "Don't get me wrong. Andy's a good guy, Sage. He's ten times better than Jonathan, and a thousand times better than—"

"Don't say it," I snapped. "I'm bad at picking men. I get it."

She fell silent. The only sounds to come from the change room were grunts and moans as she climbed out of her pantsuit and into the gown.

"Don't forget the hat that goes with that blue dress," Laken sang as she emerged from the change room and turned a couple circles, so I could get the full effect of the skirt on the taffeta gown. It looked like something Scarlet O'Hara might've worn in *Gone with the Wind*.

Day to day, it was easy to forget my sister had once modeled all over the world. Seeing her wearing that green gown with her bobbed red hair hugging her glowing face brought it all back in a rush. She was the incredibly beautiful Laken Miller. I was her frumpy sister.

"Well, fiddle-dee-dee, Miss Miller, you look stunning." I walked toward her slowly. "All we need is to do your hair and add a little sparkle."

"Merciful heavens!" Sebastian shrieked. His unmistakable voice made my skin crawl with goosebumps. "Get that hideous thing off your luscious body, woman."

I avoided Sebastian's gaze. "Oh joy. The gerbil's back."

Today he wore a black pageboy wig and carried a rust-colored handbag that went with his tan, linen slacks and matching rust shoes. The collar on his loose white blouse was open to reveal a peach chemise. The guy dressed better than I did.

"Shush," Laken whispered as she nudged me. "Stop calling him a gerbil."

"He has a pointy face and a bad attitude. It's better than calling him a rat." I huffed.

Was I wrong to adore the emerald dress? It was a vintage ball gown, after all, and this was a vintage store. Sebastian seemed to have missed that fact.

Laken shot him a scowl. "This gown is gorgeous, and I plan to wear it for the fashion show."

"Darling, whatever did you do to deserve such punishment? Hamlet, put that thing in a barrel and burn it," he commanded.

Hamlet's mouth opened as though he was about to argue but didn't dare.

"Don't you touch it." I held up my index finger as I stepped between Laken and Sebastian. "That gown is my merchandise and it's not up to you to decide what I do with it."

Sebastian adjusted his Hermes scarf then pushed a strand of black hair over his left ear. "Dear girl, why did you bother to hire me? I can never get a word in edgewise."

"I didn't hire you. Laken did. I don't even know who you are."

"Ooch." Hamlet gasped, then covered his hot pink lips.

Was he hiding a smile, or aghast that I was so clueless? It was hard to tell, especially since his hand wasn't exactly tiny and dainty. I'd seen the floaty blue dress he wore before. My sister had one just like it. The expensive, designer version. From the stitching, I knew Hamlet's dress was a knock off. We had a black one just like it in a box. I narrowed my eyes to estimate his size.

He blushed when he noticed me staring and adjusted the strap of his hot pink purse.

As I busied myself straightening the lacy blue dress on the mannequin, I smiled in amusement.

"I thought you might sleep late after the long drive yesterday," my sister said. There was disappointment in her voice as she returned to the change room.

Sebastian shook his head. "Honestly, the mattress in that so-called luxury hotel room was like sleeping on a bed of granite. Besides, we have a great deal of work to do, my darlings. This place either needs to be repainted immediately or—"

"—burned to the ground," I finished. "You said that yesterday and, no, it doesn't."

I resumed dressing the mannequin to keep my hands busy. Mostly, so I didn't throw anything at him.

"It also needs a salesgirl with basic social skills," he said.

That time, I faced him. "May I remind you that I'm not a salesgirl. I own this place."

He tapped his thin, pink lips. "Hm, that's interesting, considering Laken owns the building. I'm quite sure you work for her, not the other way around. Heaven knows you fall short of sharing her fashion sense let alone her common sense."

"Listen you..." Gerbil sat poised on the tip of my tongue as I took a deep breath. I was ready to explode but had no idea what to say that wouldn't provoke more of his condescension. This felt like a repeat of yesterday. Was the guy on drugs or simply living in his own warped world?

Laken handed me the gown. "Sebastian, let's go through the positive suggestions you had for Sage's store. Besides the paint. Which stays."

"Unless you want to paint it yourself with one of your wigs," I muttered as I carried the dress into the kitchen.

As I hooked the hanger on the rack we'd set aside for the fashion show, I recalled my vow to give the gerbil—a.k.a. Sebastian—a second chance. Things would go smoother if I kept my mouth shut. Less talking. More listening.

If I didn't blow my top first, that was.

I peered inside the small room that stretched beneath the stairs. Gill had used it as a pantry. It wouldn't make a good office unless we tore out the shelving. Even then only a desk two feet by two feet square would fit. It would make a great panic room if I needed to hide. All I'd need was a lock on the inside. Wishful thinking. The best idea would be to use it for extra stock, so our shelves didn't overflow. That was one suggestion Sebastian wouldn't offer.

Returning to the front, I caught Hamlet watching me. He turned away quickly, but not before I had a bad case of the heebie-jeebies. What was up with that guy? If Sebastian was like a gerbil, Hamlet acted more like a crab. Skittish, yet could likely cause serious harm if he wanted.

I checked my phone in case I'd missed a message from Andy. There were no texts at all. Not even from Jonathan.

Sebastian wandered through the store waving one hand as he spoke. "The lighting is horrible, the clothing outdated, and there is a severe lack of espresso." He paused and sniffed. "What is that smell? It's musty and horrid like something died. Quickly, someone fetch me an espresso to hide the smell.

"Forget it," I told him.

"Oh, and I find your salesgirl lacking in manners."

"You've mentioned that three times now," Laken said.

"And you still haven't done a thing about her."

"Why don't you tell us what you really think," I muttered, but didn't take his bait.

Nor did I—or anyone—rush to get him an espresso. I finished dressing the mannequin in the blue dress before I moved her to stand near the front window. I avoided Sebastian's vulture-like gaze as I returned for her male counterpart.

"Don't forget about the windows," Hamlet reminded him. He had a softer voice than I expected.

Laken and I exchanged glances before she frowned and asked, "What about the windows?"

Sebastian strolled toward the large windows and French doors which overlooked the ocean. He stopped next to the mannequin in blue. "The view is divine, darling, but you don't want people to window-shop. We need them to stroll inside filled with curiosity. To come in and discover the...uh..." He wrinkled his rodent-like nose. "Merchandise."

I liked this guy less every time he opened his mouth.

"Halloo," a woman in her mid-seventies called out as she burst through the door. She wore a hot pink tracksuit and blue running shoes with matching blue eyeshadow. A fashionista's nightmare.

"Hi, Enid," I flashed her a smile and was happy I hadn't left yet. If anyone could put Sebastian Hayward the Third in his place, it would be Enid Walsh, Glitter Bay's most infamous gossip columnist.

"One of your regular thrifters, I presume?" Sebastian asked, making a face.

Laken leaned her elbow on my shoulder. "How about that? Looks like I don't have to call Enid after all."

Enid peered over her red-framed glasses. "Oh, sweetheart, you are in the right place. Sage and Laken will help you find some descent clothes. They might even be able to donate those horrible things you're wearing to charity."

"This'll be good," my sister whispered.

Sebastian looked down at his double-stitched shirt and tailored slacks. "I will have you know these are Calvin Klein linen slacks and Gucci shoes."

"I see," Enid said as she patted his arm. "It was nice of those boys to give you their hand me downs."

I wanted to turn away before I burst into laughter.

Sebastian's face reddened. "Tell me this woman is not actually that stupid."

As I bit my lower lip, Laken leaned closer and whispered, "Enid's covered more fashion shows than Sebastian's ever been invited to."

Hamlet took a step forward. "I will have you know Sebastian Hayward is one of the top designers in California. He has created clothing for some extremely important people."

Enid's eyes brightened. "Oh really? Shouldn't he be in Paris or New York then?"

"Anywhere but here," I muttered.

Sebastian nodded. "Yes, I should."

"Then what are you doing in Glitter Bay?" she asked.

"Laken and I go way back," he said. "She begged me to come to this sleepy town to turn this horrid thrift shop into a thriving business."

"Horrid thrift shop?" I shouted.

My sister grasped my arm. "Down girl."

Enid brushed past Sebastian to hand me a round, plastic container. "Here, Sage. I thought you could serve these at the fashion show. They're vegan cookies. Just pop them in the fridge. How are the plans coming along?"

"Pretty good actually—," Laken started.

Sebastian cleared his throat. Loudly. "Pardon me, madam. How dare you prance in here and interrupt our meeting?"

"Oh, shush, little man. I'll just be a minute." Enid waved a hand as she approached Mata Hari in the glass case. "Ooh, what is this divine costume and where have I seen her before?"

Hamlet beamed as he took a couple steps toward her. "Oh, that's a replica of—"

Sebastian let out a squawk. "Is everyone in this awful place devoid of manners? Madame, you are not only rude, but you look like you were dressed by a hoard of drunken bag ladies."

Enid burst into laughter. "A hoard of drunken bag ladies? That's a great line. I'll have to use it in my blog."

I huffed as I broke out of Laken's grip. "Oh, that's it. I'm going to finish packing. You need to do something about him and his toxic ego."

Sebastian stared. "Do you mean there are more of these icky things in another location? I can only imagine what that one looks like if this is a step up."

"You've never heard of a vintage boutique, have you?" I asked.

"Yes," he hissed, "but I thought it was the punchline of a bad joke. Have you ever heard of Goodwill or arson?"

"Murder, maybe." I closed my eyes, too angry to count to ten. "I have better things to do than be insulted every five minutes."

Enid patted my shoulder. "Don't be upset, dear. He's like a parrot. All ruffled feathers and regurgitated chatter. Would you like company?"

"Only if you want to get put to work. I have packing to do."

"Not a chance. I'm on my way to do an interview." She turned to Laken. "Once you get that yappy little dude off his high horse, could you tell him I'd like an interview?"

"That yappy little dude has a name," Sebastian snarled. "I am Sebastian Hayward the Third from the House of Hayward in Hollywood and I don't give interviews to just anyone."

Hamlet folded his arms across his broad chest. "No, he does not."

"Who's that?" Enid cast me a sideways glance.

"Hamlet. His protégé." Before I left, I made sure I had my phone and keys in the pocket of my overalls. "Oh, Enid, can you take your box of dresses back? I'll be glad to take them on consignment, but only if you have them cleaned and lose the mothball scent."

Sebastian snorted. "Mothballs? Is that what the obnoxious stench is?"

I kept my thoughts to myself as Laken giggled.

"Sure, I'll pick them up after my interview. I'm meeting some kid on Front Street who found a tree fungus that looks like Elvis." She jerked her thumb toward Sebastian and said, "I'll interview this guy when I get back."

"Why, in my right mind, would I give you the pleasure of an interview?" Sebastian asked. "You've done nothing but insult me and attempt to poison me with mothballs."

"I suppose if you don't, I'll have to make things up," Enid said.

I shrugged. "She's done it before."

Hamlet tapped Sebastian's shoulder. "I'd do the interview if I were you. That woman scares the glitter out of me."

As I headed for the door, I agreed with Hamlet. Enid scared the glitter out of me too.

Sebastian turned on me with his violet eyes blazing. "Where do you think you're going? We have a show on Friday."

"And I still need to pack and move the rest of my merchandise before the landlord changes the locks. Laken will be here to put up with..." I flashed a fake smile. "To assist you."

I'd barely reached the sidewalk before Enid fell into step next to me. My first reaction was to groan, but I reigned it in and hoped she was on my side.

"Is your boyfriend at work today?" she asked.

"If you mean, Andy, he's at work, and he's not my boyfriend."

She smiled. "That's too bad. You and my son make an adorable couple. What do you know about that creepy little man?"

"Andy?" I stopped to stare.

"No, the arrogant one."

"Sebastian."

"That's the one." She hooked her arm in mine and forced me to continue walking. "Don't forget I'm a reporter, Sage, and my nose smells news."

Mine still smelled mothballs. "You're a gossip columnist. Your nose usually smells dirt."

"Same deal," she said with a shrug. "Tell me what you know about him."

This might be one of those times Enid's roving reporter skills came in handy. "His name is Sebastian Hayward the Third. He's a designer from Hollywood who owns a shop called House of Hayward. His sidekick's name is Hamlet. You'll have to ask Laken if you want any more than that. I just met them yesterday."

"Something about that guy rubs me the wrong way."

"Same here. Let me know what you find out."

"And what do I get in return?" she asked.

"Why do you need something in return? You're the one who wants to find out who he is. I just want him to go away."

She stared. "Well, you got me there. I'd love to model in that fashion show you girls are doing."

Ah-ha. There was her bargaining chip. "Talk to Laken. It's her show. I'm doing the grunt work."

"I'll let you know if I find anything juicy." Enid waved as she strode away.

I headed to the store not interested in hearing anything juicy about the creepy designer gerbil. My focus shifted to packing the rest of my merchandise, so we could move it when Andy finished work. Friday would arrive fast, and there was a lot to do.

Around four o'clock, Andy called to say there was a large accident half an hour outside Glitter Bay. If it was as bad as it sounded, he'd be at work until late. We wouldn't be able to finish moving tonight, but he promised to call as soon as he finished his shift.

When my stomach sank, I leaned on something for support. Our whole friendship thing was starting to feel more like a relationship thing. I texted Laken to give her the update, then mentioned that Enid wanted to model in the show.

She replied, *"I'll talk to her. S gave me a long to-do list. Ready to choke him. SYL."*

"See ya later." I knew exactly how she felt, which was why I'd left earlier.

By five o'clock, I looked like I'd used my t-shirt to dust every surface. In spite of my appearance, I itched to check on the new store. I needed to make sure Sebastian hadn't run amok and called in painters or did anything else I'd regret.

Dinner and a shower were next on my list.

Tired and coughing up dust bunnies, I texted my sister with my plans, then stuck my phone in my pocket. Maybe while I was there, I'd raid the fridge. Cooking was the last thing I felt like doing after packing all day.

I yawned, rubbing my eyes the entire way back to the new location until a small black sports car raced around the far side of the building. It barreled up the street past me then its tires squealed as it rounded the corner and nearly hit a red minivan.

No surprise there were more speeders in town than normal, it was mid-July and well into tourist season. Not the ideal time to move into a new shop, but who was I to argue? I forced my tired legs up the front steps, then reached for the doorknob.

One of the French doors stood ajar. A pane of glass lay shattered on the wood floor inside. Someone must've broken it to unlock the door. I peered through the gaping hole to the center of the room where the mannequins formed a circle.

"Like they weren't creepy enough before," I muttered. "Why can't Sebastian just leave things alone?"

Something else seemed out of place but I couldn't put my finger on what.

I was sure I heard the back gate squeak as I fumbled for my phone. "Laken?"

Who should I call first, my sister or the police?

A vehicle rumbled in the alley behind the store. Whatever I did, I needed to hurry.

I ducked around the side of the building and ran toward the courtyard while I called the police to report the break-in. While I didn't want to run into any burglars, I had to make sure my sister was okay.

The gate to the courtyard stood wide open, yet the back door of the building was closed. I hoped that meant whoever broke in was long gone. I used the hem of my shirt to open the door and let myself inside before I crept into the kitchen. My blood whooshed in my ears as I reached the swinging door between the kitchen and the store. I leaned my forearm against the wood and hoped it wouldn't squeak.

As I peered into the store, the only figures I spied were the twenty alien mannequins standing in a circle in the center of the room. Before I went farther, I glanced toward the door that led to Laken's upstairs apartment. Releasing the swinging door, I crossed the kitchen to jiggle the knob. It was still locked. If anyone was hiding upstairs, though, I could be in serious trouble.

Before I could check the pantry, someone shouted in the store, "Hello? It's the police. If there's anyone in here, come out slowly with your hands up."

"I'm here." I used my forearm to push the kitchen door wide again. This time I held my hands up near my shoulders as I bobbed to see the officer through the mannequin mob. "I'm Sage Miller, the one who called. Whoever broke in went out the back entrance. The gate was open, but the door was closed."

The officer nodded but didn't come any closer. "You didn't hear anyone break the window?"

As I walked toward him, I rubbed my jaw. This wasn't how my day was supposed to go. "I just got here. I've been at the other store all afternoon packing merchandise."

"Fair enough. Did you notice anything missing?" he asked.

"I haven't looked. I called you as soon as I saw the broken glass and made sure not to touch the front door." I stopped when I caught a glimpse of something between the mannequins.

The tall, glass case lay flat in the middle of the circle. The Mata Hari mannequin, still dressed in feathers and frills, lay face down on the floor as though someone had yanked her out of her case and threw her aside. Her headdress and wig lay several feet away.

Another figure lay inside the glass case.

As I wandered closer for a better look, I gasped, "Oh, no."

The officer joined me. "That's not good. Do you know her?"

My gaze landed on a white shirt, tan slacks, and a reddish Hermès scarf. "Him. That's Sebastian Hayward the Third."

Sebastian's sightless eyes stared up at the ceiling, his face ashen except for blood speckles from the wound in his chest. The once colorful scarf was soaked red.

"I take it he wasn't like this when you saw him last," the officer said, reaching for the mic on his shoulder.

"Nope. He was very much alive and obnoxious when I left."

"Not a good way to end the day," he mumbled.

I released a shaky breath and focused on taking one breath at a time. This was no time to hyperventilate. "I don't think this was how he thought his day would go either."

"You need to step outside, Miss. This is a crime scene. I need to call for backup."

"Good idea. I need to call my sister. She owns the building."

Chapter Four

❧❧❧❦❦❦

"Sage? Are you okay?" Laken asked, sitting next to me on the front step of the new Vintage Sage. She wrapped her arms around my shoulders. "What happened?"

I tried to keep calm as what I saw inside the store—MY store—sunk in. "I dropped by to check on things and Sebastian..."

"Oh no. What did he do this time?"

My body shook as I told her, "He's dead, Laken."

She cradled my face in her hands. "Dead? Are you sure?"

I shivered as her face became a blur through my tears. "I swear it wasn't me. I didn't do it." "Someone shot him in the chest."

"I know you didn't. You couldn't."

"Do you know where Hamlet is?" I asked, wiping my hand across my face.

"He grabbed a cab to the hotel before I left to pick up dinner."

Asking questions seemed to help quell my shock. For now. "How long you were gone?"

Laken shrugged. "Probably fifteen or twenty minutes. Something happened between them while I was on the phone with the tavern. Hamlet spilled coffee on his dress and was in a huff by the time I hung up. He demanded I call him a cab, then waited on the porch. Sebastian stayed inside to make some phone calls. Do you think he—?"

"Did you see Hamlet leave?"

"Yes. He got into the backseat of the cab before I walked up to the restaurant." She paused. "I didn't shoot Sebastian either if that's what you think."

I shook my head. "I don't know what to think. Whoever did had an awfully small window of time to shoot him, throw him in the cabinet, rearrange the mannequins, then run out the back. They left the gate open."

"That sounds like a lot of work for one person," my sister said, resting her head on my shoulder. "I'll call Hamlet and tell him to come back. He needs to know hear this from us."

"The police will want to talk to him." I nodded, then texted Andy, *"Unable to move things tonight. Call me when you can."*

"There goes any chance of moving tonight," Laken said, as though reading over my shoulder.

"We have no idea if Sebastian knew anyone in Glitter Bay, let alone if anyone wanted to kill him."

"It was probably a random attack," she said. "A crime of convenience. We did have all that jewelry he sent. How are we supposed to know if any of it is missing? We don't have an actual inventory."

She hadn't seen the mannequins yet. No way was this random.

"Did anyone else know about the necklaces?" I asked.

"Us, Sebastian, Hamlet, Andy…"

"No, Andy never saw them." I picked at a cuticle. "Maybe someone expected to walk into the tea house and ended up face to face with Sebastian."

Laken scowled. "Really? You think somebody shot him because there was no tea?"

"People have killed for less. Some lady did yell at Gill the other day for shutting down the tea house."

"Sage." She sighed.

"What?" I turned to look at her. "Face it, Laken, the guy had a serious attitude problem. I was ready to kill him when I first met him. Even you wanted to strangle him, and you've known him for years. What's to say someone else didn't feel the same way?"

"Sounds to me like you're the first person I want to interview," the police officer said behind us. His gaze was fixed on me. "You did find the body."

My face burned. "That wasn't an admission of guilt. Sebastian Hayward the Third was lousy at making friends. Since we met, he did nothing to win me over."

"Sebastian is—was—a clothing designer from Los Angeles," Laken told him. "He and I worked together when I was a model. I asked him to come to Glitter Bay to give us feedback on our new store. I left him here alone while I ran to the tavern to pick up dinner."

"You can't tell me some big-name designer from L.A. came here out of the goodness of his heart," he said.

Her face turned red as she hesitated. "No, I paid him. Handsomely, I might add. He showed up yesterday with his protégé and managed to alienate my sister, a server at Devil's Peak, and a cab driver all in one afternoon."

"See. I'm not the only one," I commented. "The guy has a whole non-fan club."

The officer sat on the step to my right. "Considering he's got a gunshot wound in his chest and is lying in a display case, we may need a list of all the people in town he's offended since he arrived."

"I'd love to, but aside from Sage I didn't get their names," Laken said. "The ones I know of anyway. There might be more at the hotel. I left Sebastian and Hamlet at the front desk last night. He was so obnoxious even I needed a little peace."

"I'm sure the people he offended won't be tough to track down. It's a small town." He met my gaze again. "You go to the yoga school up the street, don't you? What's your name again?"

"Sage Miller. My sister, Laken, and I own Vintage Sage." I struggled to remember his name from class. "Do you think we'll be able to finish moving things from our other location soon?"

As he smirked, a dimple burrowed into one cheek. "I'm Denny Rhodes. I'll be your lead investigator until my boss takes over. I don't think you'll be moving anything for a while. Not until we're done with the crime scene, anyway."

Laken extended her right arm across my chest to push me back, so she had a direct view of the officer. "Excuse me? We have a fashion show on Friday at seven for our grand opening. We still need to move in our merchandise, build a runway, and find extra chairs."

Officer Rhodes shrugged. "You might need to move your show."

"Over my dead body," my sister yelled, then cringed. "Scratch that."

I met the officer's gaze. "Please don't prolong the agony. I want everything over as soon as possible."

My sister draped her arm around me. "You'll have to excuse Sage. She loves old clothing, but not the rest of the fashion business. Particularly Sebastian."

"Close." I grimaced. "I like vintage clothing and accessories. People and trends are not my things."

Rhodes frowned. "Yet you own a clothing store. Laken, could you give Sage and I some privacy? I have a few questions."

"Sure. I'll go let Sammy out." She stood and brushed off her slacks, then touched my shoulder. "Do you want me to leave your dinner here?"

"No, thanks. I lost my appetite when I saw..." I waved my hand toward the store.

Laken nodded then left.

"Who's Sammy?" Rhodes asked once she was gone.

"Her dog. He's home in the kennel. Well, unless he's eaten it since we left earlier." I waited until my sister was half a block away before I asked, "What do you need to know?"

"How well did you know Sebastian Hayward?"

"The Third." I grimaced. "Sebastian Hayward the Third."

He wrote something in his notebook as the medical examiner's car pulled up. The two men nodded as the medical examiner went inside.

I closed my eyes against a surge of tears. "Laken introduced us yesterday. She used to work with him in L.A. and invited him here to help us with the store."

"What did he help you with?"

"Nothing. He told me to burn the place down and start over." I paused. "Oh, and about my career choice. He said I should work in a horse barn."

Rhodes chuckled. "No wonder you didn't like him."

I stared at the ocean. "What was there to like? He hated the color I spend days painting on the walls, the clothing I sell, and he wasn't all that crazy about me. I guess he expected me to be a model like my sister. When it came to our show, he wanted Laken to walk down the runway in outfits he chose."

"Was it his show or yours?"

"Mine and Laken's. At least that's what I thought."

"It doesn't sound like you're thrilled about doing this fashion show anyway."

I shook my head. "I don't like it when people make decisions for me. I've had years to learn to roll with my sister's quirks, but Sebastian..."

Officer Rhodes stood, then dusted off his slacks before he examined the broken pane. "Who had motive and means to kill him?"

"How would I know? Every time he was here, I'd leave before I said or did anything stupid. When he showed up at my house last night, Laken took he and Hamlet out to dinner, then to the hotel." I took a deep breath. "He was Laken's friend. and I didn't want to cause any problems between them. My sister would know who had any grudges."

A white cab with blue lettering pulled up in front of the building. A half minute later, Hamlet stepped out and ran a hand through his shoulder-length blond hair. Instead of the blue dress, he now wore pale gray slacks and a soft yellow blouse. Odd that he'd gone back to the hotel to change clothes, although Laken did say something about him spilling coffee.

"Actually, you can ask that guy. That's Hamlet, Sebastian's latest protégé. This is the first time I've seen them apart since they got here, which is lucky for him."

Hamlet paused to pull out his phone.

"That's his name? Hamlet?" Rhodes smiled as he met my gaze. "Stick around, Sage. I might have more questions for you."

"It's not like I can go anywhere. I need to lock up." A sudden thought struck me. "Hey, Enid Walsh was supposed to come by this afternoon. She was going to interview some guy about a tree fungus, then planned to interview Sebastian."

"The gossip columnist? What time did she get here?"

I shook my head. "I have no idea. Like I said, I was at the old store all afternoon. I reported the break in when I got here."

"So, you said." Rhodes touched the brim of his hat, then walked down the sidewalk.

Hamlet was in such a rush to put away his phone that he dropped it into the grass. He seemed wary as Rhodes spoke in low tones. They walked side-by-side toward Vintage Sage. From the sudden ashen pallor of Hamlet's face, I guessed Rhodes told him what happened to Sebastian. His chin quivered as he closed his eyes.

After a long minute, Hamlet wiped away tears as he strode toward me. My heart raced at the anticipation of a confrontation.

He pointed a long finger in my face. "How could you?"

"Hamlet, I didn't do anything. I came back to check on things and found…" My heart broke as his face crumpled.

When I met Rhodes' gaze, he seemed torn. Like he wanted to go inside but didn't want to leave the two of us alone.

"Why don't you sit down and catch your breath?" I suggested patting the wood next to me. "The officer has work to do."

"I want to see Sebastian," Hamlet insisted.

"No, you don't." My voice came out raw and raspy. "I saw enough for both of us."

Hamlet pursed his lips and hesitated before Rhodes scurried into the building. He sat next to me before he pulled out a tissue to dab at his eyes, careful not to smudge his smoky gray eyeshadow or thick black mascara. The guy wore false eyelashes better than I ever could.

He gazed at the cresting ocean and seemed to gather his thoughts. Finally, he spoke without looking at me, "Did you kill him?"

I shook my head. "No. I saw the broken window and found him when I got here."

"You found him?" He gasped as he studied me. I must've looked frightened because he pulled me into a strong hug. The scent of citrus wafted off him as though he'd recently showered. "You poor thing. That must've been horrible."

My hands began to shake again. "Yeah. I'm okay."

"Was your sister here?" He released me from his grip.

I wiped my eyes with my arm before he handed me a tissue. "She left when you did and returned after the police arrived."

"She was going to pick up dinner for us. Seb…" Hamlet couldn't say Sebastian's name either. "He was making calls for the fashion show to get models and such. Since I'd spilled coffee on my dress, I decided to take a break and change before dinner."

"Didn't you find anything in the store that would fit you?" I pointed over my shoulder with my thumb as I glanced toward him.

Hamlet forced a sad smile as he patted my knee. "You poor naïve girl. You have a few stunning pieces, but if I even touched one Sebastian would lose his mind. The concept of reselling clothing, vintage or not, was a criminal offense that set his veneers on edge."

"Even the Calvin Klein and Donna Karan designs?"

"Absolutely, darling." He sighed. "Those are on my shopping list though, especially now that he's… You know."

We sat in silence while I strained to hear the voices inside for snatches of any clues about the murder. How dare Laken leave when Hamlet and I needed her?

"I called him an arrogant goat," Hamlet said, sobbing softly.

"What?" I blinked like I'd just arrived from another world.

His lip quivered. "Those were the last words I said to him. After all the nasty things he said to you and Laken, I just couldn't stop myself. While Laken ordered dinner, he started to carry on about taking over to do things the right way. He loved your location and the building, so he wanted to—"

"Sage? Can I have a word with you?" Rhodes stood in the doorway behind us.

"Yeah." I touched Hamlet's arm and told him, "I'll be right back."

Rhodes pointed at Hamlet. "Don't go anywhere. You're next."

I paused in the doorway grateful someone draped a shiny emergency blanket over the glass case where Sebastian Hayward the Third resided.

"We've dusted the mannequins for prints but need to take the cabinet and the body to the lab in Seattle. There may be trace evidence we don't have the tools to find."

I grew queasy as I stared at the reflective blanket. "No problem. The cabinet's only been here since Monday. I'm not attached to it."

Rhodes cleared his throat. "I'll need your fingerprints to eliminate you as a suspect."

I wrapped my arms around my stomach. "That makes sense. My prints are on everything in the store. Same with Sebastian's, Hamlet's, Laken's, and the guys who moved it here from the shop on Rodeo Drive."

His eyebrows shot up. "Rodeo Drive? I'll need the name of the shop as well as the delivery company, the driver, and anyone else who helped."

"Why?"

"Same reason. To eliminate them," he said, then winced. "I didn't mean that the way it sounded. I meant as suspects."

"I got that. Do you want my statement right now?"

"Absolutely. I thought we could walk through everything you did when you first got here this afternoon." He stepped aside for one of the crime scene crew who scowled at him.

"Right now?" I inched toward the door with no desire to be in the building.

"We might as well do the outside stuff first." Rhodes led me out the front door then down the sidewalk to the street before he turned to Hamlet. "You stay put. I'll talk to you next."

"That was harsh," he said.

"You're a murder suspect, remember? I'm not in a mood to be nice."

When Hamlet opened his mouth to argue, I shook my head. Rather than speak, he waved me away with a flick of his wrist.

"Thank you." Rhodes took me by the elbow. "Which direction did you come from when you approached the building?"

I pointed to the right. "I was at our old location all day. It's across from the new pub. Not in the best part of town. When Gill decided to sell the tea house, my sister snapped it up."

"That's interesting." Rhodes walked me up the street toward downtown Glitter Bay.

The way he said "interesting" made me cringe. "Why's that?"

"Right across from the beach. Full view of the ocean. Steady traffic flow, especially when people have to drive past here to get to the Devil's Peak." He cast me a sideways glance. "The sudden move to a building like that from where you are now is enough to make people notice. They might think you killed a fashion designer to get it."

I growled beneath my breath. "First of all, Laken bought it weeks before Sebastian was even a blip on my radar. Right after Tilly San Vicente died. Secondly, my sister was a fashion model, who has earned more money than you or I will ever see short of winning the lottery. When she divorced her movie star ex-husband, she ended up with millions more. Anything else?"

Rhodes cleared his throat. "Nope. I'm good."

We were about two blocks from Vintage Sage when he instructed me to turn around to recreate my earlier arrival. As I turned, I collided with Hamlet. I let out a yelp and took a half step back, clutching a hand to my chest as if it could stop my racing heart.

"What's going on?" Hamlet asked, placing his hands on his hips.

"I told you to stay put. Why are you following us?"

He whimpered. "I didn't want to be left alone with a dead body ten feet away."

Rhodes blew out a frustrated breath. "It's more like fifty feet and there are five people inside to hold him down if he comes back to life as zombie."

My eyes widened. "That's not funny."

"I concur," Hamlet said, taking my other arm. "Now I refuse to go back alone just because I'll have nightmares. What do we do next?"

Rhodes sighed and told him, "You need to be quiet. Sage is about to tell me exactly what happened when she approached the building earlier. Did you see anyone? Were there any sounds or vehicles in close proximity?"

"That's leading the witness," Hamlet stated.

I shook my head. "He's prompting my memories."

"Are you going to Mirandize her?"

"That's not necessary," Rhodes said.

"Are you sure?" Hamlet asked. "They do it all the time on television."

"I'm positive. Sage is a witness, not a killer. I simply need to ask her some questions."

"That you know of."

"Cut it out." I clapped a hand over my eyes, then tried to recall everything I saw and heard on my way to the store. Before I found Sebastian. "There was a black car that sped around the building from the far side. It nearly hit a red minivan in the intersection. I also heard the back gate squeak when I got closer."

"Which was first?" Rhodes continued to lead Hamlet and I down the sidewalk.

"The black car," I told him. "If that's the case though, the two weren't related. That doesn't tell us where the killer went."

Hamlet held up a finger. "Or killers. Maybe there were more than one and they went separate ways. One drove and the other met him somewhere else. That's enough to confuse any witness." He grinned. "I saw that in a *Columbo* movie. Have you ever watched *Columbo*, Detective?"

Rhodes snorted. "I'm not a detective, and you are not helping."

I cupped my hands on either side of my face to block them both from view. It was difficult to tune them out while they bickered. The black car had raced past me and around the corner nearly hitting the minivan. Was I calling the police on my way to the back of the building when I heard the gate squeak? The more I thought, the more confused I became.

As if in a trance, I began to walk toward the new Vintage Sage location trying to recall the car, the gate, and... I froze. There was another sound. A bigger vehicle, like a truck or a delivery van that I'd ignored since I was focused on the gate and finding my sister.

"There was another vehicle. A truck," I said, turning to face Rhodes.

"Are you sure?" he asked.

Hamlet grabbed me by the shoulders, He stood so close his stale coffee breath warmed my face. "What kind of truck? What did it look like?"

I tried to take a step back, personal space and all that, but he held on tight. "I didn't see it. I heard the gate, then the second vehicle. It reminded me of the delivery van that dropped off our cabinets."

"Before or after the gate opened?" Rhodes stood to my right.

I shook my head. "Right around the same time, I'd say."

Hamlet groaned. "How are we supposed to crack the case? You need to focus, young lady."

"That's hard to do with you in my face." I shrugged his hands off me as I pushed between them.

"Maybe you can't remember because there's nothing to remember," Hamlet said. "I wouldn't be surprised if you killed Sebastian. You haven't liked him since day one."

I spun to face him. "I didn't kill him. Why don't you believe me?"

"Because I'm in shock. He was my boss and the only friend I had." He stormed toward the store, climbed the front steps, then stopped at the door. His entire body sagged before he sat on the top step with his head in his hands.

"I'll go check on progress," Rhodes said, walking beside me. "We'll search behind the building. Maybe the killer dropped something or left a clue on his way out. Is your sister coming back, or do I need to track her down?"

"I'll call her." I whispered as my hands started to shake again.

Two things had changed by the time we returned to Vintage Sage. Sebastian's body was on its way to Seattle in the glass case. Kind of like a morbid, modern version of Sleeping Beauty. Laken had delivered two large cups of chamomile tea. She texted to say she'd gone to the station to give her statement.

I was left alone to sip my tea on the front step.

As alone I could be with Hamlet next to me.

Chapter Five

As the sun set over the Pacific, Officer Rhodes drove a melancholy Hamlet to his hotel. Sebastian and the Sleeping Beauty case were on their way to Seattle. Laken stopped by the store and took Sammy to the beach, leaving me alone with Mata Hari while I straightened up.

Still rattled after finding Sebastian's body, I stopped every two minutes to look around. I was suddenly afraid of every little shadow. Mostly because I swore I saw a couple of those shadows move.

What if Sebastian hung around as a ghost until the police figured out who killed him?

It made sense. He hated me enough to haunt me for years.

I picked the fingerprint dust-stained mannequin up off the floor and stood her upright against the wall. She started to fall over as soon as I let her go. I lunged to grab her before I laid her on one side to take a better look. Not only was she missing the base to stand properly, but one of her ankles was cracked and a metal rod stuck out of her right foot. I'd need to fix her when I cleaned her up. Preferably before the fashion show.

Since she didn't have a proper base, I couldn't stand her with the others, nor could I leave her lying there. Under the circumstances, the sight of another body on the floor—fake or not—would be lousy for business. I carried her into the kitchen. The only place I could keep her standing upright was inside the pantry next to the small washroom in back. I'd planned to store extra merchandise there anyway.

"Welcome to purgatory," I said, leaning Mata Hari against the far wall before I replaced her hair and headdress. "Sorry about this. You deserve better, but until I get your case back or fix your leg, this is the best I can do."

I closed the pantry door, then found a piece of thick cardboard to duct tape over the broken pane until I could call someone to replace the glass. On my way to the door, I caught a whiff of mothballs. Enid forgot her box of dresses after her non-interview with Sebastian. I grabbed a notepad and jotted a reminder to call her to pick it up before it ended up in the courtyard in the trash. As I set the pen down, I remembered to add a note to call the glass guy.

Laken and Sammy returned as I locked the front door. While her dog sniffed around on the porch, my sister hugged me. "All good?"

I gazed at the stars twinkling over the ocean as though nothing abnormal happened that day. "As good as they can be."

We walked in silence back to my house before Laken volunteered to reheat whatever she'd bought home for dinner from the Devil's Peak Tavern. She nudged me outside to the back deck to relax. While I sat numb in the moonlight, a tear rolled down my cheek. Not that I missed Sebastian, but the sight of him inside the glass cabinet wouldn't leave me alone.

"Here." My sister wrapped my hand around a glass of white wine. "How are you doing?"

As I blew out a sigh, Sammy licked my bare toes. I reached to stroke his head. "I expected to see him again, just not like that. Hamlet's freaked out. He's convinced I killed his mentor. I feel sorry for the big lug."

"Me, too." She stepped into the house for a minute, then returned with our meals. "I ordered you the usual. Portobello mushroom with veggies and rice. Is that okay?"

"You know that's my favorite. Thank you. I should be looking after you. He was your friend."

"But you found him," she said. "Anyway, your meal was easy. I got so frustrated trying to order food for Sebastian and Hamlet that I swore all the way to the restaurant. Neither of them liked anything I suggested. Not that they were listening, they were too busy butting heads."

Poking at my food, I asked, "What about?"

"I'm not sure. After you and Enid left, the two of them started to whisper and give each other weird looks. I ignored them and ordered dinner before Hamlet asked me to call a cab."

I raised my eyebrows. "What did you order Hamlet for dinner?"

"He didn't leave because I ordered salmon with rice pilaf and a garden salad if that's what you mean. He had the same thing the night before, so I figured it was safe."

"I'm just curious why you didn't send his food to the hotel with him tonight," I told her as I cut into my portobello.

"I forgot."

"That's fair. He's a big boy. He can fend for himself. How did Enid's interview with Sebastian go?" I toyed with a piece of mushroom.

"Oh, that." Laken rolled her eyes. "Enid asked him one question before he demanded she leave the property."

"What did she ask?"

She speared a piece of asparagus. "I don't know. I sent them into the courtyard for privacy. Sebastian stormed back into the store two minutes later sputtering about what an awful person she was and how he demanded to speak with her editor to have her fired."

"Did Enid follow him back inside?"

"Yes," Laken said, "but before she could open her mouth, he told her the only way she'd ever publish a single word about him would be over his dead body."

I reached for my wine glass. "That's eerily prophetic. It sounds like Enid did her research as usual. I can't see her killing him though. You didn't happen to tell her Sebastian was coming before he arrived?"

"You know how hard it is to keep secrets from that woman. Besides, she overheard me on the phone with him last week."

"And didn't stop poking at you until she got answers." I chuckled, then sipped my wine. "She did promise to let me know if she found anything juicy. Did you call her about the show?"

"Yes, thanks for the heads up. I'll talk to her. Although, I'm surprised she wasn't hanging around the store after you found Sebastian."

"Yeah. She's usually right in the thick of things, isn't she?"

"I have to recruit a couple more models anyway. Depending on how many we get, we'll either need two or three outfits for each. Do you mind choosing a couple for Enid?"

"Yeah, sure." I glanced at my phone when it dinged but didn't reach for it.

"Did you hear from Andy tonight? I'll bet he had a tough evening. There was a big accident south of town."

"Yeah. Five cars, two fatalities, and ten injuries." I blew out a long breath. "He called before he left the hospital. He was going home for a hot shower and sleep but promised to help move the rest of our stuff tomorrow."

Laken curled a strand of red hair around one ear. "That's a good idea. Eat your dinner then you can do the same. A bubble bath and a good night's sleep will do you good."

I closed my eyes still able to picture Sebastian Hayward the Third lying in that glass cabinet covered in blood. My appetite wavered even more.

"Who'd do something like that?" I whispered. "I know the guy was a jerk, but why shoot him? That's so...cold. A good punch in the face can go a long way, you know."

My sister spit sparkling water onto the deck. "Sage! I thought you were all peace, love, and crystals."

"Not this week. That guy rubbed me the wrong way. I should feel bad for him, but I just can't do it. Even if that puts me near the top of the suspect list." My favorite dinner seemed more bland than usual. Either I was mired in shock, or the mushroom needed some serious seasoning.

"You disliked him. You didn't shoot him." Laken shook her head. "Besides, where would a crystal-packing, chakra-aligning hippie like you even get a gun?"

"Search me." I stabbed a piece of cold, rubbery mushroom. I ate it anyway. "What if he haunts the store?"

Laken held up her hands. "I don't think you need to worry about that. He hated the place too much to hang out for eternity."

"Are you sure? Hamlet said Sebastian loved the store so much he wanted to take over." I met her confused gaze, then shrugged. "Have you checked in on him? How's he taking things?"

"He had a meltdown when he got to the police station to answer more questions," she said. "They won't let him leave town, so I imagine we'd better get used to having him around until they clear him."

"Maybe you can keep him busy helping with the fashion show."

She raised her glass of sparkling water. "That's a good plan. Maybe we can find out what happened to the House of Hayward. Sebastian had to be up to something shady."

I tapped my glass against hers. "I'm happy to help, but only because he was your friend."

"I know. Thanks for that, Sage."

Before I went to bed that night, I rinsed a handful of crystals under running water in the bathroom sink before arranging them on my window ledge. The full moon wasn't until Friday the thirteenth—there was an omen if I'd ever heard one—but it never hurt to have a little extra mojo the way this week was going.

I also needed to figure out how to ward off ghosts. Just in case Sebastian decided to stick around.

Spreading out a soft piece of blue velvet cloth, I placed a rose quartz on it to support my budding relationship with Andy. Smoky quartz to help me stay grounded. Moonstone to enhance my intuition so I could help figure out what happened to Sebastian. It would also enhance our success and good fortune with the new store. Jade for prosperity and abundance. Lastly, I placed one last crystal for prosperity, a citrine. I had a feeling we could use a little backup.

Jonathan teased me mercilessly about my crystals, smudging, and essential oils. Andy might not think much of them either, although he'd asked about my crystals when he saw them in my shop.

Friday the thirteenth. Right after the fashion show, I'd smudge the crystals, the store, and the house to clear any residual negative energy. For now, I needed some serious sleep.

I crawled into bed next to Muumuu who rolled onto her back. When she started to purr, I stroked her soft gray belly and closed my eyes.

Chapter Six

Before dawn Wednesday morning, I tucked my crystals in their usual box after a long night of bad dreams. I crept down to the kitchen to feed Muumuu and get coffee started. After Sun Salutations on the back deck, I trotted up the stairs to get ready to face the day.

Laken was still asleep, and Jonathan hadn't texted since before I found Sebastian's body, which seemed odd. I savored the peace while I took a long shower, then dressed in a pair of khaki cargo pants, a tank top, and a loose, flowery blouse.

I reached for my clear quartz earrings. Since attracting positive energy hadn't worked out so well yesterday, I planned to ward off negative energy today.

Sammy scratched at the other side of Laken's door as I walked past. He raced me downstairs to the patio doors, so I let him into the backyard, then fed him before I poured my coffee into a stainless-steel travel mug.

Since we were both up early, I took him for a long walk on the beach to enjoy the sunrise and the salty air. Digging my bare toes in the sand made me feel a million times better. I even found several glittering pieces of seaglass, which I saved to make a gift for Laken's new apartment. Roaming the beach, breathing the salty air, and watching boats sail out of the marina made things feel right with the world again.

Until I dropped Sammy off at the house and made my way to the new store.

The sight of the cardboard in the broken pane sent the events of the previous day flooding back like a tidal wave. The glass case was still in police custody, and I was alone in the store to make peace with the whole situation.

That's when I did what any rational woman would do. I broke out a bundle of Palo Santo to smudge the store and clear out negative energy then sat cross-legged on the floor to focus. At least the police had moved most of the mannequins to one side to get the cabinet out. Still, I didn't dare close my eyes.

"Sebastian," I started, then paused. "If you're hanging around, please know Laken and I will do our best to find your killer. Of course, if you want to just tell me who did it, I'd be happy to save time so you can get out of here. Just don't cause trouble. I need this store to work no matter how much you hate it."

I sat on the floor until one of my legs fell asleep but received no reply. Just as I managed to wake up my leg, Laken arrived with Sammy in tow. She paused in the doorway to sniff the air.

"Hey. You okay?" she asked.

"All good. I just had words with Sebastian."

"Of course, you did. You do know he's dead, right?"

I grimaced. "Trust me, I remember. I told his spirit not to cause trouble and asked if he'd give us a hand tracking down his killer."

"Okay then," she said backing away. "I'm going to let Sammy out back then organize the clothes for the show. Enid and a couple other ladies are coming by for fittings."

"Great. I'll call about getting the glass replaced in the door." I put my abalone shell and feather in the kitchen before pulling out my phone.

I left a message for the glass repair guy, asking him for an estimate. As I hung up, it occurred to me Jonathan hadn't texted lately. Maybe he'd finally moved along. I shrugged, then I filled a bucket with water and cleaner to attack the fingerprint dust.

Enid ran up the front steps half an hour later. She wore bright yellow pants, an orange blouse, and shiny earrings that looked like fishing lures. "Oh, Sage! I heard what happened to that Sebastian guy. Are you girls okay?"

I glanced up from scrubbing a dark patch on the counter. "Yeah, we're fine."

She squinted. "Cute earrings. Are they some sort of hippie crystal thing?"

"Quartz. It wards off evil."

"Are they working?" She strolled toward a box beside me.

"I'll let you know."

"Fingerprint dust is brutal to get rid of," Enid said. "Vacuum it first, then spray it with dish soap diluted in warm water. It'll take a little elbow grease."

Laken and I exchanged glances, before my sister said, "I don't want to ask how you know that off the top of your head."

"I write more than the news. Did the killer take anything?" Enid opened the box and handed me an article of clothing to hang.

"No, I haven't noticed anything missing, but between Laken going to pick up dinner and me arriving, the killer didn't have had much time to search after they rearranged the mannequins."

She snapped around to face me. "Why would a killer rearrange mannequins?"

I realized I shouldn't have armed her with that information. I moved the water bucket aside. There was no point trying to clean up while Enid was rooting for information.

"Yeah. That part's kind of weird, isn't it?" Laken shot me a scowl as she emerged from the kitchen. "Hey, Enid, I didn't get to ask how your interview with Sebastian went yesterday."

"Oh that." Her jaw tightened and she rolled her eyes. "How did you meet that guy? He was an odd little man."

My sister leaned on the cabinet. "I've modeled his designs in a couple fashion shows. He'd opened the House of Hayward and hadn't hired an assistant yet. Back then, he personally designed and sewed every garment and wasn't quite so jaded."

Translation: He wasn't a jerk yet.

"Why did you roll your eyes?" I asked. "Didn't the interview go well?"

Enid hesitated, which wasn't like her at all. "I got to ask one question before he walked away in a huff."

"What did you ask?" I reached for an empty hanger.

She handed me a cream lace blouse. "Why he shut down the House of Hayward."

Laken gawked. "Shut it down? What are you talking about?"

"Didn't he tell you? His shop's for sale and the building's empty."

I stuck the empty hanger back on the rod and asked, "Where'd you hear that?"

"I'm a reporter. I have a knack for finding things like that out. All it took was a few minutes of research on the internet."

Laken shook her head. "No way. He would've told me. We've been friends for nearly ten years."

"I'd guessed from his ruffled feathers that he hadn't brought it up," Enid said. "I hoped he'd speak up. I even left to give him a chance. Instead, he went and got shot."

I couldn't stop my surprised laugh. "Yeah, the nerve of him."

She huffed as she shot me a scowl. "You know what I mean. Where did that fancy lady in the glass case go? She looked familiar. I wanted to take a few photos for my story."

"Mata Hari? She's hanging out in storage for now. I need to fix her," I told her. "Whoever shot Sebastian threw her on the floor and broke her leg, then put him in her case."

Enid raised her eyebrows. "The cops didn't mention that little tidbit."

"Oops." I winced. So far I was a geyser of information.

My sister toyed with her phone. "Enid, where did you hear Sebastian was closing his shop?"

She took Laken's phone and tapped a few buttons. "It's not exactly a secret. I'm surprised you haven't kept up with your friends since you've been here. I looked him up last week after you said he was coming to town."

I folded my arms across my chest. "You told Enid about Sebastian, but not me?"

"You're right. I'm a lousy friend and a worse sister."

"Oh, please." I tried to ignore her guilt trip. "Laken, you've had a lot to deal with lately. You've fought cancer, got divorced, and moved in with me. I didn't see any of your so-called friends step up to help."

"Until now. If course, I did have to pay Sebastian to show up," she said, glancing to where the glass cabinet had stood. Her voice rose an octave as emotion overwhelmed her. "Now he's dead. What if that's my fault?"

Enid patted her shoulder. "Now, now, honey. Put the cuckoo back in the clock. What if your pal Sebastian was just a big jerk and his murder had nothing to do with you?"

I covered my mouth as I met my sister's gaze.

Enid pulled a piece of folded paper from her purse. "My editor had me put together an obituary. This isn't the version he got. This is what I wrote after more research."

"Oh boy," Laken muttered.

I took the paper from Enid, then read aloud, "Fashion designer, model, and owner of the former House of Hayward, Sebastian Linwood Hayward the Third passed tragically from a gunshot in Glitter Bay, Washington. He was the protégé of Franco Cristiano and—"

"The former House of Hayward," Laken whispered. "I can't believe he didn't tell me what was going on. I could've helped."

"Let her finish." Enid held up a finger.

I continued, "Born Howard Sebastian Kaden—"

"Howard? That phony!"

"He was predeceased by his parents, Roger and Jenna Kaden, and his brother, Mark. In lieu of flowers, donations can be made to..." I flipped the paper over, then returned it to Enid. "You didn't finish."

She shrugged. "The rest was in the official version. Donations go to a fund for wannabe designers that a friend of his heads up."

"What friend? Whose decision was that?" my sister asked.

"No idea, but he must have a will somewhere."

Laken snatched the page. "There are so many things wrong with this I don't even know where to start."

"I thought you'd say that which is why I printed copies of everything," Enid said as she reached into her purse for another handful of papers. "Your friend wasn't only rude he was as fake as his made-up name."

Shaking my head, I told her, "I knew there was something off about that weasel."

I inched away when my sister threw me a glare. I wasn't as surprised as she seemed. Most of the people who used to be part of her inner circle seemed a bit off, including Hamlet who had to be hiding something.

My sister took Enid's evidence as she retreated to a paint-splattered chair. She read in silence for several minutes. "It's true. He was shutting down the House of Hayward."

"Worse. He was in foreclosure," Enid said. "The guy was broke. The building is up for sale, and I have no idea what happened to his designs. The news articles didn't give many details. I tried to dig for financial records but haven't come up with anything."

"Hamlet might be able to help. Have you heard from him today?" I itched to bring our computer from the other store to do my own digging. If only I had a car instead of a bike.

Laken checked her phone. "He's on his way with something to discuss."

I chuckled. "He probably wants to honor Sebastian's wishes to repaint Vintage Sage."

"Or dedicate the fashion show to Sebastian's memory," Laken muttered as she flipped through the papers in her hands.

"Dedicate the fashion show to the dead guy," Enid said. "What's she talking about?"

"No idea. I've kept my distance as much as possible. The guy drove me crazy."

"To the point she told Sebastian off this morning *after* he was dead," my sister told her as she blinked back tears, which made me feel worse. "If I knew this was Sebastian's last hurrah, I might've agreed to use one of his designs in the show."

"Except that we don't have any," I reminded her. "Besides, we sell vintage clothes, not runway fashions."

Enid chuckled. "Be happy you don't have any. Have you seen his designs? Forget fashion show, we'd end up with a Halloween pageant."

"Are they that bad?" I asked.

"Some of them. Not all the attention he got in Hollywood was good," Laken said. "Why didn't Sebastian tell me the House of Hayward was bankrupt?"

Not sure what to say, I bit my lip. "He did sell us his alien mannequins, his display cases, and a bunch of cheap jewelry. Maybe that was a cry for help."

"He told me he was renovating. Why would he lie? We've been close friends since we both started in the business."

Enid pulled over another chair to sit next to her. "Maybe he was embarrassed."

"Maybe." More like he didn't want to look like a failure in Laken's eyes.

Hamlet strolled inside wearing a flowery green dress and tan flats. Rather than the straight platinum blond wig, he wore a sleek black bob. Today, he carried a similar yellow purse to the one Sebastian had when they arrived—as well as an obvious sense of importance.

He slid off his sunglasses and asked, "Why are we sitting around, dollies? We have a store to organize and a show to prepare for."

I got the eerie feeling he was channeling Sebastian. I didn't like it, especially not after I'd burned sage and yelled at him earlier. "Good morning to you, too."

Laken went to give him a hug. "Is there anything we can do for you?"

Once my sister pulled away, Hamlet straightened his dress while clearing his throat. "I'm fine. I'm ready to get to work."

"Sebastian died yesterday," I said. "Don't you need time to grieve?"

"Darling, I sat in the teeny, tiny, hotel bathtub last night with two bottles of chardonnay and a cheesecake. I'm bloated and my eyes hurt, but I need to carry on and mourn in my own way. Is that okay with you?"

Speechless, I shrugged, then opened one of the few boxes I hadn't unpacked yet. Hopefully, we could move the rest of our merchandise once Andy finished work. The scent of mothballs accosted my nose making me sneeze.

"Hang in there, sunshine. Hopefully, he'll be gone by Saturday." Enid patted my shoulder, then gagged. "What's that horrid smell?"

"The box of dresses that you need to get out of here."

"Oh. Oops. Do you think he's guilty?" she asked.

"Hamlet? I don't know what to think. He seemed as shocked as the rest of us." I handed her the box. "Don't forget this."

"Let me know how things go." She took the box before she strolled over to give Laken a hug before she left.

While Hamlet wandered through the shop to check the clothing on the racks, I vacuumed. After a few minutes, I realized he was glaring at me. I switched off the vacuum and asked, "What's wrong?"

"Why haven't you hung the House of Hayward designs?"

Laken pushed a hanger into a flowing purple dress covered with purple sequins that came straight from the seventies on a hanger. Someone must've worn it to a disco or a wedding. "For one thing, we don't have any."

"Of course you do, darling," Hamlet gushed. "It's no wonder Sebastian didn't like you. His feelings were hurt because you hadn't displayed them."

"What are you talking about? We don't have any of Sebastian's designs in our shop," my sister insisted as she placed her hands on her hips.

Hamlet shook his head. "Where are the keys for the cabinets, you silly geese?"

Laken pulled them out of the counter drawer. "We looked in those."

"Not all of them," I reminded her. "We got sidetracked when you and Sebastian arrived."

Hamlet opened the base of the glass-topped cabinets. Inside each cabinet someone had carefully stacked several tissue paper-wrapped bundles. "You didn't even unwrap them. The poor darlings can't breathe."

I met my sister's stunned gaze and mouthed, "Breathe?"

Laken held up both hands. "Nobody told me. How were we supposed to know?"

"Oh, I don't know. Open all the cabinets," Hamlet snapped.

Curious, I reached for one of the bundles before I did something harsh like smack him.

Hamlet slapped my hand as he huffed. "Go wash your hands, young lady. House of Hayward designs are delicate and should be treated with the utmost respect."

"I liked you better when you didn't talk," I told him, then headed to the kitchen.

"Sage..." Laken started, then turned on Hamlet. "Okay, buddy. Why did we end up with all the clothes and jewelry from the House of Hayward? Which we now know is bankrupt."

Pausing at the doorway, I glanced back to see Hamlet's face grow red bordering on purple. I guessed I had less than sixty seconds to wash my hands and get back out to the showroom before Hamlet spoke, collapsed, or Laken threw something at him. Either way, I didn't want to miss the show.

I hustled into the kitchen, washed my hands, and dried them on my pants as I ran back to the storefront and asked, "What did I miss?"

"Nothing yet," Laken said.

"There's a lot you don't know," he told us as he lowered his gaze and fluttered his inch-long, fake lashes.

"You need to fill us in before we call the cops, so they can haul you off for more questioning."

He shuffled toward the paint-splattered chairs we'd kept from the tea house and sat. "My name isn't Hamlet McTavish. Not anymore. That's my dead name. My father was a Shakespearean actor and wanted me to follow in his footsteps."

Shocked, I stared. "Your dead name? You're dead, too?"

"Only part of me." He puffed up his chest like he was about to mock me, then blew out a long breath. His shoulders sagged before he said, "Hamlet is dead to me. I no longer use that name. That wasn't the real me."

"What name do you use then?" Laken asked, sitting next to him.

"Quinn Evans. I've been altering my previous life to live as the woman I am inside."

"Quinn. I like that name," I told him.

Wide-eyed, he glanced from me to Laken as if expecting a different reaction.

My sister nodded. "Sebastian mentioned you were transgender."

"He did?" I asked.

"He *mentioned* it?" Hamlet squawked. "You make it sound like I have a cold sore. Like it's not that important. This is earth-shattering, sister. It is not an easy process to become a woman, let me tell you."

We both stared at him for a long moment.

When he glanced from me to Laken, he finally chuckled. "I guess you understand that in a way I don't."

There were so many things I could've said. Instead, I touched his arm. "Would you like us to call you Quinn?"

Hamlet's mouth opened. His green eyes grew shiny with tears as a small smile played on his lips. He cleared his throat. "Yes, please. Call me Quinn. I'm a woman and I'd prefer to be treated as such."

I met my sister's gaze.

"We'll be happy to," Laken said, then paused. "Have you told anyone else?"

Quinn's chin quivered. "No one but Sebastian."

"I can imagine how that one played out," I muttered as I got up to grab a box of tissues.

"It was awful." She sobbed.

"Is that why you called him a goat?"

Quinn shook her head but struggled not to smile. "Too soon."

"Thank you for trusting us." My sister hugged her. "I know that wasn't easy, especially under the circumstances."

"Sebastian wasn't exactly supportive." Quinn touched a tissue to her face before placing her head in her hands. "He wanted me to be more like Mishel, which is why he called me Hamlet. I was expected to wear the same flashy suits and do all his thinking for him. Well, until he disagreed with me."

"Who's Mishel?" I asked.

"The guy I replaced."

"Since you've been here, you've worn dresses and act nothing like Mishel."

"I hoped Sebastian would finally accept me the way I am," she said. "It wasn't working."

I scowled and told her, "He doesn't sound like such a great boss. How long did you work at the House of Hayward?"

She dabbed her eyes. "Off and on for about a year. It was supposed to be my big break into the design world. Mishel was a genius at marketing and schmoozing people to get their designs into shows.

Once people realized Sebastian was washed up, they shunned him. He blamed the problems on me."

"Except that gave Sebastian a motive for wanting Mishel gone. Not vice versa."

Laken shook her head. "According to the papers, Mishel leaving the House of Hayward was the final straw. If Sebastian had issues designing or getting his fashions noticed, he would've begged Mishel to come back."

"True." I sighed. "Or he would've hired someone even more talented to take Mishel's place to create designs that would rock the fashion world to make Mishel jealous."

We both looked at Quinn.

"Which is totally not me," she sobbed. "Sebastian hired me away from another designer out of spite. He hated my designs, but I'm a great seamstress. I also took care of his customers, so he humored me. When I couldn't create a stellar clothing line like Mishel, he threatened to fire me."

Laken rubbed Quinn's back with one hand. "Things couldn't be that bad."

"The House of Hayward is bankrupt and Sebastian's dead," Quinn said, her voice crackling. "They can't get much worse."

"Maybe you're right."

"Sage!" my sister snapped.

I held up my hands. "Sorry."

"No, the boho girl's right." Quinn took another tissue. This one she folded neatly before she touched it below her eyes in another attempt to salvage her streaked makeup. "It's time I show you why the House of Hayward bobbed horrendously before it sank like a boulder."

Chapter Seven

Quinn tucked her dark hair behind her ears and got down to business. She opened the cabinet with the stacks of tissue-wrapped bundles, then chose one of the top packages. Peeling off the tissue, she revealed some yellow and orange spotted fabric.

"This is the House of Hayward's Conservatory Collection," she announced. "Not my finest hour."

I took a step back while she unfolded the fabric with a flourish. The dress was a simple A-line that reminded me of a monarch butterfly.

My sister smiled. "That's not so bad. A lacy black shawl would—"

Quinn held up a finger then draped the fabric over the mannequin. "Let me finish, darling."

She reached for another package and unwrapped out a colorful swatch of fabric. With a few tugs and the wave of a hand over the material, she created a foot wide red, yellow, and orange butterfly.

I winced as she attached it to the left shoulder, but couldn't summon any words that wouldn't earn me a scorching look from her or my sister.

"That's—," Laken started.

"One more piece." Quinn gently removed another package from the cabinet. While I watched, she refreshed a dented black fedora adorned with yellow, orange, and tufts of black netting. With steady hands, she placed it on the mannequin's head, then stepped back, holding her hands out. She looked at us like she'd created a magnificent masterpiece.

"Anyone else need a cup of tea?" My sister's voice was an octave higher than normal. "I'm going to the kitchen."

I tried not to wince as I turned away. "I'll join you. We'll let you finish in peace, Quinn. Would you like anything?"

"Fine. I'll do this all on my own," she said as she held up a black cape spotted with vivid orange sequins. "Just bring me a cup of something soothing that won't stain the fabrics."

The second the door swung closed and hit me from behind, I glared at my sister. It was a struggle to remain at a harsh whisper. "What have you done?"

She looked as horrified as I felt. "I am so sorry. I had no idea they were—"

"It's not the fashions, Laken, although those are pretty bad. I'm tired of the secrets. Hamlet is now Quinn, who just showed us why your buddy Sebastian's design house crashed and burned. Our store is next." I plugged in the kettle and took two packages of tea and three mugs from the cupboard. "I hope that butterfly is the worst of them."

My sister peered out the kitchen door, then told me, "You should work at home today."

"How bad is it?" I nudged her aside.

Quinn had draped a second mannequin with a simple, short black dress layered with a gauzy, ankle-length red jacket with glittering black spots.

"Omigod." I gasped. "She wants women to dress like bugs."

"What do you mean?" my sister whispered.

"First a butterfly, now a ladybug. I don't want to know what else is in there, but I have the urge to get a flyswatter."

As we whispered, Quinn took a black pill hat from a wrapper. She puffed up some attached black tulle as well as two fuzzy pipe-cleaners that resembled antennae with glittering black balls on the ends.

"Oh crap." Laken whimpered. "Sebastian wanted me to model those on Friday. If I'd seen them before yesterday, I would've killed them both." She paled as she met my gaze. "I didn't mean to say that."

"You've worn worse. I've seen the photos," I reminded her. "Remember the guy who dressed you in aluminum foil and plastic wrap for his show?"

"That was mylar and clear vinyl. It was Sebastian's space phase."

I covered my mouth before I burst out laughing. "Wow. He must've hated you from the start. I'll get the tea. You keep an eye on Princess Cockroach."

"Princess Cockroach?" My sister raised her eyebrows. "I have a feeling Hamlet or Quinn or whoever he or she is might actually enjoy that nickname."

"I know. Awkward, right? *She* asked us to call her Quinn. We need to honor that." I began to pour hot water over our tea bags, then hesitated. "I wonder if she told the police about being Quinn rather than Hamlet."

Laken shrugged as she let Sammy inside for a treat. "I'm sure that cop will show up with more questions. It would be good for her to be able to talk to people without shame. I could smack Sebastian for the way he treated her." She covered her eyes. "Never mind. If you do see his ghost kicking around, send him my way. I have a few choice words for him."

"You got it."

My phone dinged as we carried three steaming mugs back into the store and set them on the counter, far away from where Quinn unwrapped her delicate fabrics. I remained at a distance to check my messages while my sister crept closer for a better look. Before Quinn could screech about keeping the dog away, Laken tied his leash to the hook on the counter.

"Are you okay?" Jonathan was back.

I wondered if he knew about Sebastian, then sipped my tea and watched Quinn.

Sebastian Hayward the Third was one of those designers who created lines of clothing for women the size of my pinky finger. Compared to my sister, I was more like a stubby thumb. The Conservatory Collection fabrics were limited to anything gauzy, flowing, sheer, and glittery. Quinn, mad with her newfound power, demanded we dress every mannequin in her House of Hayward designs before the fashion show.

"No way," I told her, folding my arms across my stomach. "This is my store, and I'm dressing them in vintage outfits. That's why the shop is called Vintage Sage."

Quinn scowled. "If you put these outfits on hangers, they'll lose their shapes. They need to be draped on proper dress forms, so they're not ruined by disrespectful people like you."

"I'm disrespectful? Do you need a mirror, dude? Lady."

"Okay. That's enough, you two." Laken pointed to the cabinet. "How long have those outfits been in there?"

"Since you asked Sebastian for his furnishings. You already knew—"

"Got it." My sister cut her off.

"What's going on? What did you already know?" I asked.

Quinn laughed. "Oh, come on, Sage. You do know this whole fashion show idea was Sebastian's idea, right? He suggested it to Laken, so he could show these off. Thank you for calling me lady, by the way."

"You're welcome." I snapped, then turned on my sister. "Is there anything else you want to tell me?"

When Laken tapped her long, peach nails on the countertop, Sammy jumped against her leg. "I need to take him for a walk. When I get back, we can order lunch."

"Laken..." I followed her to the door, then stopped and stomped over to Quinn. Despite being almost a foot shorter than the woman in the A-line dress, I growled. "Tell me what you know, or I'll kick you in the shins."

Her green eyes widened. "You don't have to be mean. What do you want me to tell you?"

"Don't play dumb with me, Quinn."

"I'm not playing," she said, then sighed.

"I want to know more about Sebastian and what happened to the House of Hayward."

She reached for another bundle. "You know the fashion industry. One bad line can ruin a design house."

"I don't buy that. I'll bet Sebastian ruined his own reputation with that bad attitude long before he ever hired you. What was he hiding?"

As Quinn unwrapped a piece of glittering black fabric, her chin quivered.

Placing my hands on her shoulders, I marched her to a chair and forced her to sit. "Start talking or I'll call that nice police officer who questioned you when Sebastian died."

She reached for the box of tissues. "Ever since Mishel left and took nearly half of everything. Sebastian became even more angry and nastier than ever. We'd create lovely new designs and prepare for a show only to have someone else come up with similar styles."

"Mishel?"

"Who else, darling?" She paused. "Sage. If you're good enough to call me Quinn, it's only fair I call you by name as well."

Suddenly, we seemed to be starting over on even ground. I sat next to her and looked her in the eye. "Thank you. Do you think Mishel was spying on you and Sebastian?"

"I couldn't prove anything, but I did suspect him."

"Where did he go once he left the House of Hayward?"

Quinn averted her gaze. "Mishel bragged he was going to start his own design house and leave Sebastian in the dust. When his funding fell through, he was forced to grovel and get another designer to hire him."

"He must've been humiliated."

"Worse than that," she said. "He was convinced Sebastian sabotaged him. Sebastian and the investor were friends."

This was one time I wished I knew more about Laken's quirky modelling friends, even though it was one circle I'd never want to be a part of. "Who was going to fund him?"

That's when Quinn pressed her lips together so tightly that they turned white.

Worried she'd get up and leave, I softened my voice and told her, "I'm either going to keep asking questions until you break, or Laken will talk to people she knows. Either way, the truth will come out."

She bowed her head and seemed to shut down.

I rose from my chair, then strolled across the room with an itch to check out the rest of the House of Hayward designs. Surely they couldn't all be that bad. Quinn didn't budge from her seat after I'd unwrapped three more items I guessed were dresses. She even remained seated when Laken and Sammy returned from their walk.

When Laken unhooked Sammy's leash, he headed straight for his water bowl. She sidled over to me and whispered, "What did you do to Quinn?"

"All I did was ask for answers. Now she won't talk at all."

Laken groaned. "Oh, brother. Why are you sitting there acting sorry for yourself? You should be helping Sage set up the store. We need some great ideas to pull off this show."

She fluttered her lashes like she'd burst into tears. "Your sister was interrogating me, and I didn't like it."

"Then start talking." I crumpled a handful of tissue paper and threw it at Quinn's head. My aim was to get her to laugh. It only half worked. The sound it made when it hit her head caused me to smirk and her to frown. "Sorry."

Quinn waved her hand half-heartedly. "I deserved that."

"No, you didn't," I told her. "Laken, Mishel left the House of Hayward to start his own place but lost his investor. He blamed Sebastian for that. Since then, someone's been copying House of Hayward designs and selling them as their own."

Quinn's face and neck grew blotchy then reddened as she swiped at one eye. She didn't bother to argue.

Laken shot me a scowl before she approached Quinn. "Who was Mishel's investor and what did Sebastian have to do with them backing out of the deal?"

The blotchiness extended into Quinn's ears and further down her chest. "Chick Jansen."

"Oh, brother." My sister covered her face with one hand.

I'd heard that name before but struggled to remember where.

"My ex-husband's PR guy," Laken said. "Emery had nothing but bad publicity long before I left him. Most of it was his own doing. Me divorcing him while I fought cancer didn't help any. Even Chick had a challenging time giving him a good image after that."

I chased Quinn off her chair in the middle to sit next to my sister. "Why would Chick invest in Mishel's designs?"

My sister shrugged. "They met at a party at our house before I left L.A. and hit it off. Emery knew Sebastian because he'd tagged along to some of my shoots. I thought they got along well, except that Emery called him 'The Poof.'"

"That's rude."

Quinn crinkled her nose as she began to pace. "And very stereotypical."

"That's what I said, but Emery loved how mad it made me. The name stuck." Laken blew out a breath. "It got weirder. Sebastian was one of the people I caught Emery with."

I gasped. "Oh. Ouch. That must've rocked your friendship."

"We didn't speak until lately."

The click of Quinn's low heels on the hardwood mesmerized Sammy who leaned his head forward to stare while she thought aloud. "Mishel ran into Emery on the set of a movie. When Mishel told him how much he wanted to leave House of Hayward to start his own line, Emery had papers drawn up. He became Mishel's silent partner."

"How did Sebastian get involved?" I asked.

"Emery made the mistake of asking him what was needed to start up a design business," Quinn said. "Furnishings, fabrics, those sorts of things."

"Did Sebastian tell you that or did you overhear them?" Laken met her gaze.

Quinn bowed her head.

My sister scowled. "Were you one of Emery's groupies?"

"Laken, stop," I snapped.

"No, I... I'm feeling faint," Quinn whispered. "I missed breakfast."

Once more, I steered her to a chair and sat her down. "We'll get you lunch. Right after you tell us everything you know about Sebastian and Emery."

"I'd like to hear that, too." Officer Rhodes stood in the doorway. "I see your move is still at a standstill. If I didn't have to work today, I'd offer to help."

"Thanks." I forced a smile.

Laken put her hands on her hips. "Our friend Hamlet, who now officially goes by Quinn Evans, was about to tell us what she knows about my ex-husband financing Sebastian's former protégé Mishel."

"Quinn Evans? Pin in that." Rhodes raised his eyebrows, then held up a finger and turned to Laken. "Who's your ex-husband?"

"Emery Samson."

His smirk vanished. "The actor?"

I nodded. "That's the one."

"My wife likes his movies. I'm not a fan."

Laken snorted. "Me, neither. He's a much better actor than he is a human being. Apparently, he pulled out on backing Mishel who then lost his business. Quinn thinks Sebastian had something to do with that."

Quinn growled before she spoke. "I don't just think he did, I was there when Sebastian told Emery to cut Mishel loose before he got dragged into an even bigger scandal."

Considering my sister's entire marriage and divorce were based on scandal, I could see why Emery might be tempted to cut his losses. "What bigger scandal?"

"Sebastian accused Mishel of stealing his designs," Quinn said. "He told Emery that was the reason Mishel left the House of Hayward.

"Was it?" Rhodes asked.

Her cheek twitched. "No. It was the other way around. Sebastian was the one who stole Mishel's designs. His creativity had dried up and he needed his protégé to keep him afloat. With Mishel gone, Sebastian had to find someone to help revive the House of Hayward before it sank."

Rhodes made a note in his book. "That's when he hired you."

"Yes, and I'm sure he regretted it every day."

Laken fingered one of the bug dresses. "These outfits are Quinn's designs."

Quinn sighed. "The Conservatory Collection was our last shot to keep things going. Now Sebastian's dead, and I can't help wonder if I had something to do with that."

Rhodes frowned. "Is that a confession?"

"No!"

"Why do you feel responsible?" I asked.

"Because I didn't speak up. I just let everything go down in flames."

"So no confession?" Rhodes tapped his pen on the notebook.

Quinn shook her head as she returned to the cabinet. "Like It told you, I went back to the hotel to change clothes after I got coffee on my dress."

Rhodes gave up and left with Laken and Sammy when they went to pick up lunch.

Quinn continued to unpack her designs in silence. She puffed up a shiny green hat using her fist. The hat went with a hummingbird outfit she'd tugged onto a mannequin. It was nice to see some of the alien mannequins dressed. They were slightly less creepy dressed as bugs.

I leaned on the counter wishing I could pull the thoughts out of Quinn's head. Finally, I told her, "I'm sorry you've gone through all of this. What are you going to do now?"

"Sebastian promised I'd have a job here for a while." She paused and met my gaze. "But now I have to rethink everything. I guess I could go back to school or find a job in a club."

"What kind of club?"

Her face reddened while she straightened an invisible wrinkle on the hummingbird outfit. "I used to be a drag queen. That's how I met Sebastian in the first place. He loved the costumes I designed for the queens. A lot of them wanted me to design more outfits, but I chose to be noticed for something besides my five o'clock shadow."

I doodled on the notepad. "Why not do the obvious then?"

"What's that?"

"Design and sell costumes for drag queens." So much for obvious.

As Quinn met my gaze, her whole demeanor changed. She drew her shoulders back and puffed out her chest, then grinned. "Aren't you just the most adorable little genius."

"Thanks. I think."

"What about you?" she asked. "Did you always want to own a boutique?"

I pulled out a second notebook and handed it to her in anticipation of a sketching frenzy now that she had fresh motivation. "I dreamed of owning a vintage clothing store since I was little. I loved playing dress up with Mom's clothes, especially the ones she kept in the back of the closet in case they ever came back in style."

"I still have a few of those. I even made some for my sister's dolls."

I chuckled. "When I was ten, I created a line of clothing for our dolls out of aluminum foil. I nearly fell over laughing when I saw pictures of Laken modelling Sebastian's space line."

"I remember those," Quinn groaned. "Was that the end of your budding fashion design career?"

I shook my head. "No, I switched to medical gauze, sequins, and glue. The contact cement was a big mistake and cost our dog a patch of fur. The doll I used it on is still wearing it."

"That's hilarious. How old were you?"

"Twelve. Mom was not impressed. Grandma Sadie laughed so hard her dentures fell out." I didn't mention I'd seen the doll in Laken's bedroom when she moved in with me. I was touched she'd hung onto it all those years.

Quinn fingered the notebook. "I can't figure you out, Sage, but I definitely adore your moxie. Friends?"

"Friends."

While we waited for Laken to return, I opened the cabinet with the necklaces we'd found. "Hey, maybe some of these will work with your designs."

"How did you...? Those necklaces are..." her voice trailed off.

"What's wrong?" I asked.

"I can't believe that gerbil did that!" Quinn shouted. "He promised to give me some of those in return for coming here. When they disappeared, he blamed Mishel. Then he insisted we needed the money and that he'd sold them."

"You didn't know he'd shipped them here?"

"No, that's what we were talking about before..." Silence hugged us like a cashmere shawl for a moment before she continued, "I overheard him tell the insurance company the jewels were stolen, so I asked him which it was. Did he sell them or did someone steal them?"

"How much did he owe you?"

Quinn closed her eyes and released an agonized sigh. "Thousands. Sage, I have nothing left. I sold my valuables to pay for my treatments. I've been lucky to have friends who gave me second-hand clothes and wigs. They taught me about makeup and how to dress. Thanks to Sebastian, now I'm a pariah. I can never go back to Los Angeles."

"What do you mean?" I opened a box containing a silver necklace with blue stones.

"Sebastian told everyone my designs ruined him," she said. "Now that both he and the shop are gone, I won't be able to pay back the loans my friends gave me."

Quinn reached into the cabinet then unwrapped some gray-blue fabric. As she gazed from the fabric to me, a quick "huh" escaped her. She unfolded a gown and held it in front of me. "Honey, with your gorgeous red hair and those turquoise eyes—which I hate you for in a good way—you'd look stunning in this."

I studied the form-fitting dress all the way down to the flare of fabric at the bottom. It was a shimmering mermaid gown. Simple and unadorned. I wrinkled my nose. "What kind of bug is that one?"

"It's a cocoon, my dear, which is why this dress is so perfect for you. I'd love to see the beauty you're hiding emerge as a butterfly."

"I'm no butterfly." I laughed, and turned back to the boxes of jewelry. "And I'm certainly no model. I'll stay in my cocoon, thanks."

"You seriously don't think you're as beautiful as your sister, do you?" she asked.

Her question caught me off guard. "She's the supermodel, not me."

Quinn draped the gown over her forearm before she reached into the cabinet again. She grabbed my arm, then marched me to the change rooms. "Put on the dress, gorgeous lady. I want to see you shine."

I tried to squirm out of her grasp, but she was stronger than me. Finally, I blew out a defeated breath. "Fine. Give it to me."

She squealed as she piled the fabric onto my outreached arms.

Alone in the change room, I studied myself in the mirror trying to see what Quinn saw before. Turning my back on my reflection, I slipped out of my torn jeans and tank top. Since the gown had no straps or sleeves, my bra had to go as well. Within seconds, my comfort zone tumbled behind me in the dust.

"Stop stalling, darling. I want to see."

"I'm not stalling. I'm hyperventilating."

When she yanked open the curtain, her eyes grew wide, and her mouth made a little red "o."

My face burned. "I told you I'm no model."

"Honey, it's like I designed that dress just for you," Quinn whispered.

When I tried to return to the change room, she barked, "Wait. Don't move."

Quinn ran across the room as fast as she could, and rifled through the necklace boxes. She draped a glittering diamond and turquoise necklace across my bare chest and fastened it. "That's exactly what it needed. The stones even match your eyes."

When the front door opened behind us, I turned expecting to see Laken. "Andy. What are you doing here?"

Dressed in his paramedic uniform, he stood in the doorway. "Sage? I... You... You look incredible."

"See," Quinn said as she nudged me. "The cute guy gets it."

"Thanks." My face had to be as red as the light blinking on Andy's shoulder mic.

Quinn beamed. "Sage is wearing this in the fashion show we're having Friday. All that's left is to do her hair and makeup. I told her this was a good look for her. Guess I was right."

Andy grinned. "You absolutely were."

"Please tell me this hunk is your boyfriend." she whispered. "He's so hot."

"We're friends," I told her, squirming in the sausage-casing dress.

She winked. "Well, I for one love a man in uniform, especially a speechless one."

"You mean the strong, silent type?" Andy seemed to shake off his surprise. He chuckled as he strode toward us his gaze still riveted on me. "You didn't answer my texts. I came to see if you were okay."

"We're fine, thanks." I met his gaze sure my knees had turned to rubber.

"Sage, you really do look amazing," he said.

I forced a smile. "Thanks to Quinn. This is her design."

"Quinn?" Rather than ask the obvious question that flitted across his face, he nodded. "Pleasure to meet you. I'm Andy Briggs. I'm impressed you got this girl into an outfit that's not baggy and covered in paint or dust."

Her cheeks glowed pink. "You're welcome. Now man up and ask her on a real date. I'll even give you some privacy."

I groaned. "Quinn."

"Thanks, but I can't stay. I just popped in to say hi." Once Quinn left the room, Andy whispered, "Wasn't his name Hamlet the other day?"

"I'll explain later."

He smiled. "About that date."

"Andy," I started, then sighed.

"You really do look incredible, Sage," he said, looking me up and down. "I want a front row seat for the fashion show. I'll pay extra just to watch you walk down the runway in that dress."

"I can't guarantee I wouldn't fall flat on my face. I'm not a model. Laken is."

"You should do it anyway," he whispered, touching the diamond and turquoise necklace, then my jaw. My heart started to beat faster. "In fact, you should be the last person down the aisle. You'll bring down the house."

Laken cleared her throat. "I agree, but it's called a runway."

Andy backed away from me, his cheeks reddening.

My sister stood in the doorway with a couple paper bags and a cardboard tray holding our drinks. "Oh wow, Sage. Who threatened you to make you try on that gown?"

Quinn flung her arms open wide as she burst through the kitchen door. "The designer did, darling, who else?"

"Doesn't she look amazing?" Andy asked.

"With a little makeup and a great hairdo, you'll steal the show," Laken said, leading Sammy toward the counter where she set down our lunch.

"Told ya." Quinn spun me around to give them the full effect of the knee to floor flare.

As I turned, Sammy snuffled the hem of the long skirt, then glanced up at me before wandering toward Quinn.

Tired of being the center of attention, I turned away to return to the change room. "I need to get out of this thing. I'm suffocating."

"Sage, wait," Andy called out. When I turned, he snapped a photo grinning wider than I'd ever seen before. "No one will believe this without proof."

"I'll send them to you."

My eyes grew wide. "Them? How many pictures did you take?"

"A few." Andy walked toward me, then stopped and grimaced as his mic crackled. "Gotta go. See you later?"

"Yeah." I watched him leave the store, pausing to wink back at me before he closed the door.

Laken's eyes shone. "You have to close the show wearing that gown. I'd be thrilled to do your hair and makeup."

"Oh no, sweet thing," Quinn told her, draping an arm across my shoulder. "This girl's all mine. You worry about your other models. Sage is my muse. Get your own."

My sister laughed as she reached for the bags on the counter. "I have no idea what happened while I was gone, but I'm glad you had a bonding moment. Quinn, you get the salad with pecans, feta, and grilled chicken. Sage, yours has chickpeas, berries, and nuts. I got the chicken Caesar."

"They all sound yummy." Quinn leaned toward me and whispered, "I'll trade you."

I shook my head as I closed the curtain behind me. "I'm vegetarian. The chicken's all yours."

"Good to know. Next time, I'll ask for the vegetarian salad."

I struggled to devise ways to get out of modeling the cocoon dress, which was as hard as trying to get out of the dress itself. Either I needed a pair of scissors to snip some seams, or I'd still be wearing it come Friday. After shimmying and hopping in place, I managed to slither out of the curve-hugging fabric and into my own clothes.

Comfortable in my cargo pants and tank top once again, I locked the front door before we headed to the courtyard. Laken and Quinn chatted about the fashion show until Quinn mentioned designing clothing for drag queens. Laken was all for it.

While they chatted, my phone dinged. Andy sent three images of me wearing the cocoon dress. I admit, the dress made me look so good, I showed the pictures to Quinn and Laken.

Quinn grabbed my phone and typed in her number. "Send them to me. As the designer, I'd love to share them on my social media. As long as you're okay with that."

I nearly choked on a chickpea.

"Go for it," Laken said. "We could use it for advertising."

"I thought we were trying to attract customers," I muttered.

"Oh, please." Quinn groaned, then threw a wadded napkin at me.

After lunch and a relaxing dose of sunshine, I finished unpacking the jewelry while Quinn dressed a mannequin in another piece of bug-inspired clothing. We'd barely finished organizing the store when Andy returned.

"Hey, ladies." He seemed disappointed that I'd changed clothes.

"Andy and I are going to finish moving stock," I chirped, excited to get the moving portion of things over with. "Anyone else want to help?"

Quinn took a step toward me. "Sure, I—"

Laken cleared her throat. "Quinn and I have a meeting with the models. I guess we'll see the two of you later."

"Right. I'm needed here," she said, shooting Laken a frown before checking her fingernails.

"Okay, we'll stack everything in the corner, so we can deal with it tomorrow." I waved to the one corner we'd purposely left empty. Right near the door, we didn't have to haul things far.

"Sounds good," Laken said, giving a finger wave. "Have fun."

Since I'd heard that same falsetto many times before, my gut told me something was going on. What was my sister up to this time?

Chapter Eight

Cameron Dale's Corvette pulled in front of the old store just as I unlocked the door. We were blessed with the pleasure of his company because Laken was meeting with the models. No matter. I was happy for an extra set of hands to lift the heavy items.

Dust flew up from the front counter as I set a box on top. I fanned it away with one hand while I pulled open the top drawer. As I emptied it of pens, paperclips, and sticky notes, one of the notes stuck to the back of my hand. My breath stuck in my throat as I read, *"Ran out for coffee, be right back. D."*

Delia.

Everywhere I looked, several items suddenly became reminders of my former business partner. The silver hairbrush and mirror set we'd discovered at an estate sale sat on top of a well-cared for white dresser. I'd never found the heart to sell either.

"Come on, Sage, put a price on it," Delia insisted several times. "We can easily get a couple hundred dollars for that dresser."

Then Jonathan came in one day and swept me off my feet—

Those darn emotions threatened to overtake me again. I sucked in a sharp breath and muttered, "Cut it out. I've got work to do."

The rest of the time we emptied the store I put Delia and Jonathan in the past. The future held a behemoth of a store that I needed to fill.

Whatever we didn't use, I could sell online once we opened the new location. Then I'd concern myself with finding more items to sell.

For now, I had to finish packing.

It took Andy and Cameron two trips to haul the fixtures to the new location. I didn't bother to unpack since we'd all had a long day. Thankfully, Cameron took the time to help me set up the till and the computer. The whole time, he checked his phone as though worried he'd miss something. Like a date with my sister.

"You might want to call the bank in the morning to make sure your point-of-sale machine is working before the show," Cameron said, reaching for his phone again. "I'm sure you'll make a lot of sales. I have to pick up Laken for dinner.

"I have a feeling you might be stuck entertaining Quinn tonight. I think she's in need of some company after Sebastian's death."

He shrugged, then lowered his voice while Andy moved the white dresser into a brighter spot and asked, "What's with you two? Anything I should know about?"

"Things are good. Thanks for your help, Cameron. You guys have fun."

"You, too." He winked.

Once Cameron left, Andy waited near the door toying with his truck keys. "Are you sure you don't need a hand with anything else? I'm free tonight."

My eyes burned as I brushed dust off my clothes. "Nope, we're good. I'll get Laken and Quinn to help unpack the rest tomorrow. What I need now are dinner and a shower."

He met my gaze. "You still haven't told me about Quinn and Hamlet."

"You're right." I yawned as I led Andy out of the store. "Why don't I buy you dinner? I can fill you in while we eat."

"Great idea," he said, while I locked the doors. "Let's try that new pub."

"You mean the one across from my old location?"

"That's the one," he said. "Don't worry the guys there aren't exactly your main clientele."

"You've already been there?" I asked. raising my eyebrows.

Andy looked away. "After our shift last night. We all needed a stiff drink."

I touched his arm. "Sounds like it was a really bad one."

"Two little kids died. There was nothing we could do." He helped me into his truck. "Those are the hardest."

We parked in front of my old store, then walked across the street to the pub. As we reached the front door, he held up his index finger. "By the way, they have Buffalo Cauliflower and a couple great vegetarian options. I made sure to check before I dragged you over here."

I flashed a wide smile. "Aww, that's sweet. You'd better be careful, Briggs. I'm starting to think you like me."

"Who me?" He winked, then led me to a table near the bar and held out my chair before he sat across the table. Once we'd ordered drinks, along with veggie burgers and sweet potato fries, he took my hand. "Okay, fill me in. Who is Hamlet-slash-Quinn and what's the latest on Sebastian?"

I hesitated. "I told you Sebastian was murdered yesterday, right?"

Andy set his cell phone face down on the table. "I half-read your messages, but it was a crazy shift, and nothing registered. I read them again this morning to make sure I didn't miss anything. That's why I stopped to check on you. I'm glad I did. That dress..."

"What about it?" I asked as my face grew warm.

"You looked amazing in it."

"Thanks." Heat trickled from my cheeks to my chest. "Anyway, Sebastian's protégé—"

"Hamlet, right?"

"Sort of."

"Now I'm confused."

"She came back this morning."

Andy frowned and asked, "She who?"

"Quinn. She plans to stick around to fill in for Sebastian since Laken hired him for the next six weeks."

He frowned. "Help you do what? You've run Vintage Sage on your own for years."

"Sebastian wanted us to repaint the walls, redecorate, and replace me. Laken wanted to put him in charge of the fashion show to keep him busy. The man drove me crazy."

"Of course he did. You've done everything since the day you opened that store. I would've been ready to..." Andy sat back as our drinks arrived. "Where does this Quinn person fit into things?"

"That was Hamlet's bombshell today," I told him, then took a sip of my wine spritzer before I met his gaze. "He's transgender and wants us to call him...her... Quinn. Now that Sebastian's gone, she feels safe to come out."

He took a swig of his beer and stared at me for a long minute before he said, "That must've caught you guys by surprise."

"A little. A lot. The funny thing is once Quinn told us the truth she's become easier to deal with. She got me to model that dress, which I never would've done without her pushing me." I hesitated. "She designed it, and I can't believe she wants me to model it in the show."

Andy shook his head with a sigh and took my hand again. "Why not? Sage, you're a beautiful woman. I'm proud of you for even trying it on. I know it's out of your comfort zone, but I can't wait to see you walk down the runway wearing that gown. It's a huge change from khakis and a tank top." He grinned. "By the way, I want a front row seat."

"Which is why I'm not gonna do it."

"Because I asked for a front row seat?"

My ponytail swept my shoulders as I shook my head. "Laken's the model, not me. I'm much happier backstage. It makes me uncomfortable when people watch me do anything."

"Even me?" he asked, giving my hand a squeeze.

"Even you."

"So you don't like when I watch you eat?"

"Definitely not." I laughed.

"I'll be sure to stare at the pepper all night then."

All night? My heart skipped a beat. "You don't have to do that."

Andy winked, then focused on tearing bits of the label off his beer bottle. "Was it weird when Hamlet...Quinn told you?"

"About becoming a woman?" I shrugged. "Yes, and no."

He hesitated. "I have to admit this whole trans thing is weird for me. I've never known anyone... who's changed like that."

"I get that. I had a couple friends in Seattle who went through the same change after years of bullying and not feeling good in their own bodies. Once they changed their lives, they were happier. I think people like Quinn are brave for listening to their gut and being on the outside the way they feel inside."

"Now that I can understand," Andy said, then asked, "Do you know what I like about Quinn?"

"What's that?"

"She looks at you and sees what I see."

I chuckled. "Dust in my hair and rips in my clothes."

"You're one of those women who has no idea how stunning she is."

"Stop teasing."

He reached to give my hand a quick squeeze. "I'm not joking, Sage. You're smart, you're beautiful, and you're amazing. Maybe Quinn's not the only one who needs to change her life."

"What do you mean?"

"That you should open up to possibilities."

I was saved by the arrival of our food. My stomach gurgled while I added mustard to my veggie burger. If I stuffed food in my mouth, I wouldn't have to acknowledge Andy's comment, let alone how uncomfortable it made me. Living in the shadow of a supermodel had wreaked havoc on my self-esteem for years.

Andy met my gaze over our food. "I didn't mean to embarrass you. Lucky for me, my brother didn't become a brain surgeon like my parents wanted, or I'd feel the same way."

"What does your brother do?" I picked up a sweet potato fry.

"He dropped out of medical school to become a cop in Yakima," he said. "He thinks he's better than me because he carries a gun and handcuffs. I just remind him that if he gets shot, I can save his life."

I chuckled, and had to dab a spot of sauce off my lip. I glanced to see if anyone saw me make a mess. Near the back exit, Quinn sat with a thin, dark-skinned man who had had pale blond hair, round glasses, and a dark blazer with light-colored pants. I didn't think she knew anyone in Glitter Bay.

A few minutes later, Andy excused himself and left the table. I was too distracted to pay much attention. Who could the strange man be? Just when I decided to corner Quinn the next day, the answer hit me like a zap from a taser.

"Omigod, I'll bet that's Mishel," I whispered.

Before Andy returned, I snuck a few covert photos of Quinn with the man I suspected was Sebastian's former protégé. Depending on how long he'd been in town, he could be a murder suspect. Either way, the police would be interested to know he'd met with Quinn.

"Isn't that Quinn by the window?" Andy asked as he returned.

"Yeah. You don't happen to know she's with, do you?"

He glanced over his shoulder, then shook his head. "Never seen him before."

"Me neither, but I have a hunch he's Mishel."

"Who's Mishel?"

I caught Andy up on the House of Hayward, the stolen designs, and my concern about his tete-a-tete with Quinn.

"So he's a bad guy."

"I don't know," I admitted. "If he killed Sebastian, I'd definitely say he's a bad guy."

"But if he's in Glitter Bay by total coincidence, then—"

"Like what?" I cut him off sharper than I intended. When a couple glanced in our direction, I lowered my voice. "What could bring him to town besides Sebastian?"

Andy shrugged. "An eccentric aunt? A letter telling him he had a mission should he choose to accept it?"

I laughed and threw a fry at him. "Now you're reaching."

"Well, when you figure out what he's doing here and if he killed Sebastian, let me know."

"I will."

He grinned. "I have no doubt."

When Andy dropped me off at my house just after ten, my mind lingered on Quinn and Mishel. I had questions I hoped my sister had answers to.

Sammy hopped to his feet when I opened the front door. As he started toward me, I ran past him to search for my sister. She wasn't in the kitchen, the office, or her bedroom.

"She's still out with Cameron, isn't she?" A bit dismayed, I tripped over my fluffy cat as I headed to my office and turned on the computer.

It took a little searching but soon Mishel—no last name that I could find—stared back at me off the screen. I compared my photo to the image on my computer screen. My stomach sank. How long had he been in Glitter Bay? My bigger concern was whether Laken knew he was here and "forgot" to tell me.

Sammy whimpered from down the hall and scratched at a door.

"I'm in the office." I read as much as my brain could absorb before I turned off the computer nearly an hour later. Numb, I wandered through the house.

He followed me to the kitchen, then snorted before scratching at the door again.

"Oh, I'm sorry, baby." I reached for his leash. "You probably haven't been out in hours."

I walked him down the sidewalk toward the beach, but I didn't bother let him off the leash. It was too dark to search for him if he wandered off or got attacked by some nocturnal creature or a crab. We wandered close enough to the water that the waves rushed over my feet.

Mishel bobbed near the top of my suspect list. Was he in town when Sebastian was killed? His life had improved since leaving the House of Hayward, so I wasn't sure he had a motive to kill Sebastian. After his funding fell through, Mishel joined a larger designer who celebrated his talents and allowed him free reign to work on the department store line. I hoped his designs didn't resemble any sort of bugs, although a couple of Quinn's outfits were growing on me.

"I don't know where it is," a voice shrieked over the peaceful, rolling waves. "You need to talk to her."

The voice sounded like Quinn's. My pulse quickened.

Sammy's ears perked and twitched. He strained against the leash to get closer.

Across the damp sand, two people stood just outside the glow of the streetlights. Quinn and Mishel. When he mumbled something, I couldn't make out his words over the waves. I would've given a lot of money for Sammy's hearing right then.

"Look, those girls trust me," Quinn said. "They've paid to have me here for six weeks, so I have time. Don't rush me."

Sammy started to bark at something in the parking lot beyond them. The only part I caught was the man growling, "...before it's too late."

I scooped Sammy into my arms, then scurried back the way we came. The tone of Mishel's voice rattled me. I clutched Sammy's damp body against my racing heart. What could Mishel be after and what did it have to do with Quinn? Sebastian, thoughtful soul that he was, must've hidden something he stole from Mishel.

The necklaces?

Nope. Quinn knew about those.

We'd even gone through several boxes together.

The gold coins were a possibility, but I hadn't seen anything else out of the ordinary. Maybe I needed to go through them one by one.

Out of breath, I slowed my pace, then set him down to do his business before we climbed the stairs. The front door opened wide before I touched it, making me shriek.

"There you are." Laken's hand flew to her chest as she let out a sigh. "Sage, it's nearly midnight. You never stay out this late. You should've left me a note or something."

I coaxed Sammy up the stairs. Before I did anything else, I locked the door behind me before I leaned against it. When I met my sister's bewildered gaze, the whole story tumbled out in a babbling rash.

"Stop." Laken held up a hand. "Let me take Sammy's leash off. You sit."

In the few seconds it took her to free her dog, I managed to catch my breath.

My sister joined me on the couch. "What's going on? Start at the beginning."

"Mishel's in Glitter Bay. I saw him and Quinn at the pub that opened across from our old location. Did you know they have Buffalo Cauliflower and veggie burgers?"

Her face paled. "Are you serious?"

"Yeah, they're delicious."

"The Mishel part."

I pulled up the pictures on my phone. "After Andy brought me home, I checked online to make sure it was him before I took Sammy for a walk. Mishel and Quinn were near a streetlight by the marina, and I heard them talking."

Laken closed her eyes for a moment, then said, "I wonder how long he's been in town."

"It sounds like he's looking for something he thinks Sebastian had. All I could think of were those necklaces and the gold coins," I told her.

She nodded. "Unless he had a hiding place we haven't found yet."

"Quinn said Sebastian had promised her a couple of those necklaces. What if he sent them because of Mishel?" I thought for a moment. "I saw a few of Mishel's designs online. They're more elegant and classic than anything Sebastian ever created. Those necklaces would add a great touch."

Laken met my gaze before asking, "Do you think Sebastian shipped them to us to keep them away from Mishel?"

"I have no idea."

"It's late and I'm too tired to think straight," she said, giving me a hug. "Let's get some sleep and interrogate Quinn in the morning."

"Good plan. I'll write down some questions. If I don't, I'll never get to sleep." I yawned.

Laken led the way up the stairs while Sammy ran ahead. She paused outside her bedroom door. "I never should've brought Sebastian here behind your back, but I had no idea he'd bring trouble with him. We should be worrying about opening the store, not dealing with an opening, a fashion show, a murder, and an apprentice designer. You don't deserve any of this."

"Neither do you. At least you keep me on my toes."

"That's for sure." She gave me a hug, holding onto me like I was a life preserver.

"We'll figure out who killed him," I whispered. "As for Quinn, she's kind of growing on me."

My sister chuckled. "I know, right? Things have not been boring since she arrived. I still can't believe she got you to put on that dress. You really need to wear that in the show."

"That's what Andy said."

"Hey, the guy has good taste," she told me.

I groaned. "Let it go. It'll never happen."

"You in the show, or you and Andy?" she asked with a wink.

I washed up, then placed my crystals on the window ledge before I crawled into bed with a notebook at one o'clock. Despite the lengthy to-do list I itched to make my eyelids grew heavy. Finally, I reached for a bottle of lavender and took a deep whiff.

In her bedroom across the hall, Laken banged drawers and mumbled.

By the time Muumuu jumped on my bed I could barely form letters. She stretched out beside me on top of the covers and purred.

I put down the notebook and turned off the light before reaching to pet her. That was the one thing that never failed to put me to sleep. I drifted off in record time.

That bliss was short lived.

My sister stormed into my room and flicked on the light. "Okay, Sage, where is it?"

I forced one eye open. "Huh?"

"That envelope Sebastian gave me to hang on to," she said. "Where is it?"

"What are you talking about?" I blinked barely wider awake than earlier.

Laken huffed as if she'd told me six times already and sat on the end of my bed. "The day after they arrived, after Hamlet—sorry, Quinn—went to the washroom, Sebastian gave me an envelope to keep safe in case anything happened to him."

"Sebastian gave you an envelope in case anything happened to him?" I asked.

"That's what I just said." She frowned when Sammy joined us on my bed. "What is wrong with you?"

"Cut me some slack I was asleep. What did the letter say?" I struggled to sit up.

Laken scowled. "I don't know. I can't find it to open it now that he's..."

Muumuu hissed, not amused to see Sammy in her sacred space.

The dog groaned as he lay down and ignored her ire.

"Did he say who you were supposed to give it to if something happened to him?"

My sister flinched then shook her head as tears welled in her eyes. "I just assumed I was supposed to read it then go from there, but I didn't expect..."

"What did you do with it when you got home?" I rubbed my eyes.

"I took it, then put in in my purse," she said. "I brought him and Quinn to the house before we went for dinner at Devil's Peak. I really need to start eating somewhere else. Sebastian drove us to the hotel and threw a fit because they couldn't get separate rooms. I took a cab home, left my purse near the door, and came upstairs to collapse in bed because I was worn out after putting up with those two all day. Honestly, Sage, they argued like two-year-olds."

I held up a finger. "A-ha."

"What a-ha?" She sat back.

"It's probably still in your purse."

Her shoulders sagged. "It's not there."

I glanced at Sammy then stroked his head. "Did you check all of your purses? You do have three or four hanging down there."

"I've looked everywhere." Laken closed her eyes. "What if that envelope held Sebastian's last will and testament, or the deed to his design house?"

"The bankrupt one?"

She growled. "Yes, the bankrupt one. Sage, why can't you cut him some slack? The guy's dead. It makes me sad that you haven't liked him since you met him."

I stared at her. "You were in the room when we met right? It's hard to cut someone slack when they strut into your store and tell you everything you're doing wrong, then say you should work in a horse barn."

"That's why we hired him. For his honesty," my sister said.

"No, Laken, that's why *you* hired him." I pulled my blanket to my chin and lay on my back. "I just got blindsided because you were afraid I'd say no."

As I nestled into my pillows, my sister sighed. I rolled over, hoping she'd go to her room and let me sulk in peace. Sure enough, she got up and turned off the light. Rather than leave, though, she curled up next to me.

"Sage, you're right. I'm sorry," she said. Her voice crackled with emotion. I should've talked to you before you saw that invoice."

I let out a laugh. "More like before you ever made a deal with the gerbil."

Laken nestled her head against mine. "You're right. It's your shop. I just wanted to help. I forgot who I was dealing with."

"Him or me?"

"Sebastian Hayward the Third," she whispered. "While I loved him as a friend, I forgot he could be so awful."

There was a long silence. I was sure both Sammy and Muumuu were asleep. Even my sister's breathing became even as she relaxed next to me.

"Who do you think killed him?" I asked softly.

She moaned. "Quinn had the most to lose, but I'd love for Emery to be guilty. Mostly because I can't stand him, but..."

When she fell silent, I rolled over to face her, then leaned up on my elbow. "He's not even involved, is he?"

"Emery. Chick. They all run in the same circles. I have no idea who Sebastian was such a threat to. I always thought he was harmless."

I nodded. "Maybe Sebastian knew something that could've hurt Emery's career even more."

Laken grimaced. "Sage, the entire world knows what a joke Emery Samson is. It just depends on the degree of that knowledge and how it could hurt people."

My sister finally dozed off on top of the covers while Sammy snuggled next to Muumuu. With everyone somewhat content around me, and me stuck like a sardine in between them all, we fell asleep until Laken got cold and crawled beneath the covers.

I wasn't about to send her to her own room. I didn't want to be alone either.

My sister's revelations hadn't made me feel any better about Quinn, Sebastian, or what chaos might've made its way to Glitter Bay.

Chapter Nine

✧⟡⟡⟡⟡⟡⟡ ⟡⟡⟡⟡⟡✧

When I woke up at five o'clock that morning, Laken and Sammy were gone. So was Muumuu. My tossing and turning must've sent them all scurrying to my sister's room or the couch at some point during the night. I lay in bed with my eyes closed hoping to doze off but had no such luck when my phone dinged twice.

I ignored it as my thoughts drifted to Sebastian's murder and Mishel's sudden appearance. He and Quinn must've been commiserating—or celebrating—the loss of their boss.

After several minutes, I got up and tiptoed past Laken's closed door, then down the stairs. As usual, Sammy's crate in the kitchen was empty. No doubt he was curled on my sister's bed. Or in her closet. He had a penchant for designer clothing, and break and enter when it came to my sister's closet. He behaved in Vintage Sage, but Laken's clothes were fair game.

I plugged in the kettle before stepping onto the back deck. The sky was painted with pinks and purples, making the dew-covered grass shimmer. The sweet scents of garden flowers hung heavy in the air.

While the kettle came to a boil, I did a few barefoot Sun Salutations deck to get my blood moving. Morning yoga was why I wore tank tops and shorts to bed all summer. Since I was already in my workout gear when I got up, I had no excuse. With my mood brighter, I made a cup of Earl Gray, then padded past the living room to the hallway. My plan was to research Mishel, Quinn, and Sebastian.

I did a double-take as I backed up to peer into the living room once more.

What I didn't expect was to see Quinn Evans sprawled on my couch wearing a purple velvet sleep mask with a lilac night dress bunched around her knees. Muumuu sat on the back of the couch glaring while Quinn snored softly.

I stared for a long minute before shuffling to my office. Since I hadn't heard any commotion during the night, I guess I got more sleep than I thought. The fact Quinn was asleep on my couch didn't make me less suspicious of her. Something was going on between her and Mishel. Although I itched to find out what, I wasn't about to wake her up.

I spent the next hour getting lost in cyberspace and listening to music on my headphones, which slightly muffled Quinn's rumbling. Yawning, I rubbed my eyes then sat back to look at my notes. My handwriting was horrible so early in the morning. I opened a new document and tried to translate my own gibberish.

Mishel was Sebastian's protégé who'd kept the House of Hayward afloat for three years. In year four, he made noise on social media that Sebastian was washed up and Mishel was the brains behind the design house. Not good for business let alone friendship.

After a major blowout—Sebastian gained a black eye and was publicly humiliated—Mishel packed up his sketchbook and designs to strike out on his own. His social media sites were blanketed with hints about a fabulous new design house in town, then...

Nothing.

It was like he'd dropped out of the design world completely. Until the recent announcement from a high-end department store about their fresh new line. Since Mishel's success came *after* he left House of Hayward, would he still hold a grudge against Sebastian? As far as I knew, Mishel wasn't in Glitter Bay when Sebastian was shot. No motive. No opportunity.

Quinn was here though.

And she and Sebastian had a disagreement in front of Laken a short time before Sebastian was killed. Laken witnessed Quinn get into the cab to return to the hotel, but what if the cab driver only took her around the block? She would've had ample opportunity to return to the store, kill Sebastian, then go to the hotel while Laken walked up to the Devil's Peak Tavern, waited for their food, and wandered back.

Quinn definitely had both motive and opportunity.

When Sebastian's business failed, he blamed her. He also expected a transgender woman to act like a gay man. After the way he treated me, I imagined Sebastian humiliated her every chance he had.

The problem was, I had no idea how much time passed between Laken leaving the store and my arrival. I hadn't noticed a taxi drive away from Vintage Sage, just the black car.

Then there was the matter of whatever Sebastian sent to Vintage Sage that Mishel was looking for. Designs? A second set of accounting books? Even drugs wasn't out of the question.

Overwhelmed, I turned off the computer. Getting answers from Quinn could take some serious finessing, and perhaps a little humiliation on my part. Putting myself in her hands was the only way I'd be able to gain her trust and might need to let her turn me into model material for the fashion show. The thought made my stomach queasy.

Laken was in the kitchen staring at the kettle. She blew out a long breath before she noticed me. Sammy crunched on his breakfast kibble. Muumuu glared at them both from the hallway. She'd found a spot where she could also keep an eye on Quinn.

As I set my cup near the kettle, I nodded toward the living room. "I see we have company."

My sister ran her hand through her shoulder-length hair. "I can't believe you didn't hear her banging on the door. She was hysterical, and I couldn't get a straight answer out of her. Finally, I fed her a large glass of wine. She fell asleep before she finished it. I doubt she's slept since Sebastian died."

Alone in the living room, Quinn snorted, then mumbled in her sleep.

"I guess she didn't want to be alone," I told her as my phone dinged. Andy texted me good morning, which always made me smile.

Muumuu stretched, making a sound that was a cross between a yawn and a growl.

"Do you know what Mishel's looking for?" I asked, fingering my notes.

"No idea." Laken made a pot of tea, then set it on the table. She tugged the bottom of her nightshirt a bit lower before she sat on the vinyl-covered chair and crossed her long legs. "If that's what Quinn was trying to tell me, I couldn't understand a word. She was more incoherent than my ex when I caught him doing drugs."

"Yeah. I'm glad you met someone like Cameron. He's a good man." I handed her my notes, then opened the fridge. Luckily, we had a container of fruit and some muffins that I'd bought on the weekend.

She smiled. "Does it bother you that I'm seeing him? After all, he used to have a serious crush on you."

"That ended when he became as gung-ho on crime solving as you when Tilly died." I chuckled. Now here I was knee-deep in my own mystery. Thankfully, with no sidekick.

I placed the muffins on the table with three plates before I sat across from my sister, who was absorbed in reading my notes.

After several minutes, Laken made a little noise. "You know who I keep forgetting about? Chick Jansen."

"Emery's PR guy? He hadn't even crossed my mind." I peeled the leaves off a strawberry. "And we both know he was smack dab in the middle of all of this."

She handed me the papers. "Chick's supposed to be in Hollywood, but since everyone else involved seems to be popping up in Glitter Bay..."

"I'll do more digging after breakfast," I told her, reaching for a muffin. "By the way, I've decided to model that dress Quinn designed in the fashion show. Andy wants a front row seat to watch me walk down the runway."

Laken gasped in surprise. "I'm sorry. Did I just hear my introvert sister say she'd model a designer gown in our fashion show to impress a guy?"

"Don't make me change my mind." I picked a blueberry from my muffin and popped it into my mouth.

"I can't wait to do your hair and makeup," she said. "I've wanted to glam you up since I first moved into town."

"Well, you'll have to wait."

"Yeah, I got first dibs on making her over," Quinn mumbled, shuffling barefoot into the kitchen.

Muumuu ran off, presumably for the warm, vacant couch.

"Would you like some tea?" I asked, as I got up to get another mug.

She yawned. "Coffee? I need a strong kick of caffeine early in the morning. Tea doesn't do it. Whew, what a night."

I reached for the Keurig that Jonathan bought me for Christmas. "What do you take in it?"

Quinn stretched her arms into the air until something inside her cracked. "I take it as black as Sebastian's soul."

"Black it is." I waited for the coffee to brew and set the cup in front of her before I dared to ask, "Who was the guy I saw you at the pub with last night?"

Laken gasped. "Sage."

"What?" I feigned innocence as I reached for another coffee pod. Tea wasn't going to do it for me today either.

Quinn shrugged. "It's okay. He's just an old friend."

"I didn't realize you knew anyone in town."

Laken groaned. "Oh brother. Sage already figured out you were with Mishel. Just tell us why he's here and what's going on."

"He asked me to meet him for a drink that's all," Quinn said.

"No, that's not all," I told her as I started the machine again. "I overheard the two of you on the beach. He's looking for something Sebastian might've sent here."

"Oh no, I told Mishel this would happen." Quinn moaned. she covered her face with both hands. "I'm sorry for not telling you. Mishel hoped he could talk to Sebastian to straighten a few things out while we were here."

Laken scowled. "What things?"

"When did he get into town?" I asked.

"He showed up at my hotel right after I left your store."

"Yesterday?"

"Tuesday. The day Sebastian..." She paused. "You know."

Laken and I exchanged glances as my coffee brewed. I sat at the table not sure what to say.

My sister cleared her throat. "Are you saying Mishel was in town the day Sebastian died?"

Quinn paled. "He met me at the hotel that day. I'm not sure what time he got to town, but he couldn't have killed Sebastian. Could he?"

"Do the police know he's here?" I asked.

She gazed into her coffee. "I figured since Mishel had just arrived he didn't need to be pulled into all this."

I stared, then raised my voice and shouted, "You didn't think mentioning someone who came all the way from Los Angeles to Glitter Bay to confront his former boss who was murdered that day was important? What if Mishel showed up at Vintage Sage after you and Laken left? He could've killed Sebastian and left town. None of us would've known he was ever there."

Quinn hugged her coffee mug. "True."

"But why wouldn't he just leave town then?" Laken asked. "If you hadn't seen him with Quinn, he wouldn't be a suspect, right?"

"But I did, and he is," I reminded her. "She needs to be honest with us. How can we work with someone who constantly keep secrets?"

My sister shot me a scowl. "Go easy, Sage. She's had a rough week."

"She has? I'm the one who found a dead guy I didn't even like in my store." I stood, taking my muffin and half-empty mug with me. "I need to get ready for work. I have boxes to unpack before that show that you sprang on me. Right before the designer you hired behind my back showed up and demanded I repaint everything I'd spent days painting. The same guy who said I should work in a horse barn."

"The guy's dead," Quinn said softly. "Let it go."

Laken winced, then touched Quinn's arm. "Sage is right. That show's coming fast, and she can't do everything alone."

"Could I rummage through the stuff at your shop?" Quinn asked. "I can't go back to my hotel room, and I couldn't take many clothes."

"Why can't you go back to your hotel room?" I asked.

Her face reddened. "Mishel's there. He took over Sebastian's bed. The way he was talking last night, Chick Jansen's on his way to pick up what they're looking for."

"Which is what?" Laken scowled.

Quinn bowed her head, then sipped her coffee.

"This keeps getting better and better, doesn't it?" I shook my head. "Sure. Knock yourself out. I think we have a couple outfits that'll fit you."

"For free?" She smiled wistfully.

"Don't push it, lady."

Sammy was more than happy to hang out at Vintage Sage for the day. He'd made friends with a bunny and a chipmunk in the courtyard, which is why he was always worn out by the time we left every day. He spent his days either running through the garden or digging holes to bury things in.

Laken and Quinn unpacked boxes we moved the night before. I called to have our point-of-sale machine set up, then made sure the computer and printer both worked. Once those chores were done, I called the glass replacement guy again. Still no answer. There was even more at stake now that our till and the computer were in the store. I left another message before I did some digging.

I'd met Chick Jansen briefly when I went to see my sister in Los Angeles. I had no idea why Emery Samson's PR guy would want to make deals with fashion designers when he dealt with actors. The fact he was looking for something Sebastian sent to Vintage Sage worried me. While I'd researched Mishel, Chick was an unknown entity. To me, anyway.

It wasn't hard to find way too much information about him. All I had to do was search for Emery Samson. Chick was glued to his side like a barnacle at parties, movie shoots, and the like. Chick's professional images portrayed him in a charcoal suit with a pale gray shirt and red power tie.

"A suit?" Laken peered over my shoulder. "I've only seen Chick wear a suit once, and that was at a funeral for a movie studio executive.

Normally, he slums it in ripped jeans, a leather jacket, and high tops. Even at premiere parties."

"How well do you know him?" I asked.

My sister laughed. "Well enough that if I ever called the guy he'd hang up on me. Trust me, he's heard more than one of my tirades."

"Is he the kind of person who'd kill Sebastian?"

She pursed her lips in thought. "If a deal went bad involving a major amount of money, possibly. Personally, I can't see Mishel doing something like that, but it depends on what's at stake."

I continued to dig.

"Are you trying to solve Sebastian's murder?" Laken placed her hands on my shoulders.

"I'm surprised you're not helping, especially after what happened when Tilly died. You barely slept until you figured things out," I reminded her as I studied Chick's photo.

"Sebastian was my friend." Laken frowned. "It's tougher to be nosy when I know everyone, but I'm happy to help. Do you have any suspects?"

"Chick, Mishel, and Quinn are at the top of my list."

Quinn huffed. "Hey, I resent that. I can't stand the sight of blood let alone shoot somebody in the head."

I grimaced. "He was shot in the chest."

"I rest my case." She shrugged. "If I'd killed him, I would've known that."

"That's true."

"Good, then take me off your bad guy list."

My sister leaned closer to me and whispered, "You should talk to Enid."

"Why's that?"

"She's a pro at digging up dirt," she said. "You're just scraping the surface. Enid knows where the bodies are buried. So to speak."

With a click, Chick's face disappeared. "That's not a bad idea."

She hugged me. "Look, you and Andy worked late last night. Why don't Quinn and I work on the store and set up for the show? You can wander over to the newspaper office and chat with Enid about advertising."

"There's not much time to get things ready. I should stay and help."

Laken nodded toward Quinn. My sister might be able to get information I couldn't. Whereas Enid would be happy to talk to anyone.

"No problem." I resisted slapping my forehead. "I'll talk to Enid then pick up lunch on my way back."

The day quickly grew hot and hazy. I was grateful for the breeze blowing off the ocean. By the time I got to the newspaper office, I sweated profusely and was ready to kiss the feet of the guy who invented air conditioning.

Enid Walsh had her own little corner office. Likely to keep her away from her coworkers and the public. She had a whole blue theme going on today. Dark blue pants and a flowery gauze blouse over a blue tank top. It all matched her blue headband and sparkling eyeshadow.

She met my gaze when I walked in. "Sage Miller. I wondered when you'd show up."

"What?"

"I told you I'd find out what I could about the dead guy. If you let me model in your fashion show," she said, tapping a pen against her cheek.

I held up a finger. "Actually, you offered to find out about Sebastian. You asked me to let you model if you found anything juicy."

"Close enough."

"Did you find anything juicy?" I sat on the opposite side of her desk.

She picked up a blue folder and clutched it in both hands before asking, "Do I get to model?"

"I'll remind Laken." I texted my sister to confirm that Enid wanted to be part of the show. "Done. Does that folder contain information about Sebastian Hayward the Third?"

Enid couldn't resist sharing the dirt verbally. For the most part, she didn't tell me anything I didn't know. She'd discovered all about Mishel's abrupt departure, Hamlet-slash-Quinn's—her words, not mine—new line that brought the House of Hayward crashing down, and Sebastian's bankruptcy.

"Those are things we already know," I told her. "It's Quinn, by the way. She filled us in."

"Okay, smarty pants. Do you know a guy named Chick Jansen?" She raised her penciled-on eyebrows.

"Yes, he's Emery Samson's PR guy who broke off his deal with Mishel."

Enid blew out a breath that made her lips vibrate loudly like a horse. "Oh, that's just great. The only thing I have left is that Sebastian was seen with a woman the night before he died."

"Laken or Quinn?" I forced myself not to roll my eyes.

"Neither." That was when she handed me the blue folder.

I stiffened. "The night before he died was the same day he and Quinn arrived in town. Who was he with?"

Enid sat back and grinned. "Now I've got your attention. I don't know. The waiter at the pub never saw her before. He did say she was tall, thin, and kind of pretty. She had big brown eyes with fake lashes and a beauty mark in the shape of a bird on her neck."

I frowned. That meant there was someone else in Glitter Bay with a reason to kill him. "That's memorable. Maybe she's a model. That is how Laken met Sebastian, but I don't know who she could be. I'll ask Laken. Did the waiter catch her name?"

"No, but if this girl was a local, the barflies would know her."

"Good point." I flipped through the folder. "Did Laken ever do that interview with you about her life with Emery? I haven't seen it in the paper yet."

She reached into a desk drawer then pulled out a two-inch thick file folder. "That's because it's going to take me another week to finish writing it thanks to this murder. It's hard to pin that girl down to answer a few questions. She's either at the store or at the vet." She winked. "With the vet. You know what I mean."

I did.

I studied her desktop, which was dotted with several colorful folders. "I don't suppose you came across anything interesting about Chick Jansen while you were digging for dirt on Emery, did you?"

"Funny you should ask," she said. "His name came up every time I turned a page. He's a piece of work. Apparently, he did PR for several other celebrities as well as Emery. Two fired him a couple weeks ago. One accused him of assaulting them on a movie set. The other refused to give a statement."

"Who accused Chick of assault?"

Enid flipped through the pages. After a long moment, she handed me one from the bottom of the stack. "Emery Samson."

"Huh. Who knew Emery had standards? I wonder what happened."

"Oh, that one's easy. Chick tried to do some damage control after Emery's latest faux pas."

My stomach sank as I met her gaze. "Another one? Pretend I've been setting up a new store and dealing with a murder. What did Emery do this time?"

"He was the mysterious backer for that designer Mishel's new design house. He pulled out when Mishel refused to name his new line after Emery's girlfriend, some skinny little model who's been taking the runways by storm. Bridget? Birdie?" She dug through various stacks of paper before she pulled out a printed news clipping. "Aha! No, it's Bridey. Anyway, it's not like she's as memorable as Laken with her red hair and that killer smile. This girl looks like someone permanently ticked her off. I swear, I couldn't find a single picture of her smiling."

I studied the image of an emaciated brunette with the bird-shaped beauty mark on her neck. I'd bet a veggie burrito she was the same woman Sebastian met before he died. I pointed to the beauty mark. "Did you show this photo to the waiter at the pub?"

"Not yet," she said, her face reddening. "To be honest, it slipped my mind until now. I forgot about that mark, but it's probably why I called her Birdie. I'll follow up with the waiter."

"I could stop by there if you'd like. It would save you a trip." I traced the mark with my finger as if memorizing it.

Enid gave an absent nod. "Sure. Why not? Tell Laken I'll get her interview in print soon. Unfortunately, that designer's murder took over the front page."

"No problem. The way this is all playing out, you'll have an even bigger story anyway," I told her as I stood.

Her eyes shone like I'd just tossed her a donut. "What do you mean?"

"Nothing for sure yet. But it seems like half of Los Angeles is in Glitter Bay suddenly. They're after something Sebastian had in his possession."

"Oh really? Keep me in the loop. I'd love a good story to put my adolescent boss in his place.

I chuckled. Her boss was in his mid-forties. "Will do. It might cost you some advertising to promote the new location though."

"Uh-uh. You got it. Here." She scribbled a phone number on the back of a business card. "Call me. Text me. Whatever. Just make sure I get that scoop."

"Deal." I stuck her card in my pocket before I strolled across the street to the deli. After I perused the menu, I ordered three sandwiches and baked potato chips, then strolled over to ask questions at the pub while I waited.

Now was a good time to find that waiter who saw Sebastian with the woman the night before he died. When I showed the photo of Bridey to the staff on duty, no one recalled seeing her. The waiter who'd likely served them was on holidays for the week. That figured. Disappointed, I returned to the deli to pick up lunch.

If Laken knew anything about Emery and his girlfriend, she hadn't let it slip. Since Quinn was a part of the House of Hayward and knew Mishel, I could ask her about Bridey. The two of them had to be involved, especially since they'd both turned up in Glitter Bay. I just had no idea how this Bridey person figured into things. On the upside, my suspect list had grown.

As I walked into Vintage Sage with a bag full of food, I froze. There was a pile of empty boxes in one corner and a stack of shoes and upended furnishings in another. "What happened?"

"Unpacking. What does it look like?" Laken snapped. She hung a yellow Ralph Lauren cotton Henley dress on one of the racks. "We'll flatten the boxes to recycle and donate that other stuff."

My mouth dropped open. "I run a vintage shop, Laken. That 'stuff' is merchandise we need to sell to cover that thirty-thousand-dollar invoice you left on my desk. Where's the big white dresser?"

As the tension in the room grew, Quinn cleared her throat. "That was me. I hate the shoes and that ugly little table. We need to get rid of them. We moved the dresser into Laken's apartment since there was nowhere else to put it. What's for lunch?"

I closed my eyes and counted ten deep breaths. There was no point in arguing. First, I needed to calm down. Then I'd yell. I unpacked the deli bag before taking my food in one hand.

"I'm going to sit outside. I can't stand to look at either of you or that heap right now."

"Uh-oh, she's mad," Quinn said as I walked out the front door.

"Can you blame her?" Laken growled.

I sat on the steps in the sunshine. This promised to be a long afternoon. We still had to set up for the fashion show tomorrow, get a runway laid out, and do a run though with the models. It would all take even longer if Laken and Quinn insisted on throwing out half the stock.

"Don't be mad at your sister," Quinn said, sitting next to me. "We had some unwanted company after you left. Laken threw the boxes and shoes to let off steam. I was trying to cover for her."

Without a word, Laken stormed out of the store with Sammy. They headed toward the beach.

"Who was here?" I asked.

"Mishel. He demanded we hand over all of the paperwork from the House of Hayward and anything else that contained information about designs Sebastian might've stolen from him."

"I don't remember seeing any paperwork."

"That's what Laken told him, but he and his skinny little girlfriend didn't seem impressed." She opened the wrapper on her sandwich.

"Mishel has a girlfriend? What does she look like?"

"She looked like a stick bug with long, dark hair and big sunglasses. I hid in the kitchen when he came in and listened through the door. That girl didn't smile once." She paused. "Maybe that's why Laken was mad. I abandoned her."

Mishel's friend sounded exactly like Bridey Maes.

"Do you know what bothers me?" she asked, taking a small bite then chewing while I waited for her revelation. "I know I've seen that girl before."

I reached into my pocket to pull out the news story Enid gave me. "Is this her?"

Quinn's eyes bugged. "That's her. She's the wannabe who wanted Mishel to name his new line after her, which is ridiculous since she never liked him or his clothes."

"How do you know all that?" I bit into a sour pickle spear.

"She came to see Sebastian before we closed House of Hayward and has a big mouth," she said. "Which makes me wonder what she's doing here with Mishel. I know the girl chases money and fame, but he doesn't exactly have either one."

"You mean because of Chick?"

"Oh please. Mishel had all kinds of opportunities, but he blew them all. For him to get a deal with that department store. Someone had to pull a lot of strings."

"Who do you think has that much clout?"

Quinn shrugged. "Emery Samson? Other than him, you got me."

"Bridey is a fashion model, right?" I picked at the lettuce on my sandwich.

"Uh-huh. Rumor has it she just got a gig with the same store as Mishel."

"I wonder if they were a package deal?" I wasn't sure what I was thinking, but I needed to brainstorm out loud. "Is it possible the store wanted Mishel's designs, but only if Bridey modeled them?"

"No way." She shook her head. "Have you seen the girl?"

"Not in person," I admitted.

"Maybe they wanted Bridey, but she'd only wear Mishel's fashions. Either way, someone wanted the two of them to work together."

Quinn didn't look convinced. "Sebastian hated them both. From what I heard, Bridey was a pain to work with. Who else is there?"

"What if Chick didn't walk away from their deal?" I asked, sitting up straighter as a thought struck me. "Maybe instead of giving Mishel money outright, Chick or Emery brokered the department store deal. If Emery had both Mishel and Bridey under his thumb and somehow found a way, they could all make money. I know he's not an A-lister, but he has some clout."

"It's possible," she said. "But why?"

I finished my sandwich. "I need to talk to Laken. I'll bet she knows Bridey and how she's connected to all of this."

"I thought we were getting ready for the show tomorrow." Quinn's eyes widened.

"You're right. First things first. I'll interrogate my sister after dinner. Once she calms down."

When Laken returned from her power walk with Sammy, Quinn scurried after her. I overheard her give my sister the heads up while I crumpled my garbage. Whose side was that woman on anyway?

Once I figured out how to explain how Emery fit in, I pulled out my phone and Enid's business card. "Hey, it's Sage."

"Whatcha got for me?" she asked.

"Do you have time to do a little detective work? I'm helping Laken with the fashion show and can't sneak away."

Enid didn't even hesitate. "Fire away."

After I explained my theory about Chick, Mishel, and Bridey, Enid remained silent.

"Are you still there?"

"Give me an hour. I'll stop by to tell you what I find out."

I grinned. "Sounds good to me. In the meantime, I'll find out which outfits Laken chose for you to model so you can try them on while you're here."

Less than an hour later, we were nearly done flattening the last of the boxes when Enid ran inside. The fact she actually ran was what surprised me most. I'd known the woman for years. The only reasons I ever saw her move so fast were for good gossip or a food truck.

She pulled me toward the kitchen doorway. "I need a word with you."

"What's going on?" I asked, stumbling over Sammy who yipped at all the excitement.

Laken followed. "Hey, I'm part of this."

"Me, too," Quinn said as she stopped behind my sister.

Enid hesitated as she met my gaze and told us, "I don't know if you all want to hear this."

I shrugged. "How bad is it?"

"Who's she?" Enid pointed to Quinn.

"Quinn Evans," she said, reaching out a hand. "The designer formerly known as Hamlet. Hey, I like that."

"Well, that's one less thing to tell you. I guess Hamlet McTavish is no longer missing then," Enid sighed before going on to confirm everything we knew about Mishel and his connection to Chick. "Then there's that Bridey person I told you about."

Quinn grew so pale her blusher became a swipe of pink on a blank canvas.

"Bridey Maes?" my sister asked. "Is that troll involved in Sebastian's death? Please tell me she's nowhere near Glitter Bay. That woman's more trouble than I care to deal with."

I met Enid's guilt-riddled gaze, then broke the bad news, "She's here."

"No way. Are you sure?"

Enid nodded. "I saw her waiting in Mishel's car when he was here earlier. And someone saw her in the pub with Sebastian the night before he died. I called the waiter who served them."

"Oh brother. That figures." Laken sat on one of the chairs we'd moved along the wall. "She's the b... The younger 'girl' Emery left me for."

"That ho...peless thing?" Quinn asked as her gaze darted to Enid. "Oh, honey, you are so much better than her. That little girl wanted everything you had, so she could live your life. She went after your man, then took over your modeling jobs after you got sick. People told her she'd never be able to fill your shoes. She wanted to prove them wrong."

When we all turned to Quinn, she held her hands up.

"That's what I heard from Sebastian," she said.

"Sounds right to me," Laken muttered.

Enid reached into the tote bag that double as a purse that she'd bought at Vintage Sage last summer and pulled out more papers. "That's part of what I found. Bridey Maes O'Toole, her real name by the way, made it her mission to take over Laken's life in every way she could. She took every photo shoot, relationship, and sponsorship you backed out of."

"Talk about identity theft. At least she didn't change her name," Quinn said.

Laken frowned. "This is surreal."

I turned back to Enid. "Did you figure out why Chick pulled out of his deal with Mishel?"

"Because he's a two-faced jackal and nothing more than Emery Samson's puppet," a man spoke from the doorway. The same yellow-haired man I saw with Quinn at the pub.

"What do you want now?" Quinn folded her arms across her chest.

The tall, lean man scowled. "The same thing as you do, precious. Those designs Sebastian insisted he threw out. The ones that are worth even more now that he's dead."

"What designs?" Quinn asked.

Laken appeared just as bewildered as she was. She walked toward Mishel. "What designs are you talking about? I thought you took everything when you left the House of Hayward."

Enid shoved the folder at me with a grunt. "You know, I miss the days when I'd give people the information I'd worked so hard to dig up and they'd be impressed. Next you'll tell me Chick and Emery are in town, and I won't get to tell you about their plan for Emery's new line of clothes."

This time all eyes turned to Enid.

"What did you say?" I asked.

She threw up her hands. "Finally. Something no one else knew."

Mishel grimaced. "Emery mentioned a new line while we negotiated my design house. His ideas were so horrible I didn't think he was serious."

Enid waved a hand toward the mannequins. "Worse than those bug clothes?"

"Hey, that's uncalled for," Quinn snapped. "Those are my designs."

I stepped in between them before a fight could break out. "Okay, we know why Quinn's here. She was part of the package deal Laken swung with Sebastian."

"Correct." Quinn folded her arms across her chest and flashed a smug grin. "I have a six-week contract. I'm legit."

"So what?" Mishel asked.

I pointed a finger at him. "Why are you here?"

He placed his hands on his narrow hips. "That's between me and Sebastian."

When the others started to protest, I strode toward him. "In case you missed the news, buddy, Sebastian's dead. The House of Hayward is out of business and condensed into my store. If there's something we can help you with, speak up or leave."

Mishel stared at me for a long minute before he averted his gaze. He strolled around the store and began to finger dresses on hangers as well as a couple of Quinn's designs. "You'll never last. No one wants to wear all these old things."

"It's a vintage store, brainiac, and yes they do," I told him. "You know, I've had enough of you arrogant designers who feel free to take shots at my store. Get out."

"Most of these aren't even designer pieces, just old. This place is more like a fancy thrift store." He reached for a soft pink blouse.

Laken jumped between me and the pompous creep before I did anything rash. She pointed to the door and said, "You'd better leave before my sister gets hold of you. She's worked hard on this shop and doesn't like when people say that."

"She should get used to it. I'm sure she'll hear it a great deal."

"Oh, that's it." I struggled to get around her, but Enid and Quinn held me back.

"Come back tomorrow night," Enid said. "We're having a grand opening fashion show. Maybe then you'll see why this place is so special."

"That sounds more like a dare than an invitation," he told her, but seemed to mull the idea over. "I expect nothing less than a front row seat."

"Fifty bucks." Enid held out her hand.

Mishel snorted. "For a so-called fashion show in a two-bit vintage shop?"

So much for my deep breathing. All that calm went out the window as I growled.

"It'll be a great show with a killer finale," Laken said.

He raised his eyebrows. A moment later, he pulled out his wallet and handed her a fifty. "Very well. You have piqued my curiosity."

Laken handed him a poster. "We'll save you a good seat."

Once Mishel left the store, Quinn held up a sheet of paper. "He's on the list."

"Why did you charge him fifty dollars?" I faced Enid.

"He was being a jerk." She shrugged.

Laken checked out the list. "We've only sold one seat?"

"It's hard to sell tickets when we don't have any," Quinn said.

Laken covered her eyes. "Tickets? Oh, no! I forgot that part. Who put me in charge of this?"

"Not me," I reminded her. "Andy wants a ticket. We should give him and Brad each one. It's the least we can do for all the work they've done. Just don't seat them near Mishel."

Enid nodded. "And now that I'm a model, Gill and Abbie will come. Maybe I can even convince Gill's cheapskate daughter to show up. Do you have some tickets handy? I can take them around town and fill the house."

"Ooh!" Quinn's eyes lit up. "I could go with her. It's a good way for me to meet people if I'll be here for few weeks."

Enid scrunched up her nose. "I'd rather you didn't."

"The printer's hooked up," I announced. "I'll make some tickets. Quinn and I can take one side of the street. Enid can take the other. We'll be done in no time."

Once we'd designed and printed thirty tickets, I set one aside for Mishel, tucked two in the drawer for Andy and Brad, then we left the store. With Quinn hot on my heels like an eager puppy, I took off to all the local businesses.

"That woman sure seems to know a lot about what's going on around here." Quinn glanced back over her shoulder.

"You mean Enid?" I asked.

"She doesn't seem to like me even though I haven't done anything."

"She's a gossip columnist. You don't have to do anything. She has a nose for news."

Quinn clutched a hand to her chest. "Is that why she's following us?"

"She's what?" I started to look behind us, but Quinn nudged me.

"Does she think you and I are dating?" she asked. "I could put an end to that right now. I'll tell her about that cute guy you had pizza with the other night."

"It's okay. She knows Andy and I are friends." I didn't bother to mention Enid was Andy's mom. "Plus she's trying to help us figure out who killed Sebastian, so we kind of need her hanging around."

"That's easy. It was Bridey Maes," she said. "Everyone knows how much that woman hated him. She went out of her way to make a scene at Emery's parties even when no one did anything to deserve it."

Emery's parties. I stopped. "Wait, were you at those parties?"

"Me? Only since I started to work at the House of Hayward. Sebastian was invited because of Chick, and I was obligated to go with him."

"Why was Sebastian invited because of Chick?"

Quinn rolled her eyes like an insolent teenager. "Are you serious? Because they've had an on and off relationship for years."

"Chick and Sebastian?"

"Yeah. I thought you knew."

I tapped my toes on the sidewalk. She was making me feel much older than I was. "How would I know? I never even knew Sebastian until he got here. Why didn't you tell me sooner?"

Quinn shrugged as she checked her fingernails. "I'm sure Laken knew. She probably knows they're both in town too."

I raised my eyebrows. "Chick and Sebastian?"

"No, silly." Quinn laughed. "Chick and Emery. Sebastian's dead, remember?"

"How could I forget?" I glanced back to see if Enid was still following us. Sure ducked behind a potted plant twenty feet away. "Are they staying at the same hotel?"

"How should I know? I stayed at your house last night.

I motioned to Enid, and said, "Why don't you join us? That way you can hear better."

Her face glowed as pink as her running shoes, but she wasted no time in scurrying toward us. "What did I miss?"

"Nothing exciting," Quinn told her.

I filled Enid in on Chick and Emery's connection to Sebastian. I hoped she'd take the tidbit, then head straight to the hotel for an interview.

Instead, she seemed rooted to the ground. "Emery Samson is in Glitter Bay?"

"Yes, he is, but I need your help to see what he and his PR guy are up to. Quinn and I will sell tickets for the show and check on the donations Gill arranged. You're the best person to do the detective work."

Enid held out her hand. "Gimme the tickets. I'll take care of them. I have someone better in mind to track down Emery Samson."

Dread filled my stomach as I handed over the tickets. "Who?"

"Gill's grandson, Abbie. He's working at the hotel doing cleaning stuff."

Quinn stared. "His grandson's a maid? Good for him. Men deserve equal rights."

Enid and I gawked at her.

"Maintenance and janitorial," Enid said. "He's got keys to get into any room in the hotel. I'll bet he can find out where that big shot movie star is staying without anyone thinking twice about what he's up to."

I grew lightheaded at the thought of someone sneaking into Emery's room. He'd call the cops in a heartbeat. Or invite them to party. "Just tell him not to do anything illegal."

She waved a hand. "He does it all the time. He went to check on Sebastian's room yesterday. The place was a pigsty. Want to see?"

"Why did he go to Sebastian's room?" I asked as Enid pulled out her phone.

"Someone complained the air-conditioner wasn't working." She swiped through her text messages until she came to the one from Abbie. "Ah, there they are."

The photos showed a hotel room with three suitcases laying wide open and clothing strewn everywhere. Shoes and purses lay scattered across the carpet.

"My things!" Quinn wailed. "What did they do to my room?"

"Those are your things?" Enid asked.

She sniffled. "Some of them. The rest are Sebastian's. Were. That's just awful."

I shook my head. "Who'd do that?"

Quinn rummaged through her purse and came out with a tissue. "My guess is either Mishel or that witch he's hanging out with."

Enid tapped a finger to the side of her head as if thinking hard. "Do you have a room key?"

She wiped a tear away from one eye. "Yes."

"Good, I have a car," Enid said, shoving the tickets back into my hand.

"Whoa, what are you up to?" I asked.

Enid rolled her eyes. "We're going to get answers. It's not break and enter if we have a key."

"You're right. Let's go, sister." Quinn clapped a hand on Enid's shoulder.

I was left alone on the sidewalk with a handful of tickets while the two of them turkey trotted toward the newspaper office. After a couple deep breaths, I phoned Laken to request she join me to sell tickets before I tore them up and went home.

"I'll be right there," she said.

By the time she and Sammy joined me ten minutes later she was breathless. "I'll take the other side of the street and meet you at the bakery. I'm dying for an éclair."

My sister who used to live on rice and veggies was now hooked on baked goods. I debated telling her that her newfound romance with desserts wouldn't end well for her wardrobe.

Nah. I'd wait to bring it up after she enjoyed her éclair.

Three stores and seven tickets later, I pulled on the door of the only place in town that could replace the broken glass at my store. The front door was locked. No closed for vacation signs. Nothing. Odd.

I blew out my frustration. As I texted Andy. Hopefully, he had an idea. When a text arrived from Jonathan, I deleted it before I read it, then headed across the street to the bakery.

"Over here," Laken said, waving me to a table. "I got you an iced tea. No sugar. They don't have many vegetarian options, just an abundance of lard, cream, and butter filled goodies."

"No problem. I'm not hungry." Defeated, I slumped onto a chair and set the folder from Enid next to me. "Did you sell many tickets?"

She held out her hands. "I sold half. You?"

Finally, one bright spot in the week. "Same. I have five left. We can sell them at the door Friday and hopefully fill the seats."

"Perfect."

I sipped my iced tea to prepare for the hard question that had burned in my mind for the past half hour. "Did you know Emery's in town?"

She didn't even flinch as she licked cream and chocolate off her lips. "That's not funny."

"I know it's not. Enid told me you knew before she did. She and Quinn ditched me with the tickets while they went to the hotel."

Concern crossed Laken's face as she set the pastry on the blue plate. "You're serious. Why didn't you tell me earlier?"

"I don't know any more than you do." My gaze fell on the folder Enid gave me. "What else do we need to do?"

"Get the door fixed before someone breaks into the building."

I groaned. "I'm working on that. I can't track down the glass guy."

"I have ten models coming for a rehearsal tomorrow at noon, including Carlene from Devil's Tavern. I felt bad for her since she's the waitress Sebastian treated so badly. Their outfits are on that rack that's in the kitchen," my sister said. "All that's left is to lay out the runway, hang some twinkly lights, and set up a table for food."

I sipped my tea. "We might as well go string up the lights. I have a couple tables, but they might not be big enough."

"I'll see if Cameron can spare one. Why don't you knock off early? You've been doing all the big stuff this week, and I'm sure you could use some rest. I'll take care of the show stuff. You take a little down time. Tomorrow, we'll both be running around taking care of last-minute details anyway."

After a long moment, I shrugged. "I could stop by the police station to see if they've found anything. I'm not sure I want that glass case back, but Mata Hari needs it to stand. Maybe I'll see if Andy can rig a new stand for her if he has time."

"That's a good idea," my sister said.

I had another idea. "Since we have tickets left, I'll give one or two to Officer Rhodes. That way he can keep an eye on the suspects. He might have more questions."

Or some answers. I crossed my fingers beneath the table.

"Sure. Invite him. Why not?"

"You don't think that's a good plan?" I raised my eyebrows.

"Fashion shows are like funerals, Sage," she told me. "Half the time people just come to see if you bury yourself. We should invite as many people on the suspect list as possible. If they are looking for something, I'm sure they'll show up."

I grinned. "That's a great idea. Do you have any idea when Sebastian's funeral will be? It would be nice for us to send flowers."

My sister shook her head. "No idea. From what I hear, the coroner's withholding his body until they find his next of kin."

"Does that mean he doesn't have any family, or that no one wants to claim him?" I asked.

She snorted. "That was rude. He did lose both parents and his brother. I have no idea who's left. Who's on your suspect list? I can tell them it's a memorial fashion show."

I reached for a piece of paper. "Do you think they'll come?"

"Guaranteed."

My short list comprised of Quinn, Mishel, Bridey, Chick, and Emery. Before I could finish writing Emery's name, Laken grabbed my pen to scratch him off.

"Not a chance," my sister growled.

"But—"

"That man is not setting foot inside the store. Ever."

I bowed my head. "Okay, I'll be sure to share your theory about fashion shows and funerals with Rhodes when I give him the invitation."

Laken took another bite of her éclair. "Skip it. If I were you, I'd go home, pour a glass of wine, and dig through whatever Enid found before you talk to the police. Our local gossip may be a lot of things, but thorough is one of the best."

I reached for the blue folder. "Good idea."

Chapter Ten

Officer Rhodes didn't seem as thrilled to see me as I'd hoped. He ducked into the closest room and shut the door the second he met my gaze. For all I knew, he planned to hide in a broom closet until I left.

I approached the front desk and asked to speak with him anyway. "I'd like to give him something that might help his murder investigation."

The uniformed blonde at the desk, whose badge read, Conrad, frowned. Her hair was tied back in such a severe bun it must've hurt to smile. "Murder investigation. Do you mean that fashion designer?"

"Yes. The one who was shot in Vintage Sage. Does he have more than one murder investigation?" I glanced around the front office, which seemed rather quiet. There didn't seem to be much crime in Glitter Bay.

She made a face. "It's not that big a town. Please tell me you're not with the press. I swear if I have to talk to one more reporter, I'll lose my mind."

"No. I'm Sage Miller. I own Vintage Sage and found the body."

Her mouth fell open. "I'm sorry to hear that. I'll let Rhodes know you're here. We have a few pamphlets for Victim Services if you're interested."

She was much taller than I expected. Almost the same height as Laken. She rapped on the closed door and announced, "Your witness is here to see you."

His voice was muffled, but I heard, "I'll be right out."

"Have a seat," she said, waving to a chair with a cracked vinyl seat near the wall.

I'd barely warmed the seat before Rhodes strode out, opened the gate between us, and muttered, "Come on into my office."

"Your office?" Officer Conrad laughed. "Next you'll want me to bring you coffee."

I chuckled. Apparently Rhodes was trying to appear more important than he actually was. "I didn't think you were the one in charge around here."

"Only when the boss is out of the office." He waved me into a small room that must've done double duty as both a boardroom and interrogation room. "I imagine you have a lot of questions about our investigation. Like when you'll get your cabinet back."

I handed him a ticket. "Partly. I also wanted to invite you to our fashion show Friday night. A lot of people who had issues with Sebastian have suddenly appeared in Glitter Bay. I heard a rumor they're looking for something they think he hid in the furniture he sent us."

"Ah, so that's why we've had so many reporters calling lately," he said as he tucked the ticket in his pocket. "We've had dozens of people asking where Emery Samson is hiding and how they can get an interview."

"He's my ex-brother-in-law. I haven't seen him, but Enid and Quinn are tracking him down. Quinn shared a hotel room with Sebastian when they first arrived. When Mishel arrived, he kicked her out. If you need to speak to her, she's living on my living room couch. Quinn went to make sure he didn't steal or damage anything."

Rhodes raised his eyebrows. "And did he?"

"They haven't come back yet."

"Just for the record, that's where the chief is. He wanted to personally make sure Sebastian's belongings were brought back here."

My mouth fell open. "You mean no one did that the day he died? You took Quinn to her hotel. Why didn't you take Sebastian's suitcases before anyone else pawed through them?"

"Pawed?" he asked.

"You know what I mean," I groaned. "Quinn said Mishel arrived that same day, which makes him a suspect. He had motive and the opportunity to rifle through Sebastian's suitcase. Who knows what he took?"

Rhodes nodded. "For the record, I looked around the hotel room when I dropped Quinn off that night. She asked if I needed to take his suitcases, but..."

"But?"

"I got called to that big accident on the outskirts of town. I saw Andy when I arrived on scene, by the way."

A headache crept into the back of my skull. "So instead of focusing on the murder victim and collecting evidence, you went to the accident scene."

He grimaced. "Sage, the guy wasn't going to get any deader. Besides, we were short-staffed that night between the murder and the accident."

I gritted my teeth. "In the meantime, half a dozen people have gone through his belongings. Whatever he left could be long gone. Is this your first week on the job?"

Rhodes looked as frustrated as I felt. "No, but it is my first murder."

"Great." I deflated as someone knocked on the door.

"What?" He snapped as he reached over to open it.

Chief Orville Baxter stood outside the door with a large plastic bag in his hands. "I understand Sage Miller is here for her interview."

"Actually, I came to give Officer Rhodes a ticket for our fashion show on Friday. I thought he might like to keep an eye on the suspects, since he can't be bothered to keep track of evidence."

Rhodes narrowed his eyes.

I continued, "My sister made a comment about fashion shows being like funerals. I have a hunch Sebastian's killer is looking for something and might show up."

The chief narrowed his gaze at Rhodes. "Good idea. How many officers should we send?"

I squirmed in my seat. "I'd say two at the most, unless they want to go undercover to help us out with food and stuff."

"Two is good," Rhodes said. "I'll take Officer Conrad with me."

"Excuse me?" she asked, appearing in the doorway.

"Good," Baxter said. "Make it look like you two are finally on a date."

Her hazel eyes grew wide. "Pardon me?"

"Sarah, he's joking," Rhodes said.

"Maybe your witness can give us some insight into the contents of the victim's suitcase." The chief set the large plastic bag on the table, then walked out.

Bingo. It was hard to contain my excitement.

"She deals in vintage clothing, not murder investigations," Rhodes called after him.

"Humor me," the chief replied from down the hallway.

Officer Conrad chuckled. "Would you rather field calls from nosy reporters?"

When Rhodes slammed the door shut between them, I laughed. He rifled through a drawer, then handed me a pair of plastic gloves. "I know we have your fingerprints on file. This way I'll will know if you touched any of his things before you came here."

I waited until he opened the suitcase before standing for a better look. Some of the clothes looked like someone shook them out before crumpling them into the bag. "I know how anal Sebastian was about clothing. He would've balled them up like that. The few times I saw him, he was clean, his clothes were pressed, and he walked like he was afraid to wrinkle anything."

"Are you sure?"

"Positive. Can I take them out?" I waited for a response before I dared to reach inside.

He took a couple photographs, then nodded and took a half-step back.

One by one, I took out each item and searched every pocket before folding them neatly and laying them on the table. While I didn't like Sebastian, I respected the designer labels he'd accumulated.

I frowned. "For someone who planned to be in town for six weeks, he didn't have many clothes. Was this everything?"

"I could find out, but that would mean leaving you alone with evidence."

"The lack of clothing alone is evidence," I pointed out. "Laken hired him for six weeks. A clothes horse like Sebastian should have at least one suitcase per week. Laken said she saw eight suitcases and only three belonged to Quinn. Where are the rest of his things?"

Rhodes folded his arms across his chest. "Maybe he planned to go shopping in Seattle one of these weekends."

I scowled. "First of all, he's bankrupt. He has no store, and probably little money. With the amount of clothing in this bag, he might've had enough outfits for a week before he needed to find a drycleaner."

"Secondly?"

"The guy had a shop on Rodeo Drive. I doubt he wore the same thing twice."

Probably against his better judgement, he left the room. He knew something I didn't, but what?

While he was gone, I took advantage of my privacy to check the quality. All designer clothes. Not a single knock off. I even ran my hands over the silky lining of the suitcase in case he managed to hide anything in a secret spot. Over the years, I'd learned to recognize hidden items in just about any piece of luggage that came through my shop.

Nothing.

By the time Rhodes returned, I was satisfied there was nothing left to find. That struck me as odd. No wigs, no jewelry, no scarves except one. Had Quinn hidden the rest of his clothes or did someone else take them?

He met my gaze before he closed the door and slumped into a chair. "The chief agrees with you. He thinks there's something funny going on. I guess you'd better be on alert in case someone tries to pawn them at your store."

"Good thinking." I peeled off my gloves. At least I knew Sebastian's size and tastes. "There's a lack of clothing and accessories. He liked wigs, scarves, and jewelry, but there's none in the suitcase. No hidden compartments either."

Rhodes rubbed a hand over his face with a groan.

"Do you remember how many suitcases were in their room when he died?" I tried to recall how many were in the photos Enid showed me earlier. Only Quinn's three.

He met my gaze. "She told me four or five were his. I remember making a comment about how it would take me two trips to take them all to my car. The other guy... Hamlet said two were hers."

"Quinn," I corrected him, earning another frown.

"The accident took precedence. I planned to go back in the morning, but I dropped the ball. Now his killer could get away."

I patted his shoulder. "You might be in luck. I'll bet whoever shot him is still here. Everyone who knows him seems to make my store their next stop when they can't find what they're looking for at the hotel. I'll bet you coffee for a year that whoever killed him will be at the fashion show Friday. If they don't break into the place sooner."

"Gimme another ticket," he said. "Sarah and I'll be there. You and your sister need to stay out of trouble. If anyone brings those suitcases to your store—"

"You'll be the first person I call."

Chapter Eleven

I returned to Vintage Sage with every intention of sitting in the courtyard to read through Enid's folder, which I should've done before dropping by to see Rhodes. The front door was unlocked, which didn't surprise me. Even though the store was still closed, there seemed to be an open-door policy no one told me about.

"Hey." Laken glanced up from steaming a couple blouses. "Quinn and Enid are on their way. Emery might be in town, but he's laying low somewhere else. They're stopping to grab coffees. Did you want anything?"

I shook my head. "No, thanks. I'll make peppermint tea. I'm going to sit out back to read Enid's notes."

"Good idea," she said. "What did Rhodes say?"

"Nothing helpful. I gave him two tickets, so he and his partner can keep an eye on things."

Laken set aside the steamer hose. "That's a start, I guess."

I hesitated. "He did mention some of Sebastian's suitcases are missing. He wants us to keep our eyes open in case someone brings them to the store."

My sister's back seemed to stiffen. "Only Quinn had access to that room, right?"

"And Mishel who kicked her out. Bridey's probably with him. If Chick and Emery are here, they've probably been there as well."

Laken grabbed her phone and started texting furiously.

I pushed through the kitchen door and tossed my keys onto the counter before I plugged in the kettle. Blowing out a defeated breath, I closed my eyes and leaned my forehead against the white fridge trapping a piece of paper. I didn't need to see it to recall what it said. *"Forgive and forget."* Gill left it when he moved out. Laken liked it, so it remained stuck to the fridge.

"Not a chance." I reached for the square of yellow paper that had probably hung there for many years. I crumpled the little sign into a ball and tossed it into the trash.

Laken would be peeved. She was trying to make that her motto lately. Well, until the day Emery walked into Vintage Sage anyway. Hopefully, I wouldn't be present for that confrontation.

Once my tea was ready, I sat on a metal chair in the courtyard and meditated in the sunshine for a few minutes shuffling through a headful of questions.

Number one, if Quinn was a part of the staff for the next five weeks, how was I supposed to keep her busy? Unless the new location brought in a great deal more foot traffic, we'd spend long days staring at each other.

Number two, why would Chick bring Emery to Glitter Bay? Until we knew Emery wasn't roaming around town pretending to hide from paparazzi, Laken would be a basket case. Emery and Sebastian did know each other, but it wasn't like we were holding Sebastian's funeral here. Someone was bound to show up to claim him eventually.

I hoped.

Something Laken said came to mind as Sammy wandered over to lay in the sunshine next to me. How fashion shows were like funerals.

People came to make sure you failed. Was Emery in town to watch my sister, and me by association, crash and burn? If so, how did he hear about our show? It seemed parts of Los Angeles already knew about it long before me.

It all came back to Sebastian.

Quinn admitted the show was Sebastian's idea to begin with. Suddenly, I disliked the gerbil even more. Dead or not.

"There you are," Laken said, stepping into the sunshine. "Is everything okay?"

"I needed to meditate and gather my thoughts."

My sister laughed. "More like escape the craziness going on around here lately. I can't wait until things get back to normal."

"Do you mean after the fashion show or once Quinn leaves?"

"I don't know how to answer that," she told me, sitting on a nearby chair. "I am tired of people popping in and out of this place when we're not open yet."

I nodded. "Same here. Maybe I should shop for a set of new doors. It would be a whole lot easier than tracking down the glass guy to fix one pane."

Laken raised her eyebrows. "That's not a bad idea. Maybe Andy or Brad can keep their eyes open. I'll bet one of them knows someone who might have some available. Heaven knows, they'd both be happy to do your bidding."

"What's that supposed to mean?" I asked, knowing full well she was right.

"Oh, come on, Sage," she said. "Those two only hang around here to see you. Don't tell me you haven't noticed."

"They're my friends. I'll ask them about the doors. I think Andy's at work."

"You think?" My sister stood as she raised her eyebrows. "You're not sure?"

I rolled my eyes then followed her inside. "It's not like we're dating, Laken."

We'd barely reached the front counter to do some online door shopping when the front door opened. A tall woman with long, straight black hair stood in the doorway of Vintage Sage and peered over the red rims of her Donna Karan sunglasses. A strong wind could've blown her and her Gucci accessories away.

"Didn't you lock that while we were out back?" I asked.

"I swear I did. We need to put a rush on those doors and get new locks."

All it took was one glance at my sister's tight jaw and narrow eyes to realize I'd just met Bridey Maes. I lunged between the two supermodels to intercept an abundance of negative vibes.

I forced a smile. "Can we help you?"

"This place isn't so bad," the woman said. "The way Sebastian described it I figured it needed a quality arsonist."

"I'm the owner, Sage Miller. I'd love to show you around, but we're not open yet. Even though this does seem to be the busiest spot in Glitter Bay."

"Then why is the door unlocked?" she asked, pointing over her shoulder.

I thought fast. "Because one of our coworkers stepped out to grab coffee and doesn't have a key. We're not actually open yet. We're still setting up."

Bridey took off her sunglasses. "Since I'm here, I might as well take a peek around."

"We'd rather you leave, Bridey," Laken spoke behind me.

The woman stared before a small smiled played on her red lips. "Why Laken Miller. I heard you washed ashore in some small town." She paused and put her fingertip to her lower lip. "Or was that you were washed up and moved to some small town?"

My sister took a couple steps toward the homewrecker Emery had moved in with while she was battling cancer. "We're closed. Please leave."

Bridey folded her arms across her flat stomach and impossibly tiny waist. "Not until you tell me what happened to Sebastian. Mishel said one of you killed him."

Laken grimaced. "Huh. Since neither one of us was in the building at the time of his death, that's an interesting theory. Maybe Mishel killed him and is using you as his alibi. Since he was in Glitter Bay when Sebastian was killed, that means you were here."

"Says who?" Bridey laughed.

"Quinn saw Mishel at the hotel," I told her.

She scrunched up her perky nose. "Who's Quinn?"

"Me." Our newest employee carried in a cardboard drink tray with three cups and a bakery bag. "What are you doing here? We're closed."

"Hamlet!" Bridey gushed. "Oh, honey, are you okay? I thought I'd never see your handsome face again. Mishel mentioned this place and I just had to—"

I held up a finger. "Wait. You just said Sebastian told you. Which is it?"

Bridey's pale cheeks reddened.

"How would Mishel know?" Quinn asked. "He was never in here until—"

"Are you sure?" Laken cut her off. "Like I said, maybe Mishel killed Sebastian and Miss Perfect here is covering for him."

"No way. Hamlet killed him. He's always been jealous of Sebastian's talent," Bridey said, pointing to Quinn.

"So much for calling me honey." Quinn scowled as she placed her hands on her hips. "By the way, my name is Quinn, and I go by she, not he. The police have checked out my alibi and let me go."

Bridey narrowed her eyes. "For now, perhaps."

"Where you when Sebastian was killed? Who's your alibi?" Laken asked.

"I didn't kill him if that's what you mean." Bridey took a step back. "I was driving to this cute little town with Mishel. We had business to discuss, so I came with him. We needed to speak to Sebastian, but when we stopped at his hotel, no one was there."

Quinn held up her hand. "I was there. Mishel spoke to me, but I didn't see you. I'll bet you dropped him off at the hotel, then came here to kill Sebastian."

"Don't be gauche. I'd never shoot anyone," Bridey retorted.

Laken laughed. "Yeah, she'd never do her own dirty work."

I reached for the cup marked GT, green tea, and itched to call Rhodes. "Is it just me or does that sound like a statement for the police?"

Bridey frowned, meeting my gaze. "What do you mean by that?"

"Rehearsed. Like you and Mishel worked on your alibis after you killed Sebastian and before you went to the hotel. I saw his car leave the building that day," I announced, even though I had no idea what he drove. "By the way, who told you he was shot or when he died?"

"It was in the local papers."

Laken shook her head. "Glitter Bay's only newspaper is a weekly that comes out on Fridays."

"She could've found the information online," I said. "Did the police release his cause of death?"

Exasperated, Bridey stomped her foot as she shouted, "Well, I heard it somewhere. Good enough? Sebastian was my dear friend. I am devastated by his death, and I do not deserve to be treated this way."

"His friend?" Quinn asked. She puffed up her chest and stormed toward the model who was less than half her size. "You called Sebastian names both behind his back and to his face. You threatened to ruin him if he didn't let you model for him, which he wouldn't do in a million years. He said you're too bony."

"You're crazy." Bridey glared at Quinn, trying to intimidate her.

Quinn stood her ground. "Laken, you know the truth."

"Yes, Laken, you do know the truth," Bridey said. "You got sick, and I became famous."

"I think the word is infamous,"

"Whatever. Now tell your guard dog to back off."

My sister grinned. "Nah. I'm enjoying this. Besides, I've heard you threaten Sebastian more than once and I'd love to know why Mishel's car was near Vintage Sage when Sebastian was killed, even though you insist you two were nowhere near Glitter Bay."

"Whoever thought they saw it was hallucinating," Bridey shouted, inching toward the door as her cheeks and chest reddened. "We drove all the way from L.A. and even stopped in some hideous gas station. I have the receipt."

"How convenient." I turned away from them all. I still couldn't be sure his was the car I saw leaving the crime scene.

"Why are you here with Mishel instead of Emery?" Lake asked suddenly.

We all faced Bridey, who stared as her jaw went slack. "What?"

"He left me for you," my sister continued. "So how come you're in Glitter Bay with Mishel and not with Emery?"

"Because Emery Samson's a psychopath." She spat in disgust as if she'd swallowed a bug. "He tried to force me to quit modeling, so I could hang out with him on movie sets. What kind of monster does that to a person?"

"A control freak," I muttered.

Laken shot me a look that could've melted steel.

Bridey shook her head. "Look, I don't know what you heard, but I left that creep. I'm here with Mishel because Sebastian had something we both need only it wasn't in any of his suitcases or his room. He must've left it here."

"His suitcases." I muttered.

"What about them?" Quinn turned to me.

With the attention off her, Bridey shot out the front door. She stumbled down the steps in her four-inch heels, then looked as though she was tiptoeing up the hill toward the Devil's Peak Tavern.

"Where are his suitcases?" I asked. "The police only found one. Rhodes had it at the station when I was there earlier, but all that was in it was a handful of clothes."

Quinn held up her hands. "Don't look at me. I'm not his size."

"You saw it?"

I nodded. "I searched it. His jewelry was missing, there were no scarves or wigs, and definitely no hidden compartments. Whatever people are looking for, it's not in that suitcase. Where are the other ones, Quinn?"

"I have no idea."

"Did you put them somewhere for safe keeping?" Laken asked.

Quinn hesitated, then gasped. "Hey, it could be in his car."

"What could be?" Laken asked.

"Whatever Bridey and Mishel are looking for.

"Sebastian had a car?" I raised my eyebrows.

"How else did you think we got here?" Quinn asked.

I rubbed my face. "Since you both kept showing up in cabs, I wasn't sure."

"I don't have a license, and he said Laken would pay for it all."

My sister growled.

"Who has his keys?" I asked. "Could his suitcases be in it?"

"The police," Quinn admitted. "And I'm not about to ask if they found anything a killer could be looking for hidden inside. I thought Mishel was after the necklaces, which is why he sent them here. Bridey's tastes normally run more on the goth side when she's not on a job."

Since Rhodes only knew about one suitcase, I assumed they were somewhere else. I stared at the cabinet with the necklaces. "Unless they were meant to go with Mishel's designs for a shoot."

Laken took her cup from the tray. "No way. The department store would use pieces from their own lines. None of these would qualify."

Quinn reached for her handbag. "Still, it wouldn't hurt to search Sebastian's car."

"Not normally, but since the police have his car keys, I'm willing to bet his car is in the impound lot. There's no way to get access to either." I handed Quinn the bakery bag. "I'll ask Rhodes if he's searched the car, but I doubt he'll tell me else. The case is probably going to a detective and he's out of the loop."

"I doubt it," my sister said. "This is a small town. We're stuck with him."

Quinn took a Danish from the bag. "I could flirt with him. I'm not without feminine wiles, you know."

I met Laken's gaze, then chuckled. "You definitely have feminine wiles, but I don't think that'll help. Whatever they're after might not be in his car. It would help if we knew what they wanted. Do you think it has to do with Sebastian's designs?"

"Shall I turn my charms on Mishel to find out?" Quinn asked. "I won't bother with Bridey. She didn't like me before, and I doubt she'll speak to me after today."

Laken opened her tea. "Sure. See what you can do. It can't hurt, right?"

I kept my doubts to myself.

"Right after our tea break." Quinn took out her phone. "Are you sure you didn't find anything in the stuff Sebastian sent? No stolen gems or real gold coins?"

I shrugged. "We could double check, but I didn't see anything out of the ordinary, let alone of real value."

"We could take the necklaces out and inspect the cases," Laken suggested. "Sometimes people hide things of value in plain sight. We've found hidden things in false bottoms of trunks and the linings of suitcases before."

"True enough." I sipped my tea. "We can set them up for proper display and check them out at the same time."

"Sounds good." Quinn grinned. "You ladies take care of that. I'm going to have a chat with Mishel. If your friend Enid comes back, tell her I'm ready to spill the beans on Sebastian Hayward the Third if she wants a juicy story."

"She's a gossip columnist," I reminded her. "Don't worry, she'll find you."

Quinn laughed as she left the building.

Once Laken locked the door, she rattled it several times to make sure no one else could get in, then retreated to the kitchen to organize the outfits for the fashion show. I checked the answering machine not surprised to find no messages from the glass guy.

"Hey, Sage," my sister called out.

"Yeah." I wandered into the kitchen and yawned as my phone dinged.

Laken rolled her eyes. "You spent half the night moving the old store over. Why don't you have a nap or call Andy? Just take a break."

"There's still a lot to do."

"Go home. You look like you need a twelve-hour nap."

"We need to find out about Sebastian's car and suitcases."

"I'll ask the police about the car," Laken told me. "Then I'm going to get a manicure. Actually, a mani-pedi before the show might be what you need."

I backed away. Hanging out in a nail salon was not my idea of fun. "I'd rather head home. I'm sure Muumuu and Sammy will be happy to take a nap with me."

Once I grabbed my things, she gave me a hug, then shoved me out the back door. I stumbled home in a brain fog. Yawning, I pushed open the front door fifteen minutes later. It stuck halfway when something became wedged beneath the wood. A slipper. Sammy must've dragged it from upstairs. I huffed as I picked it up. How had he smuggled it past my sister?

She was likely on the phone with Cameron. Funny though. It didn't look like one of Laken's slippers. Maybe Quinn lost it under the couch.

As I set my purse on the bottom stair, I thought about the letter Laken was so upset about losing. Was it possible Sammy had rummaged around in her purse and took it?

Or Quinn?

I carried the slipper to the kitchen to wash off his slobber. On the way, I stepped over a blue cushion that leaked cotton tufts from small tears as well as a variety of socks and t-shirts that decorated the carpet.

"Nice work, Sammy. It looks like Laken forgot to put you in the crate when she brought you home, so you and Muumuu had the run of the place. I hope I don't find any other surprises, like anything brown on my rug." I shook my head, then took a photo of the cushion and the clothing to send my sister.

Laken called after she got my picture. "Good thing you went home. What on earth happened? Were we robbed?"

"Sammy and Muumuu happened." I sighed. "Quinn's things are everywhere."

Laken groaned. "Oh, Sage, I'm so sorry. I had a phone call when I got home and forgot to put him in the crate. Cameron keeps telling me Sammy gets bored and needs more walks. It looks like he and Muumuu had fun."

"Do you think so?"

"Quinn and I just went through a few last-minute plans with the models before we do a rehearsal tomorrow afternoon. I'm exhausted. I thought I'd come home and get some sleep, but I forgot about dinner with Cameron tonight."

"I'll take Sammy for a walk to burn off some energy."

"Thanks. You're the best." My sister gave a weary sigh as I picked up the leaky cushion. "I'll fix the cushion later. Actually, I should probably buy you a few new ones. I think I owe you about three by now."

"At least four." I chuckled. "Other than that, it's only been your clothes he's dragged downstairs and destroyed."

Laken yawned. "I started working on the programs for tomorrow night, but they aren't ready yet. I should have spent more time on this stuff earlier."

I grinned. "You mean like the tickets? It's too bad you don't have an extra week."

"Thanks for the support. I'll be home in a few minutes."

"What about your dinner plans?"

"I'll tell Cameron we have to get some extra stuff done or tomorrow becomes an even bigger disaster. Quinn must've heard you mention dinner. She's griping about her stomach growling. I'll see what I can find in the fridge here. Since you're nice enough to walk my dog, I guess I can be nice enough to bring something home to feed you."

I chuckled as I picked up the clothing. All were designer. None were Laken or Quinn sized. "Sounds good to me."

Once we hung up, I set the clothing on the kitchen counter for a better look. One check of the labels told me two things. These belonged to Sebastian, and they weren't in our house that morning. Since Sammy was inside all day, he couldn't have brought them in.

I searched every nook and cranny in my house before sitting on the living room floor. The only other person who'd ever had a key to my house was Jonathan and I'd been careful to get that back.

"Quinn must have had some of Sebastian's clothes in her bag when she stayed here." I rubbed Sammy's head. "I'll bet you dug them out of her bag and hid them, didn't you?"

The other possibility was that whoever brought these into the house was an unwanted guest. Jonathan could've made a copy of my house key, but he had no reason to since he lived in Los Angeles. I wasn't willing to freak myself out that someone had broken in.

I held Sammy's face in my hands and gazed into his eyes. "Please tell me Quinn had them."

He barked then pulled away and ran toward the door.

"You're right. A walk is a good idea. I'm a bit skittish right now. You need a walk, and I need time to think."

Sammy led the way to and from the beach at a fast trot. We were nearly at the house when my phone rang. The silly dog refused to slow his pace while I fumbled to answer the call.

"Sage," Rhodes said. In the background, he typed on a computer keyboard. "I just wanted to let you know we found Sebastian's missing suitcases."

I panted as I spoke, "They were in the trunk of his car, right?"

"Nope. The guy who took over his hotel room had them. They were locked in the trunk of his car."

"Mishel?" My step faltered in the sand. "Why did he have them?"

Whatever Rhodes was doing, the typing stopped and the door closed. "You were right. He's looking for something he thinks Sebastian sent to Laken, or gave to her when he arrived. You don't happen to know what he's talking about, do you?"

I shook my head. "No, didn't he tell you?"

"We're not that good of friends," he said. "While he was in possession of Sebastian's four other suitcases, I can't prove he stole them. He did have a key to the hotel room. There's nothing I can arrest him for just yet."

"But isn't the hotel room in Sebastian's name?" I asked.

"Actually it's in the name Hamlet McTavish."

I gasped. "That's Quinn's dead name."

He grew silent. "I know there has to be a good explanation for that. I'll go through my original notes from the murder to double check. I have a feeling I'll be able to nail Mishel with possession of stolen property. Are you sure he'll be at the fashion show?"

"Trust me. If he hasn't found what he's looking for yet, he'll be there."

Did it count that I said that with my fingers crossed?

Chapter Twelve

F riday morning—the day of our big fashion show and grand opening—my phone rang at seven o'clock. Luckily, I was relatively awake and had just turned off the kettle. I scowled as I answered with a rough, "What?"

"Yeah, hey." A man's voice was loud as though talking over some background sound that I couldn't hear. "I'm at the building you want work done in, but there's no one here."

"What?" I shook the cobwebs from my brain as I stared at the stack of Sebastian's clothing on the counter. I guessed it was the contractor who was supposed to be at work on Laken's apartment week. "Of course there isn't. It's seven o'clock in the morning. The store doesn't open until ten."

Silence, then a sheepish, "Well, I guess I shouldn't have punched that piece of cardboard out of the door to come in then. Good thing you don't have an alarm system. You should look into getting one though, and get that door fixed. Any creep could break into this place."

I cursed him beneath my breath. "Stay there. I'll be right over."

Not a good start to the day. Mine for now. His once I got to the store.

On my way past Laken's room as I stormed to my room to get dressed, I pounded on her bedroom door to tell her where I was going.

If I knew my sister, I'd need to call three more times once I got to the store.

I poured my tea into a travel mug before I slid on a pair of flip-flops and a thin, thigh-length sweater. Halfway to Vintage Sage, I remembered I was still wearing the shorts and tank top I'd slept in. Dressed for early morning yoga on the deck, but not to greet a contractor.

A heavy-set man in a faded t-shirt and torn blue jeans sat on the front step with a cigarette in one hand. His salt and pepper hair was disheveled, and he smelled smoky with a hint of rancid beer.

"Hey, sorry to get you out of bed like that," he said, "but I've gotta get his job done asap. My kid needs braces. Do you have any idea how expensive those things are?"

Considering I'd worn them for several years, I kept my mouth shut except for a terse, "Good morning to you, too."

I opened the front door which he'd already unlocked.

He coughed a few times. A deep, wet cough that made me inch away as he followed me inside. "Now either your hair grows really fast or you're a different lady than the one who showed me this place before."

"That was my sister. Laken's going to live upstairs once you finish her renovations." I paused at the kitchen door. "I'm Sage. I own the store down here."

"I'm Garnet. Are you two twins?"

"No, I'm older."

He gazed around the store before he winced. "You sure you don't need work done down here too? It could use a good coat of paint. I have a nice blue that I can—"

"What is it with you people and my paint?" I shouted as I wheeled around to face him. "If you want this job, you'll never bring up the paint color again."

Garnet held up his hands. "Consider it dropped. Lead the way, Red."

I fished my keys out of my pocket to unlock the apartment door then led him up the stairs. Gill and Tilly had made the upper floor big and bright, but Laken needed more closet space. A lot more closet space. With a door that Sammy couldn't break into. Since she also wanted a beachier feel, Garnet's pale blue paint might come in handy after all. While I doubted he was the type to worry about interior design, I guessed he could manage to install a closet.

By the time he huffed and puffed to the top of the stairs, I stood at the large window that overlooked the ocean. I turned to face him, calmer than earlier. I wasn't surprised his face was red and he sweated like a glass filled with ice water.

"What time does your crew get here?" I asked, hoping he didn't have health issues. There was no way I'd get him back downstairs on my own.

"Eight," he gasped. "I came first to make sure I knew what she wanted done."

I put one hand on my hip. "Maybe you should've called ahead to make sure she'd be here."

"Guess so." He wiped his forehead with a gray handkerchief.

My normally disorganized sister had left a long list on the kitchen counter. I glanced at Garnet before I set my travel mug down to take a picture of the list in case he lost it. His reputation preceded him, but I hoped he'd prove me wrong. For all our sakes.

"There you go."

He read through Laken's list and nodded. "Right. This is what we discussed. All I need is money upfront for supplies, then we can get started."

"That you have to get from my sister." I pulled up Laken's name on my phone and let it ring ten times. "Why don't you go grab a coffee or something? We'll meet you and your crew back here at eight."

Garnet grimaced toward the stairs. "Okay. Eight o'clock it is. But she'd better show up or she's on her own. I can't sit around waiting all day."

"Excuse me?" My mouth fell open again. For someone desperate to take the job for the money, his comment surprised me. "You were supposed to be here over a week ago but went on holidays. Suddenly, you show up at seven a.m. without notice expecting us to be waiting for you so you can get started. I think you can suck it up and wait one whole hour for us to wake up and get organized."

"For the record, I gave your sister notice. If I have to wait around for an hour, it'll cost ya." Garnet muttered beneath his breath as he headed toward the stairs. He paused at the top and sighed before lumbering down one step at a time.

"Oh, I don't think so." I called my sister once more.

She answered on the fifth ring and snapped, "What?"

"Did you happen to talk to your contractor this week?" I focused my gaze out the window on the ocean to keep my blood pressure from rising.

"Yup." Laken yawned. "He's coming next Friday to start work at eight in the morning."

I sighed. "Are you sure he didn't tell you this Friday? Because he showed up here at seven o'clock this morning and called me before I even had a cup of tea. By the way, how did he get my phone number?"

She groaned. "How should I know? Are you at the store?"

"Yup."

"And Garnet's coming today?"

"He's here now."

Sammy moaned in the background as I imagined Laken sitting upright to check her text messages and emails.

She gave a loud gasp like she'd swallowed a bug. "Oh man. Sage, I'm so sorry. With Sebastian and everything, I..." She growled. "I'll be there in a few minutes. Fifteen tops. Do you want anything?"

Breathe in with the waves. Breathe out with the waves.

"I'll stay here and wait. He already punched out the cardboard I put in the door, so I'm not leaving until you get here. I don't trust the guy him."

"Where is he now?"

"From the sounds of things, he's downstairs rummaging through the merchandise." I headed for the staircase.

"Oh, crap." Laken groaned. "I have to get dressed and find Sammy's leash. I'll be there in ten minutes."

Descending the stairs, I hugged my sweater around me as I reached the kitchen. At least Garnet hadn't ogled me when we met. Maybe there was a glimmer of hope for him after all.

He was, however, in the store examining the mannequins. He pulled at dress pleats, fondled sweaters, and even tried on a top hat. Of all the outfits, he seemed especially fascinated by the Bonnie and Clyde mannequins.

"Ahem." I cleared my throat. "Can I help you?"

As Garnet took a step back, he pulled a package of cigarettes from his pocket. He tugged one out, then stuck the filter between his lips. "You have some weird clothes in here. They look like bugs. I thought you might have something my wife would like."

I folded my arms across my stomach. "Why don't you tell her to come in once we're open for business tomorrow? We're having our grand opening fashion show tonight. She could come by to check it out if she'd like. I have a couple tickets left."

Garnet nodded as he headed outside. "Gimme me a couple free ones and I might consider it. It's been a while since we had a date night."

I bit my lip as he closed the door.

With any luck, the glass guy would show up and we could get the door fixed to keep the bugs—and the contractors—out. I also needed to look into an alarm system. I hoped Andy knew someone who could install one right away.

While the store was quiet, I made sure no merchandise was missing before I checked my emails. I was still distracted by the discussion we had when she saw Sebastian's clothing on the kitchen counter. Her first instinct was to call Quinn and ask if those pieces were in her bag.

Quinn insisted she hadn't seen any of Sebastian's things since Mishel and Bridey rolled into town. That left the vague possibility she was lying, or that someone else left them in my house. Both were unsettling. While Jonathan had finally stopped texting me, my stomach was uneasy. The whole week had taken a toll, but finding those clothes...

Just as I reached for my phone to check for messages, Laken and Sammy walked in. She handed me a large cup of coffee and a plastic container with a muffin and a pear inside. A peace offering.

Had I brought tea earlier? I tried to recall where I left it.

"I'm so sorry," she said, hugging me. "With everything that's gone on this week, I forgot about Garnet. Is he still here?"

"Last I saw, he went out to have a smoke. His crew will be here by eight. They need to use the back entrance while we prepare for the show tonight." When I glanced down at Sammy, I remembered leaving my travel mug upstairs. "If the work crew's using the back door, we'll need to find somewhere for Sammy. All commotion and tool noises might make him antsy."

Laken crouched to pet him. "Maybe I should take him home and put him in the kennel today."

I slid off my stool. "Good plan. Why don't I take him? I need to have a shower and get dressed anyway. Maybe he can help me run errands later. I have to pick up a few things and track down the glass guy."

Outside the store, the heat started to build. It wasn't even seven-thirty, yet it was quickly turning into one of those days that threatened to be capped off by a wicked thunderstorm. Considering the fashion show was in less than twelve hours I crossed my fingers I was wrong.

Sweat trickled down my back and chest as Sammy and I ran up the front steps of the house. The instant I opened the door, Muumuu scurried for cover. She wanted nothing to do with the heat wave we dragged into her regal domain.

I decided to skip the shower for now. I'd only be covered in sweat before I reached the store again anyway. It made more sense to take one right before the show tonight. I needed to get dressed before anyone else saw me in my pajamas.

My sister's text came just as I pulled on a short, loose dress to combat the heat. *"Get back here now!!!!"*

"Ugh. Now what?" I tamed my unruly hair into a thick ponytail and groaned. As I chased Sammy out of my closet and herded him down the stairs, my stomach rumbled. The muffin and fruit Laken brought me sat on the counter at the store.

"Sammy, something tells me this is going to be an even crazier Friday than expected." I grabbed a second muffin from the fridge. "I might need this today."

He wandered to his bowls, then filled up on kibble and water before he sneezed.

I tossed the muffin paper in the garbage as another text hit my phone. Laken again. At least it wasn't Jonathan.

This time I called Laken rather than rush back. "What's so urgent I can't get dressed in peace?"

"Rhodes is here," she said. "He went to the hotel to talk to Quinn this morning and found Mishel and Bridey there instead. They said she threw a tantrum and left last night. You don't know where she is, do you?"

The muffin in my stomach sank like a granite boulder. "No. I haven't heard from her since she and Enid went to the hotel yesterday."

"Oh crap." Laken groaned. "I can't leave the store. Garnet and his crew are upstairs."

I reached for a glass of water to moisten my mouth. "Oh, can you go up and grab my travel mug before it walks away? It's the one with the flowers on it that you gave me. Make some calls to the local hotels. I'll take Sammy and check around town. Maybe she just needed some time alone. Her life's gone kind of topsy-turvy lately."

"Either that or someone killed her." A tinge of hysteria crept into Laken's voice.

"Don't say that," I told her, while fighting not to jump to the same conclusion. "She could have just gone for a long walk. Maybe she grabbed a coffee somewhere or went to a different hotel."

Except we both knew she was broke.

My sister paused to speak to someone else. "Sage, you need to find her. Rhodes will drive around to see if he can spot her. If you have any ideas, let me know and I'll call him."

When I hung up, I rubbed my forehead. "Sammy, we need to find Quinn. The only place I've seen her outside the store is at the pub, but they're not open this early."

Sammy barked as if he agreed. As we headed toward the door, I stepped on something gritty. Sand from the beach last night. Just a small patch, but enough to trigger a memory.

"We saw her arguing with Mishel on the beach," I said, sliding my feet into my flip-flops. "If she has no money and nowhere else to go, she might be sleeping on the beach."

Sammy gave a yip. The beach was his second favorite place in Glitter Bay. Right after Laken's closet. He led me down the sidewalk and made a beeline for the heat of the asphalt parking lot. We hopped over a low-concrete block onto the slightly cooler sand.

That was where I stopped him. We both looked up and down the beach. I hoped to spot Quinn huddling nearby watching the waves. No such luck. If she was trying to escape someone, I doubted she'd hang out around near the marina up the beach. Not unless she was seeking someone to sail her back to Los Angeles, or somewhere exotic.

"Quinn," I shouted.

The only replies came from the seagulls.

Sammy and I turned to the left. He waited while I studied the large, jagged rocks below the Devil's Peak Tavern looking for any anomaly. On days when I wanted time alone to think, I'd walk among the rocks to find a quiet spot. Crossing my fingers, I steered Sammy toward them while darker possibilities fluttered through my mind.

One, we could find Quinn sitting quietly among the rocks sorting out her future.

Two, someone might've shot her and hidden her body.

Three...

I glanced up the cliff to where the tavern perched. It was the highest spot in Glitter Bay and the site of many suicides as well as a couple murders since the town was incorporated. I swallowed hard and tried to slow my pace.

Sammy, however, barked and seemed to be on a mission. He yanked me along behind him as he ran along the beach. Had he picked up her scent?

"Slow down before I lose my shoes, Sammy." I tugged on the leash.

Rather than ease his pace, he dove forward nearly yanking me faced first into the sand.

"Please let her be okay," I whispered.

A few feet from where the boulders began, there was a stretch of stones smaller than the others along the rest of the beach. I regretted wearing flip-flops the moment I stepped on the loose rocks, especially when I nearly lost my balance.

One of the larger rocks appeared to have blood smeared over it.

"Quinn, are you out here?" I asked.

Sammy snuffled near the waves while I listened for other sounds.

"Quinn? It's Sage." She probably couldn't hear me over the surf, but it was worth a try. The waves rolled in and out several times while I listened for a response.

Nothing.

My stomach did a front somersault making me regret eating that muffin.

"Quinn," I yelled louder, but still got no answer.

Sammy and I picked our way between boulders while we climbed over the smaller rocks. My loose skirt flipped up in the breeze a couple times. The second time, my foot slipped off a rock as I tried to smooth my dress down. My knee scraped against a boulder when I lost my balance, and sucked in a sharp breath. I definitely wasn't dressed for search and rescue.

"That woman better be here, or I'll—"

My words were cut off by the sight of beige fabric sticking out from between two rocks. The ends were soaked by the reaching fingers of the waves and covered with a smattering of pebbles, seashells, and watery pink.

I gasped. "Oh, please, no."

Sammy noticed the fabric, too. He headed straight into the ocean and tugged me with him. Although the water was cold, it was easier to walk in the shallows than on the rocks.

The beige chunk of fabric turned out to be an entire hotel blanket. A bluish foot stuck out from beneath one corner and rested on the pea gravel just out of reach of the waves. Vivid thoughts of Quinn coming into Vintage Sage with Sebastian for the first time, telling us about her transition, and ordering me to try on her cocoon dress flashed through my head. If Quinn was dead, chances were I'd completely fall apart even though I barely knew her.

Sammy glanced back as if to ask what I was waiting for.

Blowing out a shaky breath, I gave a nod. He beat me to the lump beneath the blanket, then shoved his nose beneath it and snorted.

An arm reached out to shove Sammy away. "Ew! Dog boogers."

"Oh, thank goodness." I clutched a hand to my chest, then shouted, "Quinn Evans, what are you doing out here? You could've been swept away by the tide or drowned. Don't you know people are looking for you?"

She sat up and blinked several times. Her hair—her real brunette curls—were rumpled and adorned with small rocks and seashells. She looked like some sort of demented mermaid. As meticulous as she was with her makeup, her mascara, eyeshadow, and blusher were smeared across her face like an expressionist artist gone mad.

"They are?" she asked.

I put my hands on my hips and got hit in the backs of my legs by a wave which nearly bowled me over. "Yes, they are."

"How did you find me?" she asked. "I didn't think anyone would notice I was missing."

"The police went to your hotel room to ask more questions. They found Mishel and Bridey, then went to Vintage Sage to see if you were with us. Luckily, Laken was so worried she called me."

Quinn yawned. "And you came to look for me."

"Of course." I sat on a nearby rock to see how bad the scrape on my leg was. It wasn't pretty, but I'd live once it stopped bleeding. "We have a show tonight and we need you."

When she didn't reply, I glanced up.

A small smile played on Quinn's lips and her eyes shone with tears. "Did you miss me?"

Choked up, I told her, "Yeah. I did. I was afraid someone hurt you, or worse."

"At least you like me more than you liked Sebastian. You haven't called me a gerbil once." She chuckled. "It was nice of you to look for me. I must look awful."

"No worse than me. You look pretty darn good considering how I pictured you'd look. I thought you were..." I closed my eyes and paused to catch my breath. "Let's go to my house, so you can shower and change. We can grab some breakfast before we get to work. We have a show tonight, remember?"

Quinn groaned as she leaned on a boulder and eased to her feet, then whimpered. Both her feet were bare and tinged blue. "A hot shower sounds fantastic, I'm freezing. Do you have something I can wear?"

"I'll come up with something." I winced at the ache from the cut on my leg as I stood, then chuckled. "We're quite the battered pair."

"Like a team from a buddy action movie," she replied with a grin.

Before I could take a step, Quinn was wrapped around me like an old fur coat. "Honey, if I was a man, Andy would have some serious competition. You're the sweetest, prettiest woman I've ever met. Except for me, of course."

"Of course. Come on, buddy. Let's get you warmed up," I told her as we waded through the shallows toward the sandy beach.

It wasn't even nine in the morning, and I'd already averted two crises. I wasn't about to ask what else the day would bring. About ninety percent of me didn't want to know. The other ten percent just wanted the day to be over with already, so I could go back to bed.

Chapter Thirteen

I yawned and my stomach growled like an alley cat by the time I ambled down the stairs to wash and dry Quinn's clothes. I'd texted Rhodes and Laken once we reached the sandy part of the beach to let them know she was safe. After I handwashed her gritty clothing and the blanket in Sammy's backyard pool, I tossed them in the dryer.

It occurred to me that all I'd eaten that day was a muffin but no coffee or tea. Although I had one of each waiting for me at the store, they were both probably cold by now. I plugged in the single cup coffeemaker and made myself a coffee. Quinn's clothes would take just long enough to dry so that I could relax for a few minutes.

Sammy, wiped out by the busy morning, lay curled up near the front door. In fact, he blocked the front door to make sure we couldn't get out again. Not even Muumuu pawing at his damp head and meowing in his ear woke him.

I nearly drooled as coffee trickled into my mug, then called my sister to fill her in on where I'd found Quinn.

My sister gasped. "She was where? Is she okay?"

"She's fine. We're at the house. I washed her clothes and she's taking a shower, so I doubt we'll have any hot water this weekend." I chuckled. "We'll head to the store when she's done. What's going on there?"

"Enid and Gill are hanging the twinkling lights, Abbie's helping Cameron roll out the runway carpet, and I'm running up and down the stairs to answer questions for the contractor. I did remember to grab your travel mug, not that any of those guys were interested in a flowery pink mug. I could really use your help here."

"Yeah, well it's not like I've been sleeping all morning," I reminded her.

"I know. I'm sorry. Garnet gave me an earful."

A sudden change of topic seemed in order. "What's Cameron doing there? Doesn't he have any patients today?"

"They were all miraculously healed." She laughed. "He had a couple cancellations, so he doesn't have to be at the clinic for another hour. His partner is dealing with emergency cases this morning."

Quinn's voice carried down the stairs from the bathroom. She sounded like Madonna singing an Elton John tune. Somehow I'd never pictured Madonna singing *Crocodile Rock*. She wasn't half bad.

"I've gotta go. I promised Quinn coffee and breakfast before we go to the store." I sipped my coffee. "Have you seen Mishel today?"

"No, but I won't be surprised if we see him and his skinny shadow show up before long," she said. "I don't want to deal with them alone."

"You'll be fine, you have Enid. We'll be there as soon as Quinn runs out of hot water in forty-five minutes or so." I crossed my fingers as I hung up.

Half an hour later, Quinn came down wrapped in my bathrobe. Her curly hair was tamed by a red ribbon I'd left in the bathroom. She flashed a shy smile. "I really need to go back to the hotel and get my makeup bag. I feel naked."

I studied her for a minute, the curve of her cheeks and the natural blush from the hot water. "This is the first time I've seen you without makeup."

"Scary, right?" she asked, gazing at the cup filling slowly on the coffeemaker. "Is that for me?"

"It is. I've had two." I handed her the bagel that popped out of the toaster. "There's peanut butter, jam, cream cheese and all that in the fridge. How did you learn to do your make-up so well? When I put it on, I look like a psychotic clown."

Quinn opened the fridge. "I was a drag queen for a while and had some great friends who taught me all sorts of tricks. Stage makeup is different from real life makeup though. I was lucky to meet people who were makeup artists in their other lives."

I set her coffee on the table. "I'll bet they can't wait to hear about your adventures here."

Sadness flickered across her face as she set jars of peanut butter and jam on the table. "Yeah. There's only one or two I'm still in touch with. They'd love it here. I've told them all about you and Laken. They're happy I have support through my transition and...Sebastian."

"Us girls have to stick together, right?" I sat across from her.

She smeared peanut butter and jam on her bagel as she sighed. "I appreciate all you've done. I'd love to teach you to do your makeup. If you let me."

"Maybe you could do makeovers at the store," I suggested. "How hard would it be to get the supplies you need?"

Quinn smiled. "Piece of cake. The problem is my lack of funds."

"We'll talk to Laken after the show and see what she thinks. There has to be something we can keep you busy with for the next few weeks."

*****

We parted ways close to Vintage Sage. Quinn decided to pick up coffee and donuts for our helpers when I stopped at the bakery for the treats they'd graciously donated for the show.

By the time I returned to the store for the second time that day, Gill had lined up several bud vases on the front counter near the till. Each contained a long-stemmed rose.

"Those look great." I set the bags on the counter next to them. "Where did you get such beautiful flowers?"

Gill eyed the bakery bags. "Some are from the courtyard. There's a rosebush in the far corner that Tilly planted when we first moved in."

I sniffed one. Tea roses. Suitable for a former tea house. "I never even thought of using them. Will they stay fresh for tonight?"

"I'll put them in the fridge for a while."

Since I was no flower expert, I held up the bakery bag. "Were you able to find some platters for the desserts?"

"I brought a box from my storage space," he said. "We'll have more than enough. Whatever we don't break, you can sell in the store later. It's not like I'll need them again."

Brad strode inside with a grin. "Hey, Sage, I hear you have a broken door."

"Yeah. Someone broke a pane of glass, and I can't get hold of the repair guy." I walked toward him, then stuck my hand through the hole. "I don't suppose you can fix that, could you?"

"Andy called me a couple days ago, but I've been busy," he said. "I have a set of doors in my truck with new locks and handles. It'll take a few minutes to install them, but they'll be sturdier than these. I had them in a barn on my property. All they'll cost you is beer and wings."

"Brad, you're a lifesaver. It's a deal." My shoulders sagged with such relief that I wanted to hug him.

Just as he returned to his truck to grab his tools an ambulance pulled up out front.

"What's going on?" Gill leaned on my shoulder. "Am I dead yet?"

I tapped his arm. "Stop it. That's Andy."

The front doors of the ambulance opened then the paramedics waved to Brad before they walked around to the back. A few minutes later, Andy strode into the building with his partner in full uniform. They each carried a ten-foot-long table.

"Where do you want them?" he asked.

I took a sharp breath, too stunned to speak.

Gill pulled out the floor map Laken had created and said, "The food will be along the corner wall to the right of the runway."

Andy frowned. "My right or yours?"

I stared in confusion too tired to figure that out, so I just pointed. "Over there."

"My left." He winked. "The lack of clear instructions tells me your day isn't going well."

"I'll fill you in later," I told him as my cell phone rang.

"Hey, Sage, it's Officer Rhodes. The lab has released the glass case. It'll arrive sometime Monday afternoon."

I closed my eyes. "Monday? But the show's tonight. How am I supposed to get my star attraction to stand up?"

"It's the best I can do." Rhodes sighed. "There's some problem with the delivery driver. Since he doesn't have a full load, he won't bring it until Monday."

"Okay. Thanks." As I hung up, I covered my eyes with one hand.

"What's going on?" Andy asked.

Brad hovered nearby as he started to take down my old doors.

"The lab released the glass case I found Sebastian in, but they can't bring it back until Monday," I explained. "I hoped to showcase Mata Hari tonight since her costume's so fabulous."

"I have no idea who that is," Brad said, shaking his head.

Cameron joined our huddle in the middle of the doorway. "I saw that cabinet in the pictures Laken showed me. I have one similar at the clinic. I use it to keep the dog treats safe, but I think we could take the shelves out and manage without it for a day."

My eyes grew wide. "Really? That would be great. Her normal base is broken, so she needs a confined space to stand up in."

Brad stuck his screwdriver in his tool belt has he took one door off its hinges. "When I'm done with the doors, I'll be happy to pick it up. You're the doc at the vet clinic, right?"

"Yeah." Cameron gave a nod.

"Wow," Andy said. "This is your lucky day, lady. I'll see you tonight."

I smiled. "I'll have your ticket waiting."

Happy that I could put Mata Hari on display, I felt much lighter. She could stay in storage until after I showered and dressed later. Despite the adrenalin coursing through my veins all day, I couldn't stop yawning. Watching Brad take the old doors off and replace them with the new ones made me even more tired.

Once Brad had tested the locks and deadbolts, he dropped a set of golden keys into my hand with a wink "There you go. Those should keep unwanted contractors out of the building."

"I certainly hope so," I told him. "How much do I owe you for the doors and installation?"

He rubbed a hand over his tanned face and winced as he thought. When he didn't reply after a few seconds, I envisioned even more dollar signs floating away.

"Consider them a gift," he said. "I had the doors in storage and the labor was nothing. One of these days, you can buy me beer and chicken wings."

"I think he's asking you on a date," Laken whispered.

My face felt like it burst into flames. I really needed more coffee. "What? I mean, thank you. For now, I can give you a ticket for the show tonight. Or two if you'd like to bring a date."

Brad gave a nod. "One will do. My dating life's kind of quiet at the moment."

Oh boy. For someone who'd sworn off dating, I was suddenly swarmed by single men. Quinn handed me a ticket for Brad while I willed my hand not to shake as I passed it to him. "I'll see you tonight then."

"I'm looking forward to it. Andy said you look amazing in that gray dress. I'm glad I'll get to see for myself," he said, then winked.

As he walked out of the store, he paused to chat with Andy and his partner. I leaned on the new door for support with my head spinning.

"Have no fear, coffee is here," Quinn sang as she came up the front steps. "Whoa. Where did all the good-looking men come from?"

When Brad and Andy smirked, I ducked to get out of their sight.

"Are you okay?" Quinn asked.

"Yup. Brad found us new doors without broken panes. Andy and his partner delivered tables. Gill supplied platters for the food, vases, and roses."

She glanced through the open doorway to the men standing near the ambulance. "I only see one big vase of roses, but boy do I see beef. It looks like Andy has serious competition."

"That's what I told her," Laken said as she walked past us on her way to the back room.

"Quinn." I shook my head as I carried the large vase from the counter toward one of the tables in the corner. "Did you grab me one of those vegan treats?"

"Why, yes I did."

"Vegan?" a man asked from the doorway ten feet away. "Since when are you vegan?"

"No." My breath stuck in my throat as my entire body seized. The crystal vase slipped from my hands. Roses and glass narrowly missed my feet as the water splashed my bare legs.

"Oh yeah," Quinn winced. "Guess who followed me home."

Emery Samson was built like a marble statue of a Greek god. Chiseled jaw, thick dark hair, and a smile that could melt the skin off a peach. He took a couple steps forward, then stopped near the shards of glass and damaged flowers. "Nice to see you, Sage. It's been a while."

"Yeah. That was by choice."

"What broke?" my sister shouted as she thumped down the apartment stairs in back.

Emery's face lit up.

I squeezed my eyes closed. "Don't come in here."

"What's going on?" Laken shoved open the swinging door and flew into the store. "Get out of here or I'm calling the—"

Just as I started to turn to stop her, she tripped on a corner of the carpet we'd rolled out for the runway and slid into me. I toppled over like a fallen tree, the kind with limbs everywhere, and landed on top of her. At least trees never had to worry about flashing their underwear at their ex-brother-in-law.

Quinn shrieked.

Emery stood there grinning and made no move to help see if we were okay. "Wow. Usually I'm the one who makes grand entrances. I didn't realize you'd be so happy to see me that you'd fall at my feet."

My sister snorted like a wild horse as she clamored to her feet and yelled, "Get out of here!"

"Is that how you greet your customers?" he asked. "Laken, honey, you won't be in business long with that attitude."

"You're no customer." Laken put one hand on her hip and pointed to the door. "Out."

He chuckled. "I'm no dog either."

"That's your opinion," I muttered, holding my skirt snug to my legs as I tried to get off the wet floor with a shred of dignity. As my hand throbbed, I realized I had a couple shards of glass stuck in my palm.

Quinn frowned. "Sorry, girls. I didn't know him coming by would be a problem."

"Yeah, well it is. Now he can leave." Laken closed the gap between her and Emery. "And if he doesn't, I'll call the police."

He held up his hands. "Come on, Laken, I haven't done anything."

"Not yet anyway."

"Hey, buddy, are you bothering the ladies?" Garnet's bulky form filled the kitchen doorway.

"She's my wife." Emery took a half-step back as he pointed to Laken.

My sister growled. "Ex-wife. Get out of our store."

Garnet lumbered toward us. While he was about the same height as Emery, he outweighed the actor by a solid hundred pounds. The surprise on Emery's face delighted me to no end. Laken didn't appear as amused, but Quinn chuckled as she leaned against the front counter to watch.

"Do you need some help to get through the door?" Garnet asked.

"Oh, please don't wreck the doors, they're brand new," I said as I picked the shards of glass out of my hand, so I wouldn't laugh.

"Quinn, call the cops," Laken said.

"I got this," Garnet told her. "My sister had an abusive husband who nearly killed her. I don't let a creep get away twice."

Emery's cool smile faded. He backed away and was halfway down the front steps before he spun around to run toward a sports car parked out front near the hydrant. A black sports car.

My pulse quickened. "Is that his car?"

"Looks like," Quinn said.

"Thanks, Garnet." Laken closed the front door and turned the shiny new lock.

Brad deserved more than beer and chicken wings. We'd negotiate a price later.

"No problem, sunshine," Garnet said. "I'm here all day. Let me know if he tries anything else."

I headed into the kitchen to grab a broom for the glass and the mop for the water and searched for something to wrap my hand in until I could find a bandage or two. I settled for wrapping my palm in several paper towels until the bleeding stopped.

As Garnet made his way back up the stairs, he muttered, "I should've wiped the floor with that guy and his fancy suit. I hate guys like that."

"You and me both," I told him. At least Jonathan hadn't shown up, nor had he texted since early morning.

By the time I returned to the store front, Laken hovered near the front door scowling at Quinn. "How long did you know Emery was in town?"

"I wasn't sure until I ran into him at the coffee shop. Enid and I never found him yesterday," Quinn said, "I know you and Sage talked about him, but I didn't realize you hated him so much or I never would have let him follow me here."

I swept up the glass and flowers while my sister paced. "Quinn, can you remind me to tell Gill I broke a vase? He probably won't care about it, but—"

"The vase?" Laken stomped her foot. "My ex is in town on the day of our fashion show, and you're worried about a silly vase?"

"And my hand." I held up my hand wrapped in paper towel that was slowly turning red. "And my wet dress and the bruises on my legs from where you collided with me. Not to mention that I flashed Emery."

"You flashed him?" Quinn's face contorted as she tried not to laugh. "I'll flag down Andy to check your hand out before he goes. I'm sure he'd love to hear the flashing story."

"What's Emery doing in town anyway?" my sister asked as Quinn called Andy inside. "How did he figure out where to find me?"

Quinn cleared her throat. "Like I said, that was my fault. He asked me about a vintage store. He said he knew the owner and wanted to say hello."

"And you know him," I said, reaching for the mop.

"And you know us," Laken said, approaching Quinn. Rather than do anything drastic, she reached for her tea. "What if Emery killed Sebastian because he's after the same thing as Mishel? Worse, what if he wants to see our show?"

"You did say fashion shows were like funerals," I reminded her.

She scowled. "You're not helping."

"Do you think he's capable of actually shooting someone?" I asked.

"Emery? Only when he's stoned, which is about seventy percent of the time."

Quinn winced. "I could tell him the tickets are a hundred dollars each. That might stop him."

Laken sat on the stool behind the counter. "Emery's a movie star. A bad one, but he does make good money. He carries ten times that in his back pocket and wouldn't bat an eye. I'm surprised Chick let him out of his sight."

Andy returned to the store with his kit in one hand. "Who got hurt?"

"Sage has glass in her hand," Quinn told him. "It was my fault. I let someone into the store that I shouldn't have. She dropped a vase, then Laken came into the room and they both fell. Sage flashed the guy, and—"

"Thank you for your discretion," I muttered.

Andy raised an eyebrow as he led me to a chair. "A vase breaker and a flasher? What am I getting into with you? Let me have a look."

I sighed. "It's fine. I covered it so I wouldn't get blood on the mop."

"Did you get cut anywhere else?" Andy asked as he knelt in front of me. He took my hand and gently unwrapped my paper towel cast.

"I don't think so."

"What happened to your leg?"

"Oh, right. I scraped it on a rock when I found Quinn asleep on the beach this morning." When he met my gaze, I shrugged. "It's been a busy day."

"You'll have to tell me about it over a glass of wine later," he said.

"Now that sounds like a date." Laken grinned as she walked away.

While Andy patched my hand and cleaned up the gash on my leg, Quinn filled him in on the night before and continued all the way to when Sammy and I found her asleep on the beach. When she mentioned seeing Emery in the coffee shop, my sister stopped her.

"Where was Chick?" Laken asked, taking the mop.

Quinn looked from Laken to me. "I didn't see him."

When Andy's mic crackled, he finished bandaging my hand quickly. "Sorry, Sage, I have to run. Take it easy, will you? I don't want to have to come back before the show tonight. I'll check it before you walk down the runway."

Laken laughed. "Take it easy? Have you met my sister? Sage is one of the busiest, clumsiest people I know."

"Only because of the move."

"Yes, I've met her," he said. "Which is how I know a couple glass shards won't slow her down. Tonight will be amazing."

I gave him a shy smile.

After he left, I stared at the white bandage. "Emery was driving a black sports car."

"That's not a newsflash," Laken said, cleaning up the mess. "He has three."

I smoothed the bandage Andy stuck on my leg as I told her, "When Sebastian was killed, a black car drove past the store. I didn't see where it came from."

Laken stared. "Say that again."

"When Rhodes walked me through what happened before I found Sebastian, one of the things I saw was a black sports car leaving the store."

"You didn't think that was important?" Quinn asked.

I turned my head so fast I got a kink in my neck. "What are you talking about? You were standing right behind me. I ran into you."

She unwrapped her muffin. "Oh yeah. Mishel drives a black car."

"So does half of Glitter Bay." Laken stuck the mop back in the water.

"There was something else. I'm sure I heard a delivery truck." I got up to walk toward the kitchen, then stopped to examine a smaller cut on my hand. "I didn't see it. It could've been anywhere, but it sounded like it was in the back alley."

Since Quinn and Laken had nothing to add, I took the mop and broom back to the kitchen. Garnet whistled like a broken kettle upstairs while I emptied the bucket. I had no choice but add Emery to my suspect list.

Laken shuffled into the kitchen before she leaned her head on my shoulder. "What are we going to do about my ex?"

"Nothing."

"What do you mean nothing?" She grabbed my arm.

"Laken, he showed up, then he left," I told her. "Technically, he hasn't done anything that we know of, so why should we worry?"

"Because he might've killed Sebastian."

"All you have is speculation. The police can't arrest him just because he drives a black car, and we hate him."

She clutched my unbandaged hand. "Sure they can. Besides, he made you drop a vase, and now you're injured. Isn't that attempted murder?"

"That's not quite how that works."

"They could arrest him for being a public nuisance or something, right?"

I shook my head. "Except I didn't get hurt until you crashed into me."

Laken frowned. "I saw him, tripped on the carpet, then slipped on the water he made you spill when he surprised you."

"Now you're reaching."

"Ugh. I know." She groaned. "Why did he have to show up? I was doing so much better without him around. I actually felt sane again."

I hugged her. "You are sane. Emery's good at making you think you're the problem. It's called gaslighting."

She checked her watch then her eyes grew wide. "Oh, no. I was supposed to drop Sammy off at the groomer ten minutes ago. We also have to pick up the food for tonight before we shower and change."

"Then you'd better hustle." I clapped my hands. "Chop, chop. Quinn and I can pick up the food, then lock up and meet you at home."

"Except your hand is cut up, the contractors are here, and..." My sister sighed as she glanced toward the staircase. "I'll send Garnet and the crew home. The last thing we need is to parade down the runway with drills and saws serenading us."

"Good plan." I doubted I'd get any rest until I collapsed onto my bed that night. A cold shower might help. And coffee.

"Sage, you have a delivery," Quinn sang out. "I'll bet they're from Andy."

"Told you he likes you," my sister said as she nudged me and winked.

I returned to the store front with Laken inches behind me. "What are you talking about?"

Quinn pointed to a large vase filled with long-stemmed, white roses. "They're so pretty. Hurry, read the little card."

My stomach flip-flopped as I froze. I didn't need to read the card. I knew who they were from, and it wasn't Andy.

Laken wrapped her arms around me as my knees wobbled. "Sage? Are you okay?"

As she led me to a stool behind the counter, I whispered, "She's back."

"Who's back?" Quinn stepped away from the flowers. "Is there something I need to know? I can throw these out if they're—?"

"Leave them. It's okay," Laken ordered. She reached for the card and opened it. "All that's on here is a circle Do you think she sent them?."

"That's how she saw our partnership despite everything. Endless. No beginning. No end. It just continues on as it always has." I closed my eyes.

Quinn opened my coffee, then handed it to me. "I'm freaking out a little. Who are we talking about?"

In the pit of my stomach, I had a hunch the mannequins circling Sebastian's body meant more than I'd first suspected. I met her gaze but couldn't speak.

"It's okay," Quinn said. "You don't know me or trust me. You don't seem to trust many people though, so I'm not offended."

I wanted to argue, but she was right.

"Sorry, I shouldn't have said that."

"No. Quinn, you're right." I told her.

She flashed a warm smile. "Somebody burned you good, huh? Was she your girlfriend?"

For once, Laken didn't say anything. She sipped her tea and let me do all the talking.

"My former business partner, Delia Reeves. We met at yoga and became fast friends. She was my partner when I opened Vintage Sage five years ago. I found out by accident that she was stealing items from estate sales and selling them in the store."

"How could you find that out by accident?" she asked.

"They both attended the same estate sale. Delia didn't realize Sage was there."

"I watched her stick a few small items in her bag. When I asked what she was doing, she said she'd pay for them, but needed a way to carry them. Since she was my friend and business partner, I had no reason to doubt her."

"How did you find out she didn't pay for them?" Quinn asked.

I averted my gaze. "The police showed up Monday morning. When I paid for the items I bought, I'd left the woman in charge my business card in case they had anything else to sell. She had a list she was checking off as people bought items. Since I'd bought a box of smaller items, she thought I'd hidden the missing pieces inside."

Quinn hung onto my every word. "Then what?"

"Then Sage suggested Delia might've seen something," Laken said.

"That explains why she's no longer your partner."

I shook my head and told her, "Delia came in while the police were there. They searched her tote bag and found one of the missing pieces. She figured if she brought them into the store one or two at a time, I wouldn't notice."

"That's cheeky." Quinn shook her head. "I can see why you have a hard time trusting people."

Laken sighed and finished the story, "Once Delia got out on bail, she bashed Sage over the head one night when she was leaving the store, then tried to burn it to the ground with Sage inside. Luckily, the guy who owned the bookstore across the street saw her when he was locking up. He called 9-1-1. Delia had connections, and a good lawyer. All she got was five years."

"And Sage got a lifetime of nightmares," Quinn said. "That bites."

My stomach sank. What if Delia was free and looking to sabotage my new location? The roses could be her way of letting me know she was back. I pulled out my phone.

"What's wrong?" Laken's eyes grew wide.

"I need to call Rhodes. If Delia sent those flowers, she might be up to something."

Quinn shrugged. "Maybe she sent them as an apology or a congrat-ulations."

"Then she should have written that," Laken said. "Do you think she'd do anything to you or the shop, Sage?"

My pulse quickened. "She's tried before. Sebastian could be collateral damage. His murder might not have anything to do with fashions or design houses. If Delia was involved, it could be plain revenge."

After my call to Rhodes, I paced the store. He promised to call me as soon as he learned anything about Delia Reeves. My heart would race until he did.

"I'll ask Gill to pick up the food," Laken said. "Quinn, do you have anything else to do today?"

"I just need some makeup to make me and Snow White look like we're still breathing. She's going to look amazing when she does walk down the aisle later."

Laken scowled. "It's a runway. You of all people should know that."

"Yeah, yeah. I was thinking about her and Andy." Quinn winked. "Are you okay, Sage?"

My sister helped me up. "She'll be fine. I'll take her home for some food and a shower. Do you mind keeping an eye on the construction guys? I told them they need to be out by four. Sage and I will be back around five to do the last-minute stuff. Just make sure to lock the doors once the crew leaves."

She nodded. "Sounds good. I'll help Gill get things organized. I have a few ideas about how to fancy up the food tables."

"Do not let Emery or anyone else inside except Gill, or you're fired," Laken said.

Quinn held up her hands. "No troublemakers allowed. No problem. No one gets in without a key or food."

I forced a chuckle. "You got it."

Laken grabbed our things, then draped her arm across my shoulders as she walked me to the doorway. Just as she reached for the doorknob, it opened, and a man stepped inside.

Chapter Fourteen

"Where do you want the food?" Gill asked as he stood empty-handed in the doorway.

"You didn't bring any," Laken pointed out.

"I'm on my way to pick everything up. Is anyone going to be here to let me in, or should I wait?"

Quinn held up her hand. "I'll be here."

I blew out a sigh and waved. "You can put everything in the kitchen. There should be room in the fridge for anything that has to stay cold. We have tablecloths on the counter and can fancy up the tables Andy brought when we get back."

"Good. I'll be back in a bit." Gill turned and left the store.

Laken held up a finger. "Before we go, I'll make sure Garnet's clear they have to clear out by four o'clock. They can come back tomorrow. I'll come early to supervise."

When she disappeared into the kitchen, Quinn joined me by the door. "You need to show me a picture of this Delia person, so I can be on the lookout. If she shot Sebastian…"

"That's a good idea," I told her. "What if she's back in town and determined to make sure my shop doesn't succeed? Or to finish what she started."

"Don't go there, Sage."

Too late. I was already halfway down that rabbit hole. "Why not? Emery's in town, and Jonathan's been texting me so often I won't be surprised if he shows up, too."

"Yeah, him and half of Los Angeles." She snorted.

My head hammered as I tugged the elastic from my hair to free my ponytail. "I just want things to go back to the way they were before Tilly died. I want Gill to run the tea house and my little shop to be back in the bad part of town again. Sebastian would still be alive and none of this would've ever happened."

"Oh, honey, you don't want any of that."

I barely heard her as I dove deep into a full-on rant, "Before I knew any fashion designers or models, besides my sister, and the local gossip columnist wouldn't give me the time of day instead of giving me hourly updates on a murder victim I barely knew."

Quinn put her hot hands on my shoulders. "But then you wouldn't have met me. Is that what you want?"

Tears welled in my eyes as I shook my head and whispered, "No."

She lifted my chin with one knuckle. "Then, as my grandmama says, 'Get up, get dressed, and show up, because nobody else can pull off being you better than you.'"

"Smart woman." I closed my eyes to absorb her words. "What you're saying is I should get this place ready for the show tonight and not worry that there might be a murderer in the audience?"

"Sorta sums it up," she said with a grin.

I blew out a long sigh. "Then how do we figure out who killed Sebastian?"

"You mean besides leaving the investigating up to the police?" Laken strolled in from the kitchen with Sammy leading the way. "I made a list of suspects to find Tilly's killer."

Quinn held up a piece of paper. "Check. I want to hear all about this Tilly woman sometime. I feel like I'm missing out."

"Believe me, you're not. Let me see that list," I said, reaching for the paper. "Chick. Emery. Bridey. Mishel. What about that truck driver, Brick? Oh, and add Delia."

Laken frowned. "What about you?"

"I didn't do it. I'm the one who found his body," I reminded her.

"Not you," my sister said, pointing at Quinn. "Her."

Quinn gasped before her voice rose an octave. "I didn't kill him. He was my boss. Besides, he owed me a lot of money."

"All the more reason for you to kill him."

I reached for Quinn's hand. "Of course, you didn't kill him. Laken saw you get into the cab and close the door."

"What did I miss here?" my sister asked.

"I'm one of you now. Your sister has accepted me into the tribe," Quinn said.

Laken frowned. "What's that supposed to mean?"

I met my sister's puzzled gaze. "It means we'll be able to work with each other for the next few weeks. Unless she gets a better gig, that is."

Quinn raised her eyebrows. "And that is probably the best compliment I'll get out of Sage today. What's next on the to-do list?"

"Sage and I need to go shower and change," Laken said. "Gill will be back with the food soon. Are you okay to keep an eye on the construction guys until we get back?"

"Depends. Are any of them cute?"

I chuckled. "Behave yourself. We'll see you in a bit."

My sister hooked her arm around mine as we walked home. "I'm glad to see you and Quinn are friends. It'll make the next few weeks easier."

"You know, even though we still have a lot to do, I'm looking forward to tonight." For the first time all week, I meant it. My heart soared all the way home.

Until I saw what awaited us on the front porch.

Jonathan Welles.

My jaw tightened and my body tensed from my forehead down when I saw my ex-boyfriend on one of my chairs with his feet up sipping from a paper cup. His dark hair was blonder and a few inches longer than when he'd left. His dark tan made his teeth whiter.

"What's he doing here?" Laken asked, stopping next to me.

My feet suddenly felt like boulders. I could barely shuffle let alone walk. "No idea. He's been texting all week, but I never answered. Maybe I should've."

She frowned. "Why was he texting you? You guys broke up."

"We did and I've been ignoring him. Yet here he is."

"Should I call Rhodes?" Laken whispered.

My stomach said yes, but I shook my head. "Let's see what he has to say for himself. If he makes any sudden moves..."

"I'll sic Sammy on him," she muttered.

Jonathan was nearly twice my size. He wasn't only a body builder but had studied jiu jitsu for years. One wrong move and I could end up in a headlock on my front lawn or worse.

"Hey, Sage," he said as he swung his legs off the table, then walked toward us. "How are things going?"

Laken stood between us. "What are do you doing here, Jonathan?"

"I came to see your beautiful sister. I've missed her."

"Yeah, I'll bet."

He turned his gaze toward me. "You haven't answered any of my texts, so I figured you were angry with me."

"Angry?" I asked. "We broke up. Why do I need to answer your texts or call you?"

He ran his hand through his hair as he shifted his weight. "Did you even read my messages? I tried to tell you about—"

Laken placed her hands on my shoulder blades and propelled me toward the front porch. "You'll have to excuse us. We have an event tonight and you're not going to make my sister ugly cry now. Come back tomorrow."

"Actually, that's what I need to talk to Sage about," he said.

"Whatever you want, it can wait. We're busy." Laken growled. "Besides, you dumped my sister for a glamorous life in L.A. and all the starlets you could handle. What makes you think she'd want you back now?"

Jonathan shook his head. "I don't want her back. I want to—"

I tried to stop, but she wouldn't let me. "Wait, what?"

"Come on." Laken continued to propel me toward the steps.

"Sage, I was trying to warn you about Sebastian." Jonathan blurted out behind us.

This time my sister froze. "What are you talking about?"

Jonathan glanced from me to my sister. "Please, can I talk to you alone, Sage?"

I folded my arms across my chest. "No. Laken and Sebastian were friends. Either tell us both, or get out of here before I call the police."

He paled as he studied us both before he reached into his back pocket. "I found this. He wants to take over your new store."

When he held out a white, legal-sized envelope, Laken gasped. I guessed it was the letter she'd nearly torn the house apart looking for.

I snatched it out of Jonathan's hand before he tried to pull anything funny. "You do know Sebastian's dead, right?"

"I heard."

"Thanks for this. Now you need to leave." I held up the envelope as I took a step back. The flap was open. Someone had already read it. Sebastian's killer?

"Sage... Please..." He bowed his head and ran a hand through his hair. "Okay. That was all I wanted. I'll see you around."

When Jonathan sauntered out of my yard, Laken grabbed the envelope from my hand before she ran into the house. I waited until he climbed into a dark blue sports car and drove off in the direction of the hotel. Away from me, Laken, and Vintage Sage.

Dark blue was close to black at a glance.

Running into the house, I locked the door, then joined my sister in the living room. She paced while she read the contents of the envelope. "Is that Sebastian's will?"

Tears filled her eyes as she nodded. "He left everything to me. Why would he do that?"

I pulled her into a hug. "Probably because you were the one person who believed in him. You brought him here to work with you after things fell apart at the House of Hayward."

"You have to believe me, Sage, I didn't know about that," she whispered.

"He tried to protect you from the ugliness. If he was still here, he'd sit down and fill you in. He just didn't get to."

Laken handed me the letter. "He thought you'd be more like me, you know."

"That I'd look like a supermodel." I smirked as I opened the folded page and sat on the couch. Sebastian Hayward the Third's final will and testament was handwritten and not notarized.

My sister wandered into the kitchen while I read how Sebastian wished to leave the House of Hayward and all of his personal possessions to my sister. The only thing he'd left Quinn was Mata Hari, or as he called her, "that ugly mannequin dressed like a dead actress."

"Do you think Quinn knew about this?" I asked.

Laken sipped sparkling water. "No idea. I wonder where Jonathan found this. I must've dropped it the other day."

"As far as I know, Jonathan's never set foot inside the new Vintage Sage. Did he even know we were moving to a new location?"

"Unless he went to get a cup of tea and figured it out."

"It's possible, but one of us would've been there."

Except when Sebastian died. I grew lightheaded.

Laken shook her head. "I zipped that envelope into the outside pocket of my purse. There's no way it could've fallen out. Someone had to unzip that pocket to pull it out."

"Who else was there when Sebastian gave it to you?"

She closed her eyes to think. "Just me and Sebastian. Hamlet—Quinn, I mean—was in the washroom. Do you believe Jonathan really found it?"

"Did you take your purse with you when you picked up dinner the night Sebastian died?" I asked.

"I don't remember," she said. "I think so. I wasn't able to go into the store to get it, so yes, I did. Why would you ask...?" She paused. "Oh, wow. Do you think Jonathan could've...?"

I blew out a long breath. "I don't know what to think. Let's get ready for the show. Maybe we'll find out how Jonathan ended up with that letter and why he's back in Glitter Bay."

My sister met my gaze. "Not to mention figuring out who killed Sebastian."

Chapter Fifteen

I'd just stepped out of the shower when Laken screeched my name from the other side of the door. My heart hammered. Did Jonathan come back or had something happened to Quinn?

Wrapping a thick towel around my torso, I opened the door enough to peer out. "What on earth is going on out here?"

My sister stood in the hallway with Sammy nipping at the belt of her bathrobe. "I have an issue with your dry cleaner. That little troll keeps ruining my clothes."

"What happened?" I opened the door wider as my long, red hair dripped.

She blinked back tears as she held up a navy-blue dress. "He shrank my favorite Chanel."

"I thought the white one was your favorite."

Her chin quivered as she told me, "Sage, I'm serious. He shrank my von Furstenberg dress too. I'm so tempted to sue him."

I laughed. "Oh, really?"

"It's not funny."

"Oh, stop being so dramatic." I rolled my eyes. "Just cut out some of those fancy dinners with Cameron, and they'll fit again."

"What are you saying?" she asked.

"Face it, Sis, you've put on a few pasta pounds. I thought you'd noticed that."

Her mouth moved, but no sound came out. After being a fashion model for years, then surviving cancer, I wasn't sure how she'd take the news. She snapped at Sammy to go lay down, then stared. "Seriously?"

"Are you okay?" I placed a hand on her shoulder in the hope of keeping her from going off like a bottle rocket into orbit.

She blinked as if trying to process the concept she'd gained weight for once in her life. "What do I do now?"

"What every other woman does when she gains a few pounds."

"Crash diet?" she asked. "I can't do that anymore. Food and I have a pretty decent relationship now." She hesitated, then chuckled. "Which is why none of my clothes fit anymore."

I hugged her. "I was going to say go shopping. To be honest, I like how you look now. All those walks on the beach with Sammy and Cameron and some good food have put a glow in your cheeks."

"And a hop in my step, as Grandma Sadie would say," Laken told me.

"That, too. It's nice to see you happy and healthy again. Now that we're expanding the store and you have a great new apartment you're moving in to, life will only get better."

"You're right. Walking and cycling all over Glitter Bay has made me feel like my old self again. And I love to shop. We could make a day of it and take Quinn to Seattle."

"Sounds good," I said. "Now go find something to wear. We have to get back to the shop to get ready for this show."

She winced. "I'm not sure if I have anything that'll fit. I may need to dig through your closet."

I tossed my long hair over my shoulder. "You hate my wardrobe. The last time you went into my closet, you told me to burn it all and start over."

"I know. I was so rude. How could you stand me?" Laken asked as she retreated to her room. "At least the pieces I picked out for you are awesome."

"Hey." I swatted at her with the back of my hand and laughed before returning to the bathroom.

*****

Half an hour later, Laken and I unlocked the new front door to Vintage Sage. I paused in the entrance to savor the mingled scents of fresh paint, cleaner, and citrus, which I guessed was Quinn's last-ditch attempt to mask them both. Once the hot appetizers arrived, the place would smell great.

The walls shone with twinkling lights while a couple fake Ficus trees sat near tables covered with black cloths and lined with battery-operated candles and glitter. White paper napkins marked where the platters went. The runway was lined with jars that held the same fake candles and more glitter, which would be a pain to clean.

All the clothing racks and cabinets were tidy moved aside for rows of chairs facing the runway on either side. Seating would be a bit squishy, but we could accommodate the thirty people we'd invited. The stage area was marked out with the same red carpeting as the runway with a microphone at the far end away from the kitchen door.

"It's so beautiful," I whispered.

"You've done a great job," Laken told me, giving me a hug. "I have to say I had doubts for a while, but the place looks great. Congratulations, Sis."

"To you, too. I couldn't have done this without you."

Sammy snuffled across the polished floor, then rolled around on the runway carpet. He'd be one of our models for the evening since I'd found a doggy tuxedo jacket and tie. Laken planned to put it on him right before they walked down the runway to start the show.

"I'll check the kitchen to see what Gill picked up," Laken said as she entered the kitchen.

I nodded, a bit distracted as I examined the white cardboard boxes on the front counter. Gill had picked up the sweets from the bakery. We had to put everything on platters. "Andy and Brad will be here soon. We could ask one of them to take care of the tickets and keep an eye on things while we focus on the show."

"Ooh, aren't you pretty. I guarantee you'll look even better later," Quinn gushed as she emerged from the kitchen.

"We're here." Gill strolled in with Enid and his grandson, Abbie. "I volunteered this guy to take care of the music. We did a sound check while you were gone. He promises not to turn it up too loud for us old people."

Abbott San Vicente, aka Abbie, tugged at the knot of his bow tie while a lock of blue hair fell across his dark eyes. "Do you want me to start the music?"

I pointed to Laken. "Ask her. She's the expert."

"Yeah, sure," my sister said, waving a hand. "Just keep it low for now, so we can hear each other."

Gill and Abbie strolled toward a small table near the stage. Suddenly, Gill stopped and muttered, "Oh joy. The Hens are here."

The Hens, as Gill called them, were a gaggle of women in their seventies and eighties who used to haunt the Sweet Eden Tea House in the afternoons. Margaret Gumble was a retired schoolteacher and her twin, Joanna, used to work in the Glitter Bay library. Both women had short white hair. Their usual tight white curls combed into soft waves for the evening.

Carol Axton, a retired accountant and the unofficial leader of the Hens, had orange hair and a blue chiffon dress. She stood in stark contrast to the twins with their cardigan and blouse ensembles.

Ursula, who I wasn't sure had a last name, wore her long, white hair loose. It hung to her waist and shrouded her thin shoulders like a cape over her gauzy blue blouse and skirt. As she swept toward me for a hug, her bangles tinkled like the percussion section in a band.

While the women admired the clothes on the racks, they chatted and teased each other. Enid swooped in to join them and soon all talk turned to Sebastian's murder. As Enid told them what she knew, she set aside a couple outfits she wanted to buy later.

"Endless gossip with that lot," Gill grumbled as he rolled his eyes.

Laken nodded. "Yeah, but sometimes that gossip can lead to a clue. Keep your ears open."

I watched the women hold up blouses and dresses while they giggled. "Somehow, I doubt any of them know anything about Sebastian's murder, or Sebastian for that matter."

"I'm going to finish with the desserts. Yell if you need anything," Gill said.

Quinn joined the Hens and tried to give helpful suggestions. Ursula latched onto her arm. The twins pursed their lips, gave them space, and went off to whisper in a corner.

Carol, on the other hand, marched toward me with a scowl. "What's the big idea having a man in drag here to sell women clothing? It's repulsive."

"Quinn is a woman," I told her. "She's working with us for the next few weeks thanks to Sebastian, the guy who was murdered. She was his assistant."

"Oh." She drew her pink lips into a tight pucker. "Well, I don't like it."

"That's a shame. She's actually a talented fashion designer and makeup artist." I paused. "She's in great demand in L.A. right now."

It wasn't a huge lie, so I didn't feel bad. Mishel and the gang had come all this way to talk to Quinn about whatever Sebastian hid.

Carol still looked down her nose at Quinn. "What has she designed?"

I forced myself not to flinch as I pointed out the bug outfits. "She's also designed the gown I'm wearing in the show tonight."

"Butterflies and ladybugs. I don't know what those other things are, but they're nothing I'd wear." She snorted. "Why couldn't you get a real designer to work here?"

I began to grow concerned that she'd say or do something to ruin the whole evening. "Carol, just give her a chance. Please. She's not what you think."

"For now," she said. "But if she hits on me, all bets are off."

"Feel free to let me know if she causes any problems." I left her side before I started to laugh. Then I spied the empty glass case Cameron delivered while we were at the house. I rushed over to make sure it was the right size. "This is perfect. We can't let Mata Hari miss the main event. She came a long way to be here."

Since the others were busy, I headed into the kitchen alone. The rack that held all the clothes for the show blocked the doorway to the storage room. I shoved it aside, then flicked on the pantry light. I caught my breath at the sight of the hidden mannequin. I'd forgotten how beautiful she was. Someone had put a lot of time and patience into doing her makeup and dressing her exactly as Greta Garbo had appeared in the movie.

"Come on, Mata Hari. It's our time to shine tonight. I'm not doing this without you." As I reached for her, something brushed my leg. I let out a shriek and fell back against the shelving.

Sammy darted out of the pantry with a loud yip as my heart hammered.

I'd barely regained my footing when Mata Hari fell against me. We crashed to the floor in a heap with me on the bottom. I was positive I heard something crack. I did a quick body scan for sharp pain, then sighed. Happily, I wasn't the one who broke, although my scraped leg and bandaged hand began to throb mercilessly.

Andy ran into the kitchen with Laken on his heels. "Are you okay? I thought I told you to stay out of trouble?"

Sammy made a hasty escape into the store as the door swung.

I groaned, still trapped beneath the glittering mannequin. "You did, but I didn't see Sammy follow me in here and he scared the crap out of me."

"Thank goodness," Laken said. "After seeing Jonathan earlier, then those flowers, I got scared when I heard you scream."

"What's this about Jonathan and flowers? Why didn't you tell me, Sage?" Andy asked. As he lifted Mata Hari off me, one of her feet fell off and landed on my skirt.

"Oh, no! She broke," I said. "We'll have to tape her up. There's nothing to tell. Jonathan showed up at the house earlier and we told him to get lost. The flowers are from my ex-business partner."

I grimaced in pain as Laken helped me sit up. When I grabbed the bottom of Mata Hari's leg, a thin cardboard tube with plastic plugs at each end fell out. "What the...?"

"What is that?" my sister asked.

Andy leaned Mata Hari against the wall and knelt next to us.

My eyes grew wide. "I'll bet twenty bucks this is what everyone's been searching for."

"Are you telling me the treasure was inside that old mannequin the whole time?" Laken shook her head. "That's impossible. Sebastian hated that thing. That's the only reason he let Quinn dress her up like Mata Hari."

"She's an antique." I reached inside the foot-long tube to pull out whatever was inside. "I found Sebastian's body in her glass case. She was lying face down on the floor and her leg was broken. I meant to ask Andy if he could fix her or rig a stand for her, but I forgot. We would've found this sooner if I'd remembered."

Since the skirt of Laken's dress was too snug for her to crouch, she sat on the floor beside me I pulled out a roll of papers. A flashdrive bedazzled with colorful rhinestones slipped out onto my skirt.

"What are those?" Andy asked.

I smoothed out the pages. "Sketches."

Laken gasped. "Hey, I've seen those before. That's Mishel's new department store line. Sebastian sent me pictures of them a couple months ago."

"Why would Sebastian have sketches of Mishel's new line?"

My sister pointed to a mark at the bottom of the page. "Because those aren't Mishel or Sebastian's designs. They're Quinn's and they're fabulous. I'll bet anything Sebastian saw them, told her they were horrible, then sold them to Mishel."

"That makes no sense," I told her. "Why would he sell them when his design house was failing? He needed a bailout and Quinn's designs could've saved him. Who'd kill him over these?"

"You mean besides Quinn if she found out?" Andy asked. "These give her motive."

Laken nodded. "Good point. Can you do me a favor, Andy? Keep an eye on Mishel and that witch he's with. I have a feeling there's something we're missing. Sage, one of us needs to stay close to Quinn. She's been pretty tight-lipped, but maybe she'll slip up and tell us what she knows."

"Which means me since she's making me over for the show." I studied the drawings, which were a huge departure from her bug designs. "Hopefully, she won't poke my eye out with a mascara wand."

"Fingers crossed. I'll keep everyone out of here while you find a good hiding spot for that stuff. Hopefully, we can figure out why Sebastian was hiding them."

"I'll give them to Rhodes," I told her. "Otherwise, I'll stress about someone finding them."

Andy helped Laken to her feet before she swept out of the kitchen, then he glanced at Mata Hari. "What do we do with the mannequin for now?"

"She needs to go into the empty cabinet out front. We can tape her foot on for now." I rolled the papers tightly, then stuck them and the flashdrive into the tube. "This is what worries me the most, besides finding Sebastian's killer. I need to get this to Rhodes. Hopefully, I can take a look at the flashdrive before handing it over."

"You want me to get Rhodes?" he asked.

I shook my head as I reached for a roll of clear packing tape. "Not yet. Can you help fix her leg? Then we need to get her into the cabinet."

He helped me, semi-gracefully, to my feet. "I can take care of that. Anything else?"

"We have to keep our eyes open to see if anyone reacts to Mata Hari's sudden presence. If anyone tries to get near her, we'll have to figure out our next move on the fly unless Rhodes has other ideas."

Andy grinned and shook his head before he leaned down to kiss me.

"What was that for?" My face grew pleasantly warm and my entire body tingled.

"I never realized how devious you were," he said, leaning his forehead against mine.

"You say that like that's a good thing."

He kissed me again. "It is if you like a good mystery. You, lady, are one interesting mystery."

"Why, Mr. Briggs, I never knew." I slid my arms around his neck.

"Well, that's a surprise since everyone else has been dropping hints like crazy."

"You're right. They have. I've just been too busy to pay attention."

He rubbed the tip of his nose against mine. "What do you think we should do about it?"

I was about to kiss him back when the kitchen door opened. Andy held me tight and kissed me anyway.

His mother, Enid, strolled in with Quinn right behind. Neither of them seemed surprised to see us locked in an embrace, I hid the tube between us as fast as I could.

"Greta!" Quinn darted straight to where Mata Hari leaned in the corner and began to fuss over her. "Sage, where'd you find her? I haven't seen her in days. I thought whoever killed Sebastian took her."

"I put her in the pantry for safekeeping. Her leg was broken, so she couldn't stand up without that glass case." I brushed dust off my skirt and met Andy's gaze.

He cleared his throat. "I was about to fix her before I put her on display. Do you want to give me a hand?"

"Do I ever!" Quinn gushed. "Greta Garbo's my inspiration. I used to dream of being able to dress her. As a designer, I mean. That's why I created my own version. Oh, the fabulous outfits I designed for that woman. I showed my sketches to Sebastian once, but he hated them and they disappeared right after that."

Quinn's voice faded as the door closed behind them.

I blew out a breath as her words lingered. Were her Greta Garbo designs the ones we found inside the tube? Just when I thought my suspect list was smaller, I was no closer to knowing who'd killed Sebastian. If Quinn had any idea Sebastian sold her designs behind her back, she would have had the strongest motive to kill him. As much as I liked her, I couldn't trust her until I knew for sure.

"Are you okay?" Enid asked.

I'd forgotten she was in the room.

She tapped the tip of her nose. "My keen sense for finding dirt seems to have stumbled across something interesting. What are you up to, Sage?"

"I think we found what the killer was after," I told her, holding up the tube.

She rushed toward me. "Seriously? Can I see?"

"I'm not sure that's a good idea. The show's starting soon and I don't have time to figure out who wanted it or why."

Enid scowled. "And you don't want to let it out of your sight."

"Am I that obvious?"

She grinned as she touched my arm. "We're a lot more alike than you think. Let me run home and get my laptop. If I look like I'm sitting in a corner writing, no one will bother me. They'll think I'm preparing my feature for the paper, which I will, just not right now. I can see what's so special about what's in that tube."

It was an internal struggle for me to trust her with the flashdrive, but I didn't have much choice. My curiosity won. I slid it out of the tube but kept the papers to deliver to Rhodes.

"We can use the computer at the front counter to take a peek before we open the doors." I told her. "You get first dibs on the scoop, but the information stays on my computer until we figure this out. If it's something bad, then I'm the one who gets in trouble, not you."

She nodded as she grabbed my hand above the bandage. "I'll just be an accessory. I get it. You drive a hard bargain, Sage. We need to hurry. People are lined up outside and the storm is rolling in, so we won't have privacy for long."

I followed her into the store and spied Rhodes across the room with a blonde in a black pantsuit. The female officer I'd met at the station, Officer Conrad. As I walked toward them, Laken waved to get my attention. I held up a finger and gave her a nod.

"Sage," Rhodes said. "I hoped we could talk before the show. This is my partner—"

"Officer Conrad. We met. Nice to see you both," I cut him off as I shoved the tube into his hands. "This is what everyone's looking for. Enid has the flashdrive that was inside and is doing a quick search. I have a hunch the killer will be here to get it back tonight."

He stuck the tube beneath his suit jacket. "Do you think they'll cause trouble?"

"We've had enough run ins with suspects all week to concern me."

"Got it. I'll keep it safe." Rhodes met my gaze then placed a hand on my upper arm. "I'll keep an eye on Enid, while you worry about the show. Officer Conrad will have your back. I'll check out the contents of this tube in a quiet place."

"Good luck finding that," I told him.

"Call me, Sarah," Officer Conrad said. "I tried to get Laken to let me model, but she figured I'd be more helpful keeping an eye on suspects."

"I appreciate that. I'm so frazzled right now. That tube was inside Mata Hari's leg. She's been in a storage room since Sebastian was killed. No one knew where to find her but me. Now that she's out in the open, they might realize there's something special about her."

"You think they'd search her in public?"

I shrugged. "My best guess is during the show while people are distracted."

"Or after your guests leave tonight," she suggested, gazing around the room. "Someone's killed once, Sage. They won't hesitate to harm you or your sister."

That wasn't what I wanted to hear.

I gazed around the room as our models followed Laken into the kitchen-turned-dressing room like flock of multi-colored haired ducklings. "Quinn said something about designing outfits worthy of Greta Garbo. The mannequin version. I have a hunch that's what we found."

She led me toward the beverage table and poured a glass of wine. "Maybe the 'why' part is on the flashdrive. Sebastian must've kept some sort of incriminating evidence. I'm sure Rhodes will know more once he gets a look."

"I hope so." I left her side to join Rhodes and Enid at the counter. I was halfway across the room when someone grabbed my arm. With a shriek, I tried to pull away.

"Relax, girl. Sheesh." Gill led me toward the Clyde mannequin. Bonnie's outfit was in the kitchen. "I thought since Enid was going to model the Bonnie outfit, maybe I should wear the Clyde suit to welcome guests."

I glanced at the silvery gray suit and laughed in surprise. "You want to wear a suit?"

He scowled. "It's been known to happen more than once."

"It's a great idea." I waved Quinn over. "Can you help Gill get Clyde's suit? I'll grab something else to put on the mannequin as soon as I talk to Enid."

Quinn grinned. "Can I pick out an outfit for now, too?"

"Why not?" I shrugged. "We're all playing dress up tonight. You might as well have fun."

"Speaking of fun. What's Enid doing at our computer?"

I thought fast. "She asked if she could borrow it to start her column for the paper so I could make sure she has all the names and information."

"That's so exciting." When Quinn hugged me, she smelled like my body wash. It took me a minute to recall she'd showered at my house that morning. It already seemed like days ago. "I'll see you in the kitchen."

"Let's get you into that suit, handsome," she said, linking arms with Gill.

Andy and Brad stood across the room wearing khakis and suit jackets with their dress shirts open at their collars. My stomach fluttered. Why hadn't I thought to ask them to model? The women of Glitter Bay would've flocked to the show. Maybe next time.

Next time? I really was tired.

Enid and Rhodes looked excited about something on the screen. I was almost at the front counter when I locked eyes with Emery Samson. It seemed he had worked his way—more like bribed his way—to the front of the line. When he winked, I scowled. He pointed to the front door and asked me to let him in.

Actor or not. He was not getting VIP treatment in Vintage Sage. Not if I could help it. He was a suspect like everyone else. Him and Chick, who pulled him back from the window as a flash of lightening illuminated the dark sky behind them.

It was a chilling reminder that there was more than one storm coming our way.

Chapter Sixteen

I slipped behind the counter to peer over Enid's shoulder and asked, "Did you find anything helpful?"

"I found ten files," she told me. "Scans of clothing sketches, inventory lists, and one I can't crack into. Do we really have to give this guy the flashdrive?"

Rhodes nodded. "This guy is a cop, Enid, and this is evidence. Legally, you shouldn't have access to it, but I wanted to see what's on here before the show. If someone does try anything, we know what's going on and have proof."

Enid's fingers flew across the keyboard faster than I expected. She opened file after file for me to take a quick look. Did Rhodes even notice she'd saved a copy of each file into our "Fashion Show" file?

"It's showtime." Gill announced. "Take your places. We have a big crowd waiting to get in."

Any stray models who'd snuck out for an appetizer or a glass of wine scurried into the kitchen. The storefront grew quiet for a minute, until a chorus of giggles erupted in the kitchen. Laken asked Abbie to turn up the music to mask the chatter.

Gill, now dressed in the Clyde suit, opened the front doors at seven o'clock to admit the line of over twenty guests. Emery and Chick entered first. They glanced my way before making a beeline toward the wine and food.

Mishel and Bridey both wore basic black. Bridey completed her look with black lipstick and nail polish. She pulled Mishel away from Emery to where Mata Hari stood.

I pretended not to watch and turned toward the male mannequin in the window that Gill had borrowed the suit from. It now wore a black shift dress, a long string of colorful pearls, and a curly, blonde wig. I chuckled. Why not? I hoped Carol wouldn't create a scene when she saw it.

"Time to shut this down." I indicated the screen as I murmured to Enid. "All of our suspects are here. You need to get into the kitchen before Laken has a fit."

"Yeah, yeah." She removed the flashdrive, then handed it to Rhodes.

He stuck it into the inside pocket of his jacket. "Don't you have to go? You're in the show, right?"

"I want to wander through the crowd first. I think our suspects are all here now," I told him. "I am the host, after all."

"Good idea. I'll join you, so you can point out the people I need to keep my eyes on."

Without actually pointing, I described Chick and Emery who lingered near the beverage table. Chick's dark gaze met mine as thunder rumbled across the water. He scowled and turned away.

I tried to hide behind the monitor.

Rhodes grinned. "That's Emery Samson? He's much shorter in person."

"Aren't cameras great?" I asked. "They can add ten pounds or ten inches."

I pointed out Mishel and Bridey who'd split up to peruse the merchandise. Each of them glanced at the crowd as though they were up to something.

"I wouldn't put it past either of them to steal something," I said.

When the door opened once, a tall, lean woman strolled inside wearing a white linen suit with a single pink rose on her lapel. My breath stuck in my chest. Her hair was done up in a perfect roll. Her ensemble screamed money and privilege rather than prison. She could've easily modeled with Laken and Bridey.

"Delia Reeves," Rhodes said.

I folded my arms across my stomach, mostly to stop my hands from shaking. "I wonder what she's doing here, especially tonight. I hope she doesn't cause trouble."

"The show starts in a few minutes. You'd better go. I'm sure you have things to do."

"Thanks. Good luck."

"You, too." He grinned. "I'd say break a leg, but..."

I chuckled as Abbie turned the music up to mask the thunder overhead. If the killer was here, they'd be happy to be able to search without anyone hearing.

He placed a hand on my arm and gave a nod. "Sarah and I'll keep things under control. I'm glad Andy and Brad are on our side."

"Me, too." I flashed Andy a smile. In return, both he and Brad raised their wine glasses. My stomach fluttered as I ducked through the crowd to avoid Delia and the others.

I paused next to Gill. "With any luck, the power won't go out during the show."

He shrugged. "We have candles everywhere, even along the runway. I doubt anyone would notice. Well, except for the music. I'll get Abbie to figure out a Plan B, just in case."

"You're amazing. Are all of the tickets we sold accounted for?"

He grinned. "Yup, including the two we sold to Emery for a hundred dollars each. We'll have to buy a couple bottles of wine with that later to celebrate."

"That sounds like a plan. I'm sure we'll have enough left over from tonight. Did you buy a whole case?"

"Laken had very specific requests." He locked the door. "Including the bottle she made me hide in the fridge for you. We both agreed you'd need it."

"I'll have to thank her later." I hugged him, then made my way through the crowd to make sure everything went as planned. Namely, the fashion show I never wanted.

Vintage Sage—my beautiful new boutique—held a sold-out crowd of twenty-five. They nibbled appetizers, perused the gently used, designer clothing and display cases filled with old watches, Sebastian's necklaces, and antique brooches. The food smelled delicious. Too bad my stomach was in knots.

A few people milled around Mata Hari, who stood between Abbie's table and the front counter. They paused long enough to read the sign Quinn printed about the replica costume she'd made in honor of Greta Garbo. No one seemed to linger for an abnormal length of time.

"You did a great job, Sage." Andy kissed my cheek and draped a possessive arm across my shoulders. "Gill said the show sold out and everyone with a ticket showed up, including all your suspects."

"Yeah." I winced. "I wish I could keep an eye on them, but Laken and Quinn roped me into modeling. I suppose I'll have a better vantage point from on stage."

He gave my shoulders a squeeze. "Brad and I are here, so are the police and Gill. Between us, we have things covered. All you have to worry about is showing off those great outfits. I'm going to get some of those appetizers before they're all gone. Do you want anything?"

"No, thanks." I hugged him, happy he was there to cheer me on. "I'm too nervous to eat."

"Break a leg, Sage," Andy whispered.

He kissed my forehead before sauntering across the room to mingle. Straight to where Emery signed napkins for guests at the beverage table. His sidekick, Chick, sipped from a tiny teacup while he glared across the room. Mishel stood several feet from Mata Hari. His scowl was nearly as deep as Chick's. His gaze never seemed to leave the mannequin. Did he know Sebastian hid the designs in her leg and was waiting for his opportunity to strike?

Bridey circled the room like a vulture as though looking for something or someone. If they were partners, I wouldn't put it past her to create some sort of diversion. I was grateful Gill bought battery-operated candles rather than real ones. A fire would seem like an obvious way to clear everyone out of the building.

"You drew in a nice crowd," a familiar voice said as the scent of jasmine perfume surrounded me. "I never thought I'd set foot in Vintage Sage again let alone see it become a beautiful butterfly."

A shiver ran down my back like ice water. I turned slowly to face Delia and asked, "What are you doing here?"

She held a glass of red one in one hand and smoothed her white linen suit with the other. "Relax, darling, I have handlers. Officer Rhodes and his partner allowed me to come say my two-bits. Neither will let me out of their sight for a second. If I so much as cough on you, they've promised to throw me in a jail far away."

Her revelation didn't comfort me. I started to walk away. "I have to check on the models. Enjoy the show."

Delia grabbed my arm. The second her bright purple nails rested on my wrist, Officer Rhodes and his partner started toward us. She relaxed her grip and held up her hand. "Sorry, I promised to behave."

"What do you want?" I asked, my hands shaking.

"Sage, we used to be the best of friends," she said. "I'm proud of you. You deserve this."

I decided to give her the benefit of the doubt. For now. When I smiled, the police held back. "Thank you. I appreciate that."

She gave my arm a light squeeze. "I know you're not happy to see me, but I'm glad to be here. I even found a necklace I want to buy later. The purple one with little flowers."

"We'll be opening the till for purchases later," I told her.

"Great. I'm looking forward to the show."

I met Andy's questioning gaze across the room and gave a shrug as I headed to the kitchen door.

Enid yanked me inside and asked. "What is Delia Reeves doing here? I thought she'd be in jail for the rest of her miserable life."

"She got time off for good behavior," I muttered as my palms sweated.

"She tried to kill you."

"Trust me, I remember. She said she's proud of me, but she's probably here to watch me fail just like Laken's so-called friends."

Enid smirked. "Well, that's her loss, isn't it? Failure's not happening. We're going to knock 'em dead and catch a killer."

"I love your enthusiasm."

"Yay! My muse has arrived!" Quinn ran up to us squealing. "Let's get you ready to bring down the house."

I didn't like her choice of words but understood the sentiment. I was reminded of Edgar Allan Poe's story The Fall of the House of Usher. In this case, the House of Miller. As Quinn led me to a tall chair standing in front of a brightly lit mirror, I whispered, "Go away, bad thoughts."

All the while, the dark clouds loomed overhead. The wind picked up and lightning lit the room at uneven intervals. The "dark and stormy night" the weatherman had predicted was rolling in quickly. As thunder rumbled overhead and the lights in the building flickered, I hoped Quinn meant we'd bring down the house figuratively—not literally.

Chapter Seventeen

Quinn did such a fabulous job on my makeup that I barely recognized myself when she held up the mirror. I studied the smoky blends of gray and turquoise eyeshadows, thick eyelashes, and soft pink on my cheeks. Topped off with my first outfit of the evening, a pale peach pantsuit that felt like buttery suede, I felt like a million dollars.

Mostly, I was grateful she hadn't used the mascara wand as a lethal weapon.

"Sage, you look amazing," Laken said, putting the final touches on her up-do. "Quinn, you could have a great career as a makeup artist. I could get you interviews with people I know."

"You are good. I don't even look like me," I told her, then tried not to laugh at the horror that crossed her face.

"Sure you do. I worked with what you have. You're naturally gorgeous. Curious and clumsy, but gorgeous."

"Now that I agree with," Laken said. "Sage, you're being a great sport about all of this. I put something in the fridge for you for later. A token of my appreciation."

"Gill told me." I stepped back to admire my sister in the emerald gown she'd modeled days ago that Sebastian told her to burn. The glittering necklace and green gemstones in her hair added the touch of bling it needed. "You look breathtaking."

"Oh, go on." She motioned for me to keep the compliments coming. "I've missed this part of shows. The excitement, the nerves—"

I winced. "The upset stomach."

Laken gave me a hug. "We'll catch them, Sage. Whoever it was, we'll get them."

"I hope so," I whispered.

My sister stepped back and clapped her hands then reached for Sammy's leash. "Let's get this party started. Have fun, everyone, you all look amazing. Be sure to smile and put some bounce in your step. I'm off to emcee the show."

"Wait, she's not modeling with us?" Enid asked.

"Not a chance." Laken poked her head out the kitchen door to cue Abbie who changed the music. "This is your night to shine, ladies. For the first time, I get to run the show, not star in it."

After the long, crazy week, the music thumped and the show was underway. My sister strutted through the kitchen door, then disappeared for her walk down the runway to a loud cheer from the audience. It was a full minute before she thanked everyone for attending to officially open the new Vintage Sage Boutique.

"Okay, ladies, just like we rehearsed," Quinn said, taking her position near the door. "Walk to the end of the runway, pause, turn, and walk toward the door. Pause again before you come back in. Once you change outfits, get back in line. After your second trip down the runway, walk back to the door then go to your spot. I've marked the floor with green tape. Sage is our closer. Once she's in place, everyone takes a bow, then we all get a big glass of wine and see if there are any of those little shrimp things left."

"Oh, dear. I just forgot everything before shrimp things," Ursula said, then chuckled.

Enid adjusted the hat that topped off her first outfit. The blue lace dress. "Sage will be the star of the show, as she should be. After all, she owns this great new store."

Everyone in the change room applauded.

A flush crept up my chest to my face. Since I had their attention, I made a quick announcement, "Could you do me one favor? When you come back after your turn down the runway, let me know if you see anyone lurking near the glass case. It's important." I paused. "Break a leg, everyone."

Margaret Gumble piped up, "Legs are fine, just don't break any hips."

We laughed as Laken announced the first model of the evening.

Carlene took a deep breath, then flashed the winning smile that made her everyone's favorite at waitress at the Devil's Peak Tavern. Well, aside from Sebastian. After all the grief he'd caused her, we owed her a fun minute in the spotlight.

As each model left the kitchen to stroll down the runway, I peered through a gap in the door. My focus was on the glass case. While Chick and Emery sat a few feet away from it, neither of them seemed distracted by it.

"No one out there looks suspicious to me," Carleen, petite and raven-haired, whispered as she returned wearing her black Donna Karan sailor pant jumpsuit. "There are a few cute guys in the audience though. I may have to work the room later."

Quinn gave her a high-five. "You go, girl. Margaret, you're up next."

Margaret Gumble, the soft swells of her white hair glittering with spray-on sparkles, pursed her lips before she sauntered out with an exaggerated sway of her hips. The beads on the fringes of the flapper dress she wore clattered around her knobby knees.

I leaned close to Quinn and asked, "Anything unusual yet?"

She raised one eyebrow. "You mean aside from a stable full of geriatric models? Nada. People were checking her out, but no one's laid a hand on her."

"We are talking about Mata Hari, right?"

"Yes." She chuckled. "Will you relax? That cop is sitting in the perfect spot. He can watch the show, the crowd, and the mannequin."

"I'm sorry, I'll trust you," I told her.

Margaret returned to change into her second outfit.

Her twin Joanne shoved us all aside with her skirts as she hit the runway in a pink chiffon gown that reminded me of Glinda the Good Witch in the Wizard of Oz.

Taking several deep breaths, I wished I was in the other room and nowhere near the stage—let alone about to walk down it. Laken was a more natural model than me. She was also a more suitable emcee than I would've been. I settled into my non-speaking role.

"Thank you for inviting me. This is fun." Carol patted my arm as she left the kitchen. The yellow Donna Karan dress she wore hadn't looked like much on the hanger, yet it hugged her curves beautifully.

Quinn held up a hand as thunder rumbled overhead. "Before you ask, nothing yet. Your boyfriend looks really good in that suit though."

I frowned. "Andy's not my boyfriend."

Enid chuckled. "That's not what I saw. My boy was wrapped around you like a shawl."

As the women in the kitchen oohed and aahed, I covered my ears.

"Your boy?" Quinn asked.

"Andy's my son," Enid said. "And I've never approved of his girlfriends. Until now."

My entire body seemed to erupt in flames.

Ursula flipped her long white hair over one shoulder and strode out of the room wearing a flowing skirt and blouse. "Don't be embarrassed. Andy Briggs is very handsome. He has a beautiful soul, just like you."

Carol huffed as she returned to the kitchen. "I miss all the good stuff. Who are we talking about now?"

"Sage is dating Andy," Margaret said, catching her up on my love life while they changed clothes.

"Guys, we've only known each other a couple months. Let's not rush things."

Carol shrugged. "So what? I only knew my husband a week before we got married."

"A week?" I stared.

Enid hugged me, careful not to rumple the peach suit Laken chose for my first outfit. "There's no rush, sweetie. I waited a lifetime for Gill. My boy's not going anywhere. He adores you."

"Thanks, but I—"

"You're up next, Enid," Quinn called.

Following her to the door, I was tempted to peek at the crowd again. Instead, I closed my eyes. It was seconds before she returned.

"Knock 'em dead, kid," Quinn said, tapping my shoulder.

"Me?"

"Come on, girl. Strut your stuff!" Enid told me.

Quinn met my gaze and said, "Attitude is everything. Stand tall, walk proudly, and own it. You got this."

I forced a smile as I walked through the door and onto runway with flickering fake candles down the length of it. For a brief instant, I felt like a real model. Until I spied Emery's lecherous grin. While I tried to focus on the glass case behind the crowd, I was distracted by Andy's smile.

My stomach fluttered as I paused at the far end of the runway. Gill elbowed Andy. I didn't have to hear them to know he was telling Andy to ask me out.

I turned to strut back up the runway and wanted to run straight out the back door. My gaze darted to Laken who shook her head slightly. Nothing yet. So far, Sebastian's killer, if they were here, hadn't made any moves.

Maybe we needed to spread the rumor that we'd found the missing designs.

I sidled up to Quinn as thunder rumbled and the lights flickered. "I need a piece of paper and a pen."

"Uh-uh." She shook her head. "Honey, what you need is to pour yourself into that dress so I have enough time to do your hair."

I blew out a frustrated breath. "Okay, then write a note for me and ask one of the ladies to hand it to Gill. He needs to spread a rumor that we found the missing designs."

Enid perked up as she fastened the suit jacket of her Bonnie outfit. "I can do it."

"You found what?" Quinn's eyes grew wide as she lunged toward me.

"It's just a rumor," I told her.

Margaret frowned. "But what about the stuff Enid saw?"

I scowled at Enid, then motioned to Quinn. "Get the next model out."

"How do you know that's what everyone's looking for?" Quinn asked. She nearly shoved Margaret out the door, before writing a hasty note. "Joanne, give this to Gill."

Joanne's cheeks turned pink. "I'd be delighted to."

"Thank you."

"Don't get carried away, it's just a note to lure a killer," Enid snapped. "That man is mine."

Carol and Ursula gasped and stared at her.

"What? It's not exactly a surprise." Enid flared her nostrils. "Who's next?"

They both paled then darted toward the door to line up.

"Get dressed," Quinn barked at me.

"Yes, ma'am." I began to struggle out of the pantsuit under Quinn's glare. I was grateful we weren't alone or she might've done something we'd both regret. I wiggled into the cocoon dress.

"Are you sure you want me to leave?" Enid zipped the back of my dress before she helped me with the necklace and a silvery lace shawl. "She looks ready to strangle you."

I nodded. "Go. I'll be fine. If she does, we won't have a finale and you'll know what to tell the police."

"Be careful." She ran to stand guard at the door when Quinn waved her over.

Quinn approached me, then spun me around so fast the flare of fabric below my knee swirled around my calves. "Let's get your hair done."

"I'm sorry I didn't tell you. There wasn't time."

"You don't trust me. I get it." She pulled and combed my hair, then added a few bobby pins with such force they scratched my scalp. A minute later, she held up a mirror. "How's that?"

I sighed. "Oh, Quinn. It looks great. You've made me look so good today."

"And yet you stab me in the back over and over again," she told me. "Sweetie, I wish you knew how gorgeous you are. All I did was highlight your natural beauty. Now you just have to go back out there and shine."

When I moved to hug her, she stepped back. "What's wrong?"

"If I hugged you now, I'd end up giving you a big old bear hug," she said. The look on her face said she was ready to choke me for keeping the designs we found a secret.

"I'm going now," Enid called over her shoulder. "Quinn, you're next."

"I'll be out in a minute." She reached for the hat and shawl to finish off her butterfly outfit. "Wish me luck."

I stopped her. "Quinn, you don't need luck. You have so much talent." I hesitated. It was time to come clean. "I saw your sketches. That's what everyone's after. The sketches you did that Sebastian said he hated."

"What are you talking about?"

"The line of clothes Mishel sold to the department store are your Greta Garbo designs. Sebastian must've sold him copies and kept the originals in case anything went wrong."

Enid gave a loud stage whisper into the kitchen. "Quinn, move it."

"Tell everyone to walk down the aisle one more time," I said.

"It's a runway," Quinn reminded me as her face paled. "Are you saying my designs are good enough for a national department store chain?"

I nodded as Laken rambled on about the Mata Hari mannequin, and asked the ladies to take an encore walk down the runway, while she stalled to cover for the gap in the show. "Of course they are."

A slow smile spread across Quinn's face as her eyes lit up. "This is the best day ever. Not only are my designs in a fashion show and a department store, but I get to model them with my best friend."

My heart seemed to explode at her words. "Yeah, I guess you do."

"Then let's rock this thing together, Sister," she said, holding out her hand. "Now all we need is to catch us a killer."

"Let's do this." I took her hand as we left the kitchen together.

When we burst through the kitchen door, Laken faltered for a brief second, then carried on with a grin as if we'd planned the double entrance all along.

For my part, I should've been more concerned with putting one foot in front of the other, especially since I'd never worn four-inch heels before. I'd also never worn a gown that tethered my knees to the point I could only take exaggerated baby steps.

While Quinn steered me down the runway, I glanced toward the glass case where Mata Hari stood with her sequins sparkling. We strutted to the end of the runway, then paused. A few people in the back row stood but I still had a partial view of the glass cabinet and was sure I saw someone crouching near the cabinet.

Then Quinn turned to me as we turned.

"Did you see that?" I asked.

Quinn whispered, "I didn't see anything. Relax. Rhodes is keeping an eye on things. We'll turn in a sec."

As my heart hammered, I forced myself not to glance back. The show was over and no one had made a move toward Mata Hari or us. Was I wrong to think they would?

"Ladies and gentlemen, Vintage Sage owner, Sage Miller, and the designer of those two fabulous gowns, Quinn Evans."

Arm in arm, Quinn and I turned to face the audience. I smiled until I noticed the door to the case opening. Someone had one hand on the glass but disappeared from view as the audience stood to applaud.

"They're making a move," I said, over the sounds of applause and rumbles of thunder.

"Let's get him," Quinn shouted.

Holding hands, we scurried down the candlelit runway as the power went out.

Chapter Eighteen

The models, audience, and the person searching Mata Hari's case were all plunged into semi-darkness. I was grateful for the dozens of candles lining the runway and shining on nearly every surface. Things would've been ten times worse in complete darkness.

Gasps and murmurs swept through the crowd as chairs toppled over. Andy leaped to his feet and raced across the room with Rhodes and Brad to grab the figure as Mata Hari fell. Her tiara clattered across the floor, the stones reflecting the dim light.

Quinn and I stopped short as Mishel, who had a seat at the end of the runway, jumped in front of us demanding to know what was going on. We glanced at each other, then tried to get past him to see who Rhodes and Andy had caught.

"You people are crazy," Emery shouted. "Will someone please tell us what's going on?"

Sarah called for backup, then stood in front of the door to make sure no one left the building.

Jonathan sputtered as he lay on the ground with Mata Hari on top of him. "Get this thing off me. I was only trying to help Sage. This is all a big misunderstanding."

"I guess that depends on what you were looking for," Rhodes told him.

His mouth fell open. "I'm not looking for anything. The case was open. I went to close it and this thing fell on me. Somebody get it off."

"I don't believe him," I said, trying to get around Mishel, who held me back.

Quinn knocked him back into his seat. "Get out of the way, little man. We're trying to catch a bad guy."

Bridey's mouth fell open. "A bad guy? Do you mean Sebastian's killer?"

"Like you're surprised," Quinn said.

"There's a killer here?" Carol shouted as she gave Quinn a shove. "It's you, isn't it? I knew there was something I didn't like about you."

"No." Quinn fell against Chick. "Sebastian was my boss."

Everyone seemed to talk and leap out of their seats all at once as Rhodes and Andy hauled Jonathan to his feet. As Brad lifted Mata Hari into the cabinet, her foot fell off with a thud on the wood floor.

"I didn't break that," Jonathan insisted. "It was already broken."

I wove through the crowd toward Jonathan. "You were here the day Sebastian died, weren't you? That's how you knew where to look for the designs."

He tried to lunge at me but Rhodes and Andy held him back. "I have no idea what you're talking about. I opened the door to take a better look and she fell on me."

"You just said you tried to close it," Rhodes reminded him.

"What designs are you talking about?" Mishel asked.

Quinn snorted. "Oh, don't act so shocked, you and the bride of Frankenstein were both in on this. How much did you pay that guy?"

He snorted. "What are you talking about?"

"Why did you kill Sebastian?" I asked, glaring at Jonathan. "Did he owe you money, or did someone put you up to it?"

"I hated what he was trying to do to you," he yelled.

Laken jumped between us and told him, "Sebastian didn't do anything. I can't believe you killed him and stuffed him in that case."

"You have no proof I was here," Jonathan roared.

"You just admitted you killed him." I stood next to my sister. "Besides, you're the only person in the store who went near that case all night, which is where Sebastian hid Quinn's designs. Why did you arrange the mannequins in a circle? Did you search them, too?"

"My designs were in that ugly mannequin the whole time?" Mishel gasped as he lunged toward Jonathan. "Where are they? I want them back. I own those."

I grasped his arm as Brad blocked him. "No, you don't. Sebastian sold you the copies, not the originals. If you had the originals, Quinn would have no proof they were her designs you sold to the department store."

An audible gasp went through the crowd.

Bridey inched away from Mishel. "You stole Quinn's designs? How could you?"

"What are you squawking about?" Mishel asked, his voice rose an octave. "You bribed the truck driver to tell us where he was taking Sebastian's things. Too bad he wouldn't let us search the truck before they left, then no one would've ever known."

"How dare you." Bridey tried to get around us to the kitchen.

With her thin frame, she managed to duck around Quinn, but couldn't outrun Brad. As he stepped in front of her to block the kitchen door, Joanne strolled over and stood next to him. As far as guards went, they were an unlikely pair. They were enough to deter Bridey.

Quinn stormed after her. "You were the model, he was the so-called designer, and Emery was the banker. What does that other guy have to do with anything?"

"I don't know." Bridey burst into tears. "I have no idea who he is."

"Yeah, we only dated twice," Jonathan said, sarcastically.

Chick headed to the beverage table for more wine.

"What are you talking about? I'm no banker for anyone," Emery announced.

"Oh, please. You're in this as deep as the rest of them," Laken said. "You helped Mishel get his new fashion line in stores. How much did that cost? Certainly not any amount of pride. Did they tell you they'd put your name on the label or Mishel's?"

"You're wrong, Laken," he growled.

"I did it all for Sage," Jonathan admitted as Rhodes pulled his arms behind his back. "I was trying to help save your store. I know how hard you've worked."

As Rhodes snapped a set of handcuffs on Jonathan, he asked, "To save her store from what?"

Jonathan bowed his head. "I overheard Emery and Chick talking on the set one day about how Sebastian planned to take over a vintage store in Glitter Bay and leave Los Angeles for good. Sebastian thought Laken owned the store and bragged about how easy it would be to take it from her since she owed him. He didn't know about Sage, and I couldn't let that happen."

Andy didn't look impressed. He clenched his fists at his sides as though ready to take a swing at Jonathan.

"Andy, he's not worth it," I warned.

Laken gasped. "Take over the store?"

"I told you he would," Quinn reminded her. "He even hired a lawyer."

"And we saw the paperwork," I said.

Mishel sputtered as Bridey left his side. "How did you...?"

Quinn shot me a sheepish glance. "Sebastian told me while Laken was ordering dinner the day he died. That's what we argued about."

I looked at Jonathan. "How much did you know?"

He seemed to search the room. "Delia has been a family friend for years. I called to let her know you were in danger. She agreed to keep an eye on you until I could get here. When I showed up, Sebastian was here alone. She can tell you."

"It really was you," I whispered. "Jonathan…"

He closed his eyes. "I tried to warn you. When you wouldn't take my calls, I confronted Sebastian. He bragged about all the things he planned to do once he took over. Ask Delia. She knows everything."

I looked around but didn't see Delia. I was afraid to turn my back on Jonathan in case he tried anything.

Quinn sighed. "He's right, Sage. Sebastian wanted a fresh start and loved the tea house. Just not the color."

"I wish you'd texted or called me back. None of this would've happened."

"You're blaming me?" I shouted at Jonathan.

"No, I…" he started then bowed his head.

Rhodes took him by the arm. "This might be a good time to stop talking and call a lawyer. Let's go."

"I don't need a lawyer," Jonathan insisted. "Delia, tell them what happened."

I struggled to breathe. "I need to get out of this dress."

Quinn draped an arm across my shoulders. "I'll come with you. Do we need to give a statement or anything? My girl here has a bottle of wine with her name on it."

"I know where to find you," Rhodes said, turning to walk Jonathan to his car as rain began to fall in huge droplets.

Laken sat on one of the chairs. "Why didn't Sebastian tell me he wanted to take over?"

Mishel shook his head. "Why else would he send you every fixture from the House of Hayward? Speaking of which, where are my sketches?"

Quinn glared. "You mean my sketches."

"I paid for them."

"But I drew them," she snapped. "They belong to me."

Across the room, Rhodes cleared his throat. "And I have them in my possession. Sage smuggled them to me before the show."

Quinn's eyes brightened as she grinned. "Beautiful and devious. Andy, you'd better move fast before this one gets snapped up."

My face burned as I walked past Brad into the kitchen. The air was several degrees cooler. It was also dark. With all the candles in the store, I'd forgotten the power was out. At least I knew which corner of the room my clothes were in.

I felt my way along the cupboards until I found one of Gill's fake candles. I had my finger on the switch when an arm snaked around my neck. The scent of jasmine accosted me.

"Let me go," I squawked. I tried to struggle, but there wasn't give in the snug cocoon dress.

"Oh, Sage," Delia breathed in my ear. "You have no idea what you've gotten into. If you think those designs mean anything, you're delusional."

"The police are—"

"In the next room. I know." She yanked me toward the back door cutting off my airway as I stumbled. "If you would've read Jonathan's texts, you would've figured it all out. That stupid circle was a dead giveaway, yet you still didn't get it. What more do you need, girl? To be hit over the head with it?"

We'd barely backed up two feet before the back door flew open. There was a loud crash before Delia and I were showered with water and roses. The lights came on as her arm fell away from my neck and she dropped to the floor in a pool of glass and water. The scent of crushed white rose petals reached my nostrils.

"That'll teach her to mess with my girls." Quinn stood over Delia in triumph with her hands on her hips. "Are you okay, Sage?"

I began to laugh with sheer relief as I plucked rose petals out of my top. "Wet and covered in glass, but I'm fine."

Laken ran into the kitchen with Andy and Sarah close behind. "Andy, you were right. She was here. No wonder no one saw her leave."

"Are you okay?" Andy asked as he hugged me.

"I'm fine," I assured him. "I was so focused on Jonathan I didn't even think about Delia. Not even after he said they were friends."

He brushed a couple pieces of glass and rose petals off my dress before he kissed me. "I still think you look amazing in that dress."

"Oh, brother. Save it for later," Laken groaned. "Let's get rid of the bad guys, so we can enjoy the rest of the night. My sister has a gorgeous new store and I'm ready for some serious retail therapy."

"And I'm more than ready for a glass of wine," I told her.

Chapter Nineteen

❦

After a good night's sleep, I was startled to see Quinn sitting on the back deck early the next morning. "Good morning. I thought you'd sleep until noon."

"Good morning. I heard Laken leave to let the contractors in this morning and decided not to waste the day. I came dressed and ready to go." She wore leggings, a thigh-length tunic she'd bought the night before, and a sparkly rainbow headband.

Sammy joined us and licked her face.

"For what?" I asked.

"Yoga. Laken told me you do some sun worship thing every morning, so I thought I'd join you. If that's okay."

"Sun salutations. Sure, that's fine. I'll go slow, so you can follow."

She clapped her hands like a giant, exuberant child. "Oh goody. How do we start?"

I showed her how to stand in mountain pose with her feet hip-width apart and her hands at her sides. "You need to move with intention, but not like a robot. Let your movements flow from one to the next."

"I would if I knew what I was doing," Quinn said, then copied me as I placed my hands in prayer position in front of my chest. "Is this good?"

"Great." After a couple breaths, I raised my hands toward the sky. "Hold this for a couple breaths, then we're going to bend down to touch our toes."

"You're joking." She snorted.

"It's the next posture."

"What if I can't reach my toes?"

I shrugged. "Then touch your knees. Or as low as you can go without hurting yourself."

Quinn gave me a thumb up as she bent to touch slightly below her knees. "I'm not actually here for yoga. I need to talk to you about something important."

"Can it wait until we're done?" I asked, moving my left leg back into a lunge.

"Nope. I'm too excited." She remained in place with her hands on her shins. "You know that tailor shop up the street from Vintage Sage? I talked to the owner the other day after you and I talked about my future. I'm going to work there part-time doing repairs for them for a few hours a day. After that, I can rent the sewing machine to create drag queen outfits like we talked about."

"Quinn, that's great." I held my lunge a little longer waiting for her to catch up.

She beamed. "Don't worry, I'll still work for you, but only part-time. I could end up a very rich woman once all the stuff with Mishel gets sorted out."

I met her gaze, not sure what to say as I lowered my hips to the deck and arched back into cobra.

She continued, so I didn't have to worry, "I contacted some friends from my club days and they're interested in seeing my new designs. You were right, Sage, I'd be much happier doing that than designing dresses for a department store all the time. That only gets me in trouble."

"I'm so happy for you, Quinn." I gave up on yoga and gave her a hug before I sat on the deck.

"There's just one teensy little problem," she said, holding up her thumb and index finger a tiny way apart.

"What's that?"

"I can't afford to live in a hotel much longer. I need a place to stay." She held up her hands. "Just until I sell a few outfits and get the money from Sebastian's estate for my designs. Then I'll look for my own place."

I'd been so distracted by the events of the week that I hadn't even anticipated she'd plan to leave. "Quinn, I—"

"I know Laken's in your guestroom, but she'll be moving soon. For now, I'd be thrilled to sleep on the couch." She sighed. "I'm sort of tidy and a great cook. You could teach me all about vegan cooking, or non-cooking. Do vegan's actually cook?"

"Yes, we do," I told her. "Quinn, I just—"

She winced. "If you're worried about me being a bit crazy, it's okay. I've never hidden who I am. Not from you and Laken, anyway."

I raised my voice. "Quinn."

"What?"

"I'm trying to tell you I'd be honored to have you for a roommate."

Her grin grew wide as her eyes shone with tears. She lunged forward and hugged me so hard that Sammy bounced back barking. "I promise to give you space when you need alone time with your boyfriend and I won't snoop." She paused. "Okay, maybe a little because I'm naturally nosy. Who knows, maybe we'll get to solve another mystery together. Aside from you finding a body and Delia trying to choke you, the whole crime-solving thing was kind of fun."

"No more murders. I've never been so scared in my life as I have been this week. What will happen with your designs Sebastian stole?"

"Officer Rhodes says they're evidence until the police sort things out. He advised me to get a lawyer and reach out to the department store. They might want to charge Mishel and Emery with fraud. Too bad they can't charge Bridey with being stupid."

I patted Sammy's back as he curled in the space between us. "I'll bet the store will still want to use your designs."

"Maybe, but I doubt they'd want a transgender woman as part of the package."

"Excuse me?" I huffed. "Quinn Evans, you are the designer. You should get the same recognition and the huge truckload of money Mishel was supposed to get. If there's one thing you've taught me, it's to own the gifts you've got. You've got more talent in one pinky than Mishel and Sebastian combined."

Her face reddened. "Yes, I do. The problem is I don't fit into the world they wanted to be a part of. That's why I like making outfits for drag queens. I'm like you, Sage, a free spirit. I want to make people look good on their terms, not because some fancy pants store dictates how they should dress and charges them a fortune to do it. Although the money would be nice. People should love their clothes, not worry about going in debt for a scrap of fabric with some designer's name on the tag."

"That's why I started Vintage Sage. To recycle those fancy scraps of fabric. I'd be a hypocrite if I didn't invite you to show your designs there. Heaven knows I have more than enough mannequins.

"And my customers would love all the bling and pretty things you sell." Quinn smiled, then met my gaze. "Now, about my wage at the store—"

I rolled my eyes. "Sammy, let's go for a walk."

About the Author

❧ ❦

Award-winning author Diane Bator began writing as a kid when she fell in love with storytelling. After ten years of working with various traditional publishers, she's created her own company, Escape With a Writer Publishing to relaunch her previous work plus many new titles. A proud mom of three, Diane loves a good joke. She's also a Reiki Master, a blue belt in goju-ryu karate, and an artist who loves stopping at odd places on road trips and creating new things from old.

Her website is https://dianebator.ca/

Join her newsletter and Escape With a Writer! https://dianebator.substack.com/